DEADLY DIVINATIONS

DEADLY DIVINATIONS

A Gideon Jones Novel

Paul Leonard Williams

EpiphanyMill Publishing

Text Copyright © 2019 Paul Leonard Williams
Cover Art Copyright © 2019 Whendell Souza

Published in the United States by EpiphanyMill Publishing, a division of EpiphanyMill LLC. Star Valley, AZ

EpiphanyMill Publishing is a registered trademark, and the BigEBooks colophon is a trademark of EpiphanyMill LLC.

Visit us on the Web! EpiphanyMill.com

Library of Congress Cataloging-in-Publication Data
Williams, Paul Leonard
Deadly Divinations / Paul Leonard Williams. – First edition.

ISBN 978-1-947691-06-3 (intl. tr. Pbk.) –
ISBN 978-1-947691-07-0 (ebook)

[1. Detective-Fiction. 2. Supernatural-Fiction. 3. Martial Arts-Fiction.] I. Title.
Library of Congress Control Number: 2022936338

The text of this book is set in 11.5 Apollo MT.
Book design by Rod R. Garcia
Edited by EMB

Printed in the United States of America

10 9 8 7 6 5 4 3 2 1
First Edition

I dedicate this book to my mother who was a wonderful example
of living your faith and taught me the importance of not just
talking the talk but walking the walk.

I miss you, mom.

The only thing necessary for the triumph of evil is for good men to do nothing.

~*Edmund Burke (1729-1797)*

Let's Dance!

~*Gideon Jones (1986)*

Special thanks to Betsy, the love of my life.

You've helped me to keep on keeping on.

Love you darlin'!

Chapter 1

La Llorona

"There is no need to hunt. He will seek you out like a moth drawn to a flame. The young have always found forbidden fruit to be irresistible."

The creature struggled against its restraints in the dark. "Release me!"

"Not yet. My spell is still incomplete. I must first bait the trap. I will go to the boy in his dreams and convince him to go to the river, enticing him with the promise of excitement and adventure."

Blake clambered out from under his covers and silently slid out of bed. He changed from pajamas into jeans and a t-shirt. He was careful not to make any noise. He didn't want to alert his parents to the fact that he was up past his bedtime. Somewhere along the way, most adults forget essential components to living a worthwhile life. Chief among them is that having fun is *crucial.* It was a shame his parents were among those who had forgotten this important fact. *If they remembered anything about having fun, I wouldn't need to sneak around like this*, Blake thought to himself. He sighed dramatically and continued with his stealthy preparations. He put a bag of cookies next to the comic books in his backpack and zipped it shut. Grabbing his flashlight, he crept silently from his bedroom. Tonight, he would meet Dave at the fort, a little treehouse the two of them had built near the river. Mom had forbidden it, saying there was no reason to play with Dave in the middle of the night. The two could meet tomorrow after breakfast. But where was the fun in that? There was no sense of adventure, no element of danger! What was mom so worried about? He was ten now, after all, not some baby. Besides, it was said La Llorona stalked the banks of the Rio Grande at night. If he and Dave were lucky, they might catch a glimpse of her!

The story of La Llorona dated back to the early 1800s. 'La Llorona' is Spanish for the weeping or wailing woman. She is the ghost of a young mother whose children drowned in the mighty Rio Grande. The legend said the woman's two small children had been playing near the banks of the river. Despite their mother's warnings not to do so, they wandered into the water while she was distracted and got swept away by the strong currents. The mother tried to save them but was too late. Devastated by the loss of her children, the poor woman walked the banks of the river day and night. Weeping and wailing, she called out to her lost children. One day she snapped and committed suicide. La Llorona drowned herself in the murky waters.

Now the woman's ghost haunts the banks of the Rio Grande, searching for her lost children. Some nights you could hear her eerie, tormented weeping and wailing. For generations now, the locals have warned their children not to play near the banks of the Rio Grande alone, especially at night, or La Llorona would snatch them up.

Blake didn't think they would actually see any ghosts, but he grabbed his aluminum baseball bat just in case. Despite his best efforts to make no sound, the door to his room squeaked loudly on its hinges. Blake froze in place, sure his mother would emerge from the shadows. Slipper in hand, she'd be ready to smack him with it mercilessly, then double his chores and ground him for a month! When she didn't appear, he decided not to look a gift horse in the mouth. He moved quickly but more silently; leaving his little adobe house and venturing out into the night to rendezvous with Dave.

After walking two blocks to the stucco wall surrounding his neighborhood, he scaled it, agile as a monkey. Blake scrambled over into the trees and shrubs on the other side, making his way down towards the river. It was late September, but summer had not yet fully given way to autumn. The evenings were still fairly mild. He wore a denim jacket anyway, mainly to protect himself from getting scratched up by the dense tangle of brambles that grew along the banks of the river. Pretending he was a famous explorer, Blake held the flashlight in his left hand and swung the baseball bat with his right. He imagined it was a machete and he was hacking his way through the jungles of South America looking for Aztec gold.

As he noisily made his way closer to the riverbank, he abruptly stopped and listened. He didn't know why, but something didn't seem quite right. He could hear the babble of the rushing river as the water rolled over rocks, but nothing else. Suddenly he realized that was it! The *lack* of noise! It was odd. Usually, there was a cacophony of night sounds: the constant chirping of crickets, the buzzing of other insects, the croaking of frogs, the occasional hoot of an owl, or the distant cry of a coyote. Now there was nothing, not even the faint sound of the wind rustling leaves.

Blake stopped swinging the bat and started to shiver, not because he was afraid, but because it was suddenly cold. The temperature dropped rapidly. Low enough that he could now see his breath. Now *that* was odd. He wasn't sure why, but he turned off the flashlight. Using the bat, Blake slowly parted the branches obstructing his vision, taking care not to make a sound and break the eerie silence. He carefully peeked out into the now ominously quiet night. The scene the parting branches revealed was truly terrifying. Crouched by the banks of the river was a grotesque and horrific thing. It must have been at least seven and a half feet tall, quite possibly eight. It had elongated arms hanging past its knees, ending in wicked-looking claws. The thing was lanky, almost to the point of being skeletal. Its skin was unnaturally white, like an insect that had crawled out from under a rock. Also, it was stretched tight like a shirt several sizes too small. In places, it was cracked and peeling or hung off its frame in long bloody ribbons. Its jaw was almost unhinged from its face and its cheeks were gaunt and corpse-like. The eye sockets were dark and sunken in, like they were hollow. It was mostly bald but had patches of long stringy black hair that clung to its scalp in clumps. The smell... Jesus! The stench of rotting meat overpowered him and made Blake nauseous.

Although Blake had been careful not to make a sound, the thing immediately looked up from whatever it was inspecting and stared right at Blake with those dark sunken eyes. It opened its mouth wide, revealing sharp needle-like teeth, and cried out. It was a shrill ear-splitting shriek, impossibly long, high pitched, and piercing. It froze Blake in place as if the terrible wail had somehow managed to physically hold him in its clutches. He was unable to break free.

The ghastly creature shambled towards Blake at an alarming rate of speed, arms outstretched. Those nightmarish claws flexed, ready to seize him in their awful grasp. Snapping out of his fear-induced trance, Blake took off like a shot. He leaped over fallen logs and ducked under low-hanging tree branches. The terrified boy zigged and zagged as he tore through the dense underbrush. Sheer terror drove him to run faster than he could have at a track meet, despite the many obstacles.

It was too dark to see. He was unable to avoid some of the branches and brambles and he paid for it with several scratches on his unprotected face. Heedless of the nasty scrapes, Blake sprinted blindly into the night, desperate to escape the horror that pursued him. In his blind panic, he didn't see the arroyo. Head over heels, he tumbled down the steep bank of the dry gulch. There was an audible crunch as his ankle snapped. Blake cried out in pain.

The boy's cry was answered by the terrible piercing shriek of the creature. Without thinking, Blake tried to run but collapsed in agony when he put weight on his injured ankle. In a panic, he scanned for the baseball bat, but he'd lost both it and the flashlight in the fall. The long, awful wail of the creature sounded once more, only this time much closer. Suddenly, the creature, with its ghostly pale skin and patches of stringy black hair, peeked its head over the bank. Its lips curled back in an evil predatory smile, revealing long sharp needle-like teeth. Gazing down at the helpless boy with those eerie sunken eyes, it let out another dreadful high-pitched wail.

Blake scrambled away on his hands and knees as fast as he could to the opposite side of the arroyo. He tried to climb up the steep bank, but the soft dirt gave him no purchase. For every two feet he clawed up, he slid a foot and a half back down. The nauseating smell of rotting flesh wafted over him and the ghastly shriek of the creature sounded once more, much louder. It was dangerously close. Sobbing hysterically, Blake redoubled his efforts and desperately clawed his way up the steep bank of the arroyo. He reached the top in elation and used a nearby tree branch to help pull him to more solid ground. Suddenly, a ghoulish white hand clamped down around his injured ankle and dragged him screaming back down into the arroyo.

"Mommy!!" Blake screamed in terror. The young boy's cries for help were drowned out by another terrible screech from the creature.

Chapter 2

Pinball & Pugilism

I sat in a dark corner of the smoke-filled bar. It kept me shrouded in shadow yet afforded an unobstructed view of the entire place. Not that there was very much to it. The place was a dive; dirty and run down. The few patrons seemed to mostly fit into two categories: rowdy bikers and disgruntled dock workers. There were a couple of down on your luck types who seemed to be doing their hardest to drown their sorrows in whiskey sprinkled in for good measure. It seemed nobody with any class frequented this establishment. Then *he* walked into the bar.

Alex Fowler. Alex was an unassuming looking fellow of average height and build in his late twenties. He looked a good ten years older because his closely cropped hair was mostly grey. Alex had recently been in an accident. A car hit him as he was crossing the street, but he seemed none the worse for wear. In fact, he was walking around; amiably greeting some of the dockworkers, shaking hands robustly, and dolling out high fives.

I put my camera to my eye and started snapping pictures. Why was this of any interest to me, you might ask? Good question. You see, Alex claimed severe injury and was unable to work because he was in a great deal of pain. These certainly didn't seem to be the actions of a man afflicted with a debilitating injury. Either Alex made a miraculous recovery, or he was an ambulance chaser.

Alex worked as an EMT and knew just the right people who would exaggerate the extent of his injuries for a cut of the insurance money. Not a bad little scam, except Alex had pulled it off too many times now. Perhaps he'd been too stingy with his cut to his accomplices. In any case, my client, the insurance company, caught wind of it. They didn't take kindly to the shenanigans and hired me to see if I could catch him in his lie. You see, I'm a private eye. Gideon Jones is my name, proud owner and operator of the White Knight Detective agency. This wasn't my favorite type of case, but hey, a man's got to pay the bills.

Alex moved. In doing so, he forced me to change positions to keep snapping pictures. This was damning evidence and I had to capture it. Unfortunately, I got too focused on getting the shot and forgot about discretion. One of the bikers noticed my clandestine photoshoot and stomped over.

"Hey! Just what do you think you're doing?!"

All eyes were suddenly on me.

"Oh, nothing. Just doing a project for my photography class," I said. "It's going to be a montage of modern-day badasses. Who's tougher than bikers?"

I was hoping the compliment would get me off the hook, but no such luck. Easy Rider was still in my face.

"Well, who said you could? You need to ask permission before you do something like that. We like our privacy."

Alex bolted for the exit. No matter. I had enough shots. "Sorry, my mistake! It won't happen again," I said, making for the exit.

"Not so fast," Easy Rider said, blocking my path. "Hand over the camera."

I am not a small man, standing six-foot-one. I'm also a regular at the gym. But I was eclipsed by Easy Rider. He was a *very* big boy, standing about six-foot-three, maybe six-foot-four inches tall. If I had to venture a guess, he weighed in at over two hundred and fifty pounds. He looked like your quintessential biker. Long hair past his shoulders, kept out of his eyes with a bandana, and he sported a big bushy beard. His sleeveless denim vest was adorned with all sorts of motorcycle club patches. His bare arms were heavily muscled and had the requisite skull tattoos. A thick leather belt, complete with a big Harley Davidson belt buckle, kept up his faded blue jeans. He had big black biker boots, and even a chain going to his wallet.

Easy Rider certainly looked the part of a big, bad biker. None of this impressed *me* very much but I could tell by the way he carried himself that Easy Rider was sure he looked intimidating as hell. For now, it was best to play the part of the scared victim.

"No need for that. I'll just get going and give you your privacy. Sorry to have bothered you."

I tried to slink past him, but he grabbed hold of my camera strap with both hands, like your stereotypical bully grabs hold of suit jacket lapels in the movies, and roughly pulled me in close.

"I *said* hand over the camera," he snarled.

It was a move meant to intimidate, but I wasn't in a particularly vulnerable position. We were too close for the biker to throw any effective strikes at me, but I'd had enough. I didn't care for bullies and I needed those pictures to get paid. There was no reason for this guy to act like such an asshole! It was high time someone taught him some manners.

Since Easy Rider had both hands firmly wrapped around my camera strap, there was nothing to stop me from grabbing hold of his testicles. I squeezed hard with my left hand. Simultaneously with my right hand, I stabbed in and pressed down with my index and middle fingers, right into Easy Rider's throat just above the breastbone. It's a non-lethal area but there is a nerve cluster there and it hurts like hell. The biker immediately released his hold on the camera. He crumpled into a heap on the floor at my feet, all the while howling in pain. Although it was satisfying to see the big guy go down, the scream accompanying the fall was too loud. Now I had to deal with all his biker buddies.

I was hoping no one had actually seen anything and only just turned our way when they heard Mr. Tough Guy squealing like a little girl. I acted like a concerned Good Samaritan. "Oh my God, he's hurt! I'll go get help!" I yelled, hoping I looked like a model citizen as I made a beeline for the exit. I'd almost made it to the door when Easy Rider cried out.

"Somebody stop that asshole! He cheap-shotted me in the balls!"

Let the record show, I *hate* bar fights. Being a fourth-degree black belt in both Judo and Karate, I'm better equipped than most to survive that kind of scenario, but I still don't like them. When dealing with multiple attackers, the danger factor ratchets up exponentially. Vulnerability comes from too many angles for my liking. Deciding discretion was the better part of valor, I dropped all pretenses and sprinted for the exit.

Mere inches from the door, I felt a hand grab my shoulder and spin me around. I didn't resist. Instead, I went with it. I brought my arms up and in around my head, cradling it in what looked like a defensive posture to ward off blows. It was, but it was also a sneaky way to deliver an elbow right into my attacker's nose.

I followed up with a quick left-right combo. My assailant lifted his arms to protect his face, so I launched a front snap-kick to his mid-section. He doubled over, so I took advantage of his less aggressive posture to maneuver him between myself and the oncoming bikers. Using him as a meat-shield might give me time to make a getaway. I backed up towards the door.

The tactic only bought me half a second before Easy Rider's friends bum-rushed me en masse. I shoved the meat-shield into a group of three and they went down in a tangle of limbs. There were two who managed to avoid the pileup. They moved in, trying to flank me in a pincer maneuver; one coming in on the left and the other on the right.

I glanced at the one to my left. He was further away, so my focus turned to my closer adversary on the right. I wasn't ignoring Lefty though. Unbeknownst to him, I could keep track of him via a mirror embossed with a Budweiser logo on it.

Righty came in with a wild haymaker, which I easily blocked and countered with a good, stiff jab. The Budweiser mirror let me know Lefty was almost on top of me, so I launched a back-thrust kick that caught him in the gut. It sent him backpedaling off at a surprisingly high rate of speed. He wind-milled his arms about wildly as he tried desperately to catch his balance, only to collide spectacularly into a KISS pinball machine in the corner. The resulting crash elicited a dazzling array of flashing lights, raucous bells buzzers, and other assorted electronic sound effects. Lefty appeared to be down for the count, but maybe he set a new high score.

Righty was still very much in the fight, although he must have been feeling quite scrappy. He came at me with another big looping right cross. Taking advantage of his all-out committed attack, I kept my hands up in a traditional boxer's defensive position; elbows pointing down, forearms facing out to protect myself. Simultaneously, I stepped inside the punch's trajectory. This put me in much closer quarters to grab hold of his punching arm and turn into him. Using all the attacker's momentum, I leveraged it into a judo shoulder throw called Seoi Nage.

Unless you've trained specifically in how to fall in such a way you protect yourself, the ground will hit you a heck of a lot harder than anyone else can. Seoi Nage is one of judo's more dynamic throws. Slammed into the ground so hard his mom felt it, it was game over for Righty.

I quickly turned my attention to the other assailants. Unfortunately, not quick enough. I glanced up in time to see a punch fly towards my face, but not soon enough to do much about it. My hands were in the wrong place to block and I didn't have time to dodge the attack. So, I clenched my jaw shut but relaxed the rest of my body and went with the force of the blow. Admittedly not ideal, but it's actually much better than it sounds.

Clenching my jaw shut kept me from biting my own tongue. Biting one's tongue is not a pleasant experience. Ever heard the phrase, 'rolling with the punches'? It's a real thing and considered to be the pinnacle of technical genius in the striking arts. The idea of rolling with punches is to move your head in the same direction as the force of a blow as you receive it, thereby taking off much of the force. That can be the difference between getting knocked out or staying in the fight.

The punch staggered me, but I was able to stay on my feet. I brought my hands up in a defensive stance again and absorbed my attacker's follow-up strikes on my forearms. To let him know I didn't appreciate that very much, I kicked his shin. It was a sneaky attack. His attention was on hitting and he never saw it coming. I wear steel-toe work boots and I know it had to hurt like hell.

The biker reflexively bent over to protect his injured shin. I leapt forward with a flying knee that caught him full in the face. All of a sudden, pain exploded in my head. Someone cheap-shotted me, probably with a beer bottle. They don't break as easily as they do in the movies. Getting clubbed with one can be devastating.

I saw stars, momentarily stunned and unable to defend myself. Another blow from a different direction hit home. I stumbled and went down. Before I could get to my feet someone savagely kicked me in the ribs. I tried to scramble away on hands and knees, but a massive blow slammed down right in between my shoulder blades. Someone hit me with a chair! Again, *much* sturdier in real life than Hollywood makes them out to be on the big screen.

Things were getting very ugly very quickly. Then, the thunderous and distinctive boom of a firearm in close quarters went off. Christ almighty! This was the end!

Chapter 3

State of Denial

I heard the unmistakable sound of someone racking a shotgun. Then, in a great booming voice, a warning was issued: "Back off right now! If one of ya so much as twitches, I'll blow ya ta hell!"

I recognized that thick Irish accent immediately. It was Father Dominic!

Father Dominic is not your typical Catholic priest. Before he was a man of the cloth, he was a member of the Irish Republican Army. Those days are behind him now. Even so, he isn't someone you want to mess with. He's a member of the Order of Saint George; a secret sect of the Catholic church tasked with protecting the flock from witches, demons, and all sorts of evil things that go bump in the night. The Order takes its job very seriously. They bump back!

Last year I took a case to find an ancient artifact called the Horn of Ryujin. Turned out, the Horn had supernatural powers. A dark wizard along with a clan of ninja assassins was searching for it as well. Father Dominic played a crucial part in ensuring the Horn didn't fall into their hands. Also, the man had impeccable taste in beer! Every now and then we get together to enjoy a few pints. Of course, the good Padre was bluffing here. He wouldn't take a human life. Without his Roman collar, the bikers had no idea he was a priest. They just saw a crazy Irishman pointing a 12-gauge pump-action shotgun at them.

"Can ya walk?"

Unbeknownst to Father Dom, he just quoted a line from *Highlander.* I saw it at the theater the day before. I replied in my best Scottish brogue, "I'll bloody well walk out of here!"

"There's no need for such language, boyo! And why are ya talking in that ridiculous Scottish accent?"

I feel my sense of humor goes unappreciated for the most part. "It's from the new movie that just came out. *Highlander.* With all the sword fights, you know? 'There can be only one'!"

"Only one what?"

"Never mind. Let's make like a baby and head on out."

"You Yanks are a strange lot."

I ignored the comment and stumbled out the door. Father Dominic brought up the rear, covering our escape with his shotgun.

"If any of ya try following us, you'll get a face full of buckshot!" Father Dominic warned. He froze the bikers in place with the gritty steel in his voice.

Once we were in the parking lot, I noticed a row of Harley Davidson motorcycles, all neatly aligned like soldiers standing in formation. I got a running start and slammed a side-thrust kick into the first bike. It fell over into the next, starting a chain reaction that sent them all tumbling down like dominos. It was my little way of letting the bikers know that twelve on one is a far cry from a fair fight. It was a pretty chicken shit thing to do and I didn't appreciate it very much. I wasted a second gloating. Sense of moral outrage sated, I took off after Father Dominic.

We drove over to Father Dom's apartment out in Tenderloin. It's a real rough neighborhood. Definitely not the place you'd expect to find a priest. But as the good Padre says, some of his duties are best conducted a safe distance away from the parish at Saint Mary's. Unlike his neighbors, Father Dominic's little one-bedroom apartment has bars on the windows and a reinforced steel front door. That wasn't the only thing that set it apart.

Once inside, it was obvious Father Dom had a unique sense of style. His little place was an odd combination of Catholicism and firearms. The furniture was minimal and a bit on the old side, but comfortable. There was a small couch and a recliner in the living room, but no TV. Crucifixes hung over the doorway and window. Bookshelves or gun racks filled every other available inch of wall space.

The contents of the shelves were an incongruous mixture of religious writings and military manuals, with the occasional box of ammunition or small figurine of some saint thrown in for good measure. It must have all seemed very strange to someone visiting for the first time, to say the least. To the uninitiated, Father Dominic probably seemed like some sort of over-armed religious nut bag fanatic, but I knew better.

The world goes to great lengths pretending they don't exist, but they do. Monsters. Everyone thinks there's no such thing as monsters, right? Hell, I believed that until I ran into one myself. You see, nowadays people dismiss them outright. That wasn't always the case. Before the modern age of electricity, automobiles, and jetliners; mankind wasn't so arrogant. In fact, if you go back before the invention of firearms it was a *given* that monsters existed!

Not a coincidence. I think monsters just learned to be more cautious once mankind was better armed. Once enough people unite behind a common goal, we become a force to be reckoned with. Add modern weaponry into the equation and mankind becomes a lot less like prey and a lot more like a dangerous adversary. So, the monsters started being much sneakier. In fact, they got *so* good at being sneaky they eventually became mere myth and legend. Whether folks acknowledge it or not, there's an entire world that exists alongside the everyday normal life of mankind. It's one that, collectively, people try really hard to ignore. Deep down, on a subconscious or instinctual level, we know it. There's a reason humans are afraid of the dark.

Mankind's strength has been in its numbers and, more recently, in technology. A sense of community and intellect make people strong, but physically we are nowhere near the top of the food chain. There *are* things that go bump in the night. There *are* supernatural predators out there. Before dismissing this as a wild claim, check the facts I have to back it up. Hundreds of thousands of people are reported missing each year. The FBI has the exact numbers. Now, if you take into consideration the population of the United States, the percentage of people who go missing is almost the exact same loss ratio experienced by herd animals on the African Savannah to large predators. No one likes to make that connection but it's true.

Mind blown? The obvious question is why hasn't anybody said anything? If you think about it, in a way they do. Sort of.

Almost every family has a ghost story. Unnatural things happen all the time. Most people have experienced something impossible to explain. They'll share the experience over a few beers among close friends, behind closed doors, but no one talks about it openly. If they don't have irrefutable proof, the best-case scenario is getting laughed at. Maybe they'll get weird looks or be shunned. Worst case scenario, they get a jacket with the extra-long sleeves and locked up in a loony bin.

The sad fact is most people don't want to accept a reality that frightening. People are more than capable of ignoring facts if the conclusions they point to make them too uncomfortable or afraid. Time and time again, history has demonstrated exactly how far people will go to ignore something if they want to. People believed the world was flat. The Earth was the center of the universe. No one believed germs existed. People laugh and scoff at Bigfoot sightings but eyewitness accounts of mountain gorillas in Africa were treated the same way until someone produced a dead body to be examined. It's sad but true. The human race is in denial and the monsters take advantage of that fact.

Luckily, not everyone has their heads buried in the sand. There are those of us who have accepted the fact that magic *does* exist and monsters *are* real. We deal with the supernatural bad guys. We fight the good fight. It's a war fought behind the scenes, in secret, but the struggle is very real. Father Dominic and the Order of Saint George are among those on the front lines. Father Dom is one of my favorite people in the world. He's a mentor and a friend, and I love hanging out with him. But the fact he came looking for me instead of leaving a message at my office was not a good sign. If Father Dominic was actively seeking me out, it meant innocent lives were at stake.

"Father Dom, thank you kindly for saving my bacon back there."

"My pleasure, boyo."

"I'm assuming you didn't show up looking for a drink."

"Good heavens no! That sorry dive can't hold a candle to the Mighty Mug!"

The Mighty Mug is our favorite watering hole. It's an old-school tavern with a wonderful selection of fine brews and spirits. Not just American lagers but pilsners, ales, ambers, porters, stouts, bocks, and double bocks. Not to mention a fine selection of whiskey, bourbon, and single malt scotch! And the food! Good God almighty, but their steak sandwiches were worth dying for!

"Work-related then?"

"Aye. I'm afraid it is."

Father Dominic handed me a cold beer from the fridge. I gladly accepted. He was old school and believed one should try to soften the blow of bad news with good brew; a real class act and my kind of guy.

"Let's have the details, then."

"There's been a string of abductions. Children have been taken.   The   Order   has   reason   to   believe   there   is   occult involvement."

Father Dominic handed me a manila envelope. Inside was a one-way ticket to Albuquerque, New Mexico, twelve hundred dollars in cash (double the amount of my usual retainer), and a photo of a swarthy individual wearing a Roman collar.

"Who's the priest?"

"That's Father Lopez. He'll be your support element this time. I'm afraid I won't be able to come with ya on this one, boyo. I'm needed elsewhere. The Order has me on a different mission, but you still have help. Father Lopez was the one who made the Order of Saint George aware that these missing children cases were not typical and that there could be occult involvement. He has a better grasp on the situation than anyone. He'll be your point of contact, and guide as it were, once you are in New Mexico. He'll be waiting for you tomorrow at the San Miguel Chapel in Santa Fe. Father Lopez is a Franciscan. He's not in the Order of Saint George, but he's a friend and has aided us before. If you turn the picture over, you'll find a pre-determined greeting and specific answer we use as a kind of challenge and password. If someone overhears, it will sound like the two of you are discussing scripture. Also, show him this." Father Dominic handed me a Catholic devotional medal of Saint Michael on a silver chain. "When you do, he will show you a similar medal. We use it as a verification of credentials. Are you ok, boyo? I'm sorry. If it were up to me, I'd tag along."

If I'm not careful, I can be easy to read. Father Dom picked up on the fact I was seeing red, but it wasn't because he wasn't coming with. You see, I'm old school. I cling to some ideas that are no longer in vogue in this modern world of 1986; things like manners, fair play, and honor. In my book might doesn't make right. You shouldn't step all over the little guy to get ahead just because you can. Chivalry was not dead; badly wounded maybe, but not dead. It's why I named my business the White Knight Detective Agency. I live my life by an ancient code and adhere to some archaic rules. Chief among them, you never **EVER** messed with women or children. Supernatural or not, I was going to make whoever, or whatever was kidnapping children pay and pay *dearly*.

"Oh, I'm ok Father Dom, but very soon someone in New Mexico won't be."

Chapter 4

Hellfire

Chumana descended the crude wood ladder down through the hatchway at the top of the Kiva into the darkness below. She was thin but not frail. Wiry would be a better description. She moved with the strength and natural dexterity of a wild thing, yet she was past her prime. Her long black hair was beginning to show streaks of grey. Crow's feet etched the edges of her eyes and frown lines wore at the corners of her mouth. She was deeply tanned and had the slightly weathered look of one who spends their days exposed to the harsh elements. Chumana had high cheekbones and her features were sharp and angular, giving her a severe look. The dominant feature of her face was her eyes; large piercing eyes that were black as coal and burned with malice and hate.

Most Kivas were sacred places, built underground out of adobe bricks, and used for spiritual ceremonies by the Pueblo Indians of New Mexico. This chamber was more akin to a dank pit. It was an atrocity. There was nothing deserving of veneration in this place. Chumana had twisted it through her dark and morbid rites. Smoky oil lamps provided dim light. Shadows, taking the shape of malevolent spirits that crawled and slithered, danced on the walls.

The pahos, or prayer sticks, normally brightly colored and adorned in feathers and buckskin to make petitions to the spirit world were charred black, entangled in human hair, and stained with blood. Kachina dolls, figures carved from cottonwood root and adorned in ceremonial robes and feathers, vividly painted according to what benevolent spirit they were a messenger of, were all missing. Instead, horrid, misshapen, and deformed figurines, all painted black. These were Nadir, fetishes of the underworld.

Once off the ladder, she made her way to the fire pit in the center of the chamber. Chumana knelt, opened a large leather sack, and took several handfuls of dried pine needles and tumbleweed for tinder. She carefully placed them into the center of the pit. Then, she struck a match to set them ablaze, all the while mumbling the beginnings of her spell. She added some of the hair she took from the children and scraps of cloth she tore from their clothes to the minuscule fire and started chanting her incantations louder, more earnest. Immediately there was a hiss, accompanied by an acrid smell. This seemed to please Chumana. She grabbed some thorny brambles piled in a corner of the chamber and added them to the tiny blaze. Slowly, she kept adding more and more wood until the little fire grew into a massive inferno.

Chumana circled the huge bonfire while chanting louder and louder. She whirled and spun erratically about, her arms outstretched. Gradually, her chanting became more like a song and her erratic movements more like a dance. As she continued to skip and prance around the fire, she started to strip, throwing her own clothing into the pyre until she was completely naked. Her figure was without an ounce of excess body fat. As she danced, she moved with a feral sort of grace. Her back arched as she spun and whirled, singing her spell. She continued, on and on, chanting and dancing, until her skin was slick and gleaming with sweat. She moved with gliding steps to a rhythm only she could hear. Her hips writhed and her arms swayed. Chumana tilted her head back as she cantillated her primal song, in a perverse sort of ecstasy building to a crescendo. As she did so, the undulating flames turned from orangish yellow to blood red.

Not only did the witch's bonfire change in color, but the normal popping and crackling sounds a fire makes were replaced with a sort of serpentine hissing. The unnatural fire began to move with a life of its own, not as a normal, flickering, campfire moves, but more like the throbbing contractions of a beating heart. With each new palpitation, the now hideous fire swelled until the flames reached the ceiling of the kiva. Once they could climb no higher, they began to twist in upon themselves, writhing like a giant mass of snakes re-forming into some new, grotesque abomination.

Soon the roiling flames morphed into a vaguely humanoid shape, but stooped, twisted, and deformed. The colossal fiery fiend that loomed over her resembled one of the grotesque Nadir fetishes except formed from molten magma, wreathed in blood-red flame. For a tense moment, it stood eyeing her with apparent disdain and slight regard. Then it spoke; a booming and eerie sound that was an odd mixture of massive boulders grinding upon each other and the hissing of a giant serpent.

"Why do you call upon me woman?" it bellowed.

Chumana immediately cast herself upon the ground at the fiend's feet in supplication. Over the years she learned the dwellers of the Nadir, or underworld, considered themselves superior to mankind. She had taught herself to grovel in a way that was pleasing to them.

"Oh, great one! Your humble servant is in need of your intercession."

The fiend laughed. It was an unsettling sound, completely devoid of mirth and full of contempt. "Ha! You begin to feel the ravages of time once more and wish to shed your skin as the snake does to regain your fading youth. Don't you, little serpent?"

"It is only to better serve you, great one."

"You know my price. The blood of the innocent."

"Cha'kwaina, the one who cries, or La Llorona as the descendants of the Spaniards call her, struggles to break free of my grasp. I cannot hold her much longer, but she is no match for your mighty power, great one."

"What concern is this of mine?"

"Cha'kwaina brings many children. You will bathe in a river of innocent blood."

The vile monstrosity paused for a moment, deciding if the promised recompense would be worth its involvement. Chumana remained frozen in place, prostrate at the fiend's feet, knowing full well her life hung in the balance. It was always a gamble to elicit the aid of demons. They exacted a high price for their support. Experience taught her demons could be placated with the blood of children.

"Very well, little serpent. Fetch me your cauldron."

With evident glee, Chumana leapt up and bounded over to the corner of the kiva where a black cauldron the size of a laundry basket sat. A cloud of flies swarmed the revolting thing as if it were days old roadkill. Protruding from the vile vessel at odd angles were six branches snapped from six different species of tree and a macabre assortment of leg bones from six different species of animal still stained with blood. Charred gore and other awful remnants of old potions encrusted the bottom and sides of the cauldron. At the center was a blackened human skull. Chumana placed the cauldron at the fiend's feet. It bent over the repugnant thing and spat into it. The fiend's spittle hissed like acid and skittered about the cauldron as if alive.

"That should give your potion the added power you seek."

Chumana prostrated herself before the fiend once more. "Thank you great one, thank you!"

"Do not bother me again, little serpent. Unless you bring an offering of innocent blood."

With that, the fiend winked out of existence, leaving only glowing embers where the great bonfire once blazed. Chumana placed the cauldron atop the glowing coals and began tossing in ingredients from her sack. Soon she would bend Cha'kwaina to her will once more. The fiend would have his blood and she would have back her youth. Most important of all, she would be able to continue to exact her revenge.

Chapter 5

The City of Holy Faith

Father Dominic gave me a lift to the airport. I travel light and only had one large duffel bag as a carry-on, so there was no luggage to check. He walked me to the gate. When we arrived, the plane was starting to board, so I turned to say my goodbyes. "Goodbye, Father. Wish me luck."

"I'll do more than just that boyo. I know the airlines don't take kindly to a body bringing firearms onboard, so I took the liberty of sending a courier to New Mexico with a little 'care package' ahead of ya. When ya meet with Father Lopez he'll have some goodies for ya."

Now that was great news. I learned the hard way that conventional small arms didn't have the desired effect on some supernatural baddies. The Order of Saint George knew this as well. They employed only certain types of firearms and used ammunition with added punch. Armor-piercing rounds with extra gunpowder to be more precise. Hearing I'd be better prepared for any terrible nasties elated me.

"Father Dom, I could kiss you!"

"Calm yourself boyo! What is it you Yanks say? Take a chill pill?"

I laughed a hearty belly laugh and gave the good Father a manly embrace with much back-slapping. "Seriously Father Dom, thanks a million."

"You're welcome boyo. Now let me give you a blessing before ya go."

I quickly got down on my knees to receive the good Father's benediction, heedless of the strange looks we were getting. I wasn't exactly the goodie two shoes, church-going type, but I had seen firsthand the real power in the Catholic rites. Faith was a weapon to be used in the struggle against dark forces. As I knelt, Father Dominic placed his hand gently upon my bowed head and recited his special prayer. I silently repeated his words, adding my own faith to his and hopefully invoking God's favor upon me and my task.

"O' heavenly Father, we ask that your blessings and protection be upon your servant as he contends with the forces of darkness. Heavenly Father, shine your countenance upon him as he dons your spiritual armor. Watch over him as he girds himself with the truth. Protect him, O' Lord, with the breastplate of justice. Help him to always firmly grip the shield of faith, with which he will be able to ward off and extinguish the burning arrows of the evil one. Be with him as he wears the helmet of the salvation of Jesus Christ and wields the sword of the Holy Spirit which is the Word of God. Holy Father, in the name of our Lord Jesus, help us to drive away forever all darkness and evil that seeks to prey upon your faithful servants. Lord Jesus, our beloved savior, bathe us in the light of your protective presence. Increase in us our faith and trust in your almighty power. In nominee Patris et Filli et Spiritus Sancti Amen."

"Amen," I echoed, making the sign of the cross. Feeling better prepared, I boarded the plane.

The flight was without incident. When the plane landed at Albuquerque International Airport, I picked up a rental car. The beige 1984 Buick Skylark sedan wasn't exactly top of the line but nice, with the sheen of a fresh wash and wax. Armed with a road map and some tourist brochures, I left the small city of Albuquerque, headed north on Interstate 25 towards Santa Fe, and my meeting with Father Lopez. There wasn't much in the way of scenery on the drive up. The terrain was comprised of drab brown rolling hills that looked like they hadn't seen rain this decade. The vegetation was sparse and made up of mostly dried grass and weeds, nearly bleached white by the sun, with the occasional prickly pear cactus sprinkled in here and there for good measure. After an hour or so, as I made my way further north, the landscape became dotted with little pinyon pine trees. Not quite dense enough to call a forest. As trees go, they weren't very tall, reaching eight, maybe nine feet in height. In my opinion, not very impressive for a tree.

At this point, there was a steady incline, steep enough to hear the engine of the rental car growl in protest as I pressed down harder on the gas pedal. I was unwilling to slow progress as the Buick climbed along the stretch of road. As I gained elevation, the trees became much more abundant, but still not very tall. If I had to venture a guess, they were rarely exceeding ten feet in height, becoming a sort of pigmy forest.

Still, the rich green was a pleasant change of pace from the dull brown landscape further south. Even the sky was an unusually bright blue, striking and vibrant. I wasn't sure if it was because there were fewer people and therefore less pollution, but the New Mexico sky was much more impressive than I was used to. The sky back home in San Francisco just couldn't compete. It seemed so drab and vapid in comparison.

As I crested the ridge, I could see the city of Santa Fe sprawled out in the valley below. As I descended into the valley and drove further along into the city proper, I wasn't wholly convinced it qualified as a city. Not by California standards anyway. It seemed more of a big town, really. There was a presence that drew you in. The tourist brochures called it 'The City Different'. I could see why. It was like stepping back in time. There was no skyline; not a single building above two stories. Almost without exception, they were in the old Pueblo Indian style of architecture, painted in earthy shades with flat roofs and stucco exteriors with rough-hewn circular wooden beams or timbers called vigas. The beams seemed to be rafters protruding through the exterior walls of the buildings for purely ornamental or aesthetic purposes.

I met Father Lopez at one such building, San Miguel Chapel. The old church seemed to be the quintessential representation of 'El Ciudad de Santa Fe', the city of holy faith. The venerable church was of humble adobe brick construction and brown stucco exterior. Atop the bell tower was a striking white wooden cross. Nothing grandiose or resplendent. Nevertheless, the small church seemed to command a certain respect, not only because of its great age but its quiet dignity, worthy of reverence. It seemed imbued with the residual effects of centuries of prayer and it now radiated a kind of aura. I couldn't quite put my finger on it, but I liked it. Somehow, there seemed to be more than meets the eye to the place. One of the tourist brochures told me that in Santa Fe the chapel is simply referred to as 'the oldest church'. Accurate, as it is the oldest church in the continental United States. Franciscan friars constructed the adobe church in 1610. Later, in 1848, an elaborate three-tier bell tower was added, followed by the installation of the seven hundred- and ninety-eight-pound San Jose Bell. According to the brochure, in 1872 Santa Fe was struck by an unusually strong storm that brought down the bell tower and the San Jose Bell along with it. The tower was repaired but the Bell is now on display inside the chapel.

I entered through the big wooden double doors in front. Once inside, I was again struck by the beauty of the place and the sense that I'd stepped back in time. I was raised Catholic, so I was used to churches and conducting myself with the requisite decorum such establishments were due. Even if I were a heathen who had never set foot in a church before, I was sure I would've felt the need to show respect. There was a simple and humble, yet elegant beauty to the place. The walls were whitewashed and adorned with wooden carvings of the stations of the cross. The stations of the cross, or 'way of the cross' as it is sometimes called, are a series of images depicting Jesus on the day of his crucifixion. Normally the stations were pictures, but in this chapel wooden carvings told the story. There are fourteen images arranged in numbered order. The faithful travel along and stop at each station, saying specific prayers and reflections. This procession is usually done during Lent on Good Friday.

There were two rows of wooden pews with an aisle down the center that led to a massive altar, which looked ancient. The altar was also made of wood. Ornately carved, it depicted several saints. The chapel was empty except for one man seated in the first pew, facing the altar in quiet reverence. I assumed it was Father Lopez but since his back was to me, I couldn't be sure.

Being raised Catholic, I knew the drill. I dipped my fingers into the little cistern at the back of the church by the doors that held holy water. Then, I made the sign of the cross as I proceeded down the aisle towards the front of the church where the man was quietly seated. I took a seat in the pew directly behind his. I broke the silence but kept my voice to a whisper as I said the first part of the covert exchange.

"People often think of Christ as gentle, docile even. But the scriptures say Jesus made a whip out of cords and with it, he drove out the money lenders from the temple."

The man turned to face me. I could see it was Father Lopez from the picture. He smiled and recited his part of the exchange.

"Yes, John chapter 2 verse 15. Did you know Jesus also told his disciples 'if you don't have a sword, sell your cloak and buy one'?"

Father Lopez spoke with a very slight accent. It was different than the one I'd heard in Southern California, but it definitely had a Hispanic flair to it. Kind of like people from Louisiana and Georgia had different accents but you could tell they were both from the South. I made a mental note of it and leaned forward. As I did so, the medal of Saint Michael dangled conspicuously on its silver chain. I continued with my part of the exchange.

"Luke chapter 22 verse 36. Yes, sometimes a weapon is needed to fight the good fight."

Father Lopez nodded his head sagely. Eyeing my medal, he said, "I like your necklace."

"Thank you. It's a medal of Saint Michael, one of the Archangels."

"Yes, and did you know he defeated Satan in single combat?" As Father Lopez asked the question, he opened his folded hands in his lap, revealing a similar medallion.

"He is one of my favorite saints. In fact, I also have his medal."

The exchange was now complete. Smiling, I extended my hand. "Pleased to meet you, Father Lopez."

The Father took my hand in a good, firm grip and shook it vigorously. "Mucho gusto Mr. Jones."

"Please call me Gideon."

"Of course. Pleased to meet you, Gideon."

I glanced around the chapel. "This sure is a beautiful little place."

"Yes, and there is much history here."

"I'm sure, but do you mind filling me in on all the details at a different locale? I skipped breakfast and I'm starving!"

"Of course. I have yet to eat lunch myself. Do you like hamburgers?"

His question caught me off guard. I assumed the priest would want to go somewhere more... New Mexican-y. "Yes, that's a great suggestion. A good burger would do me wonders."

"Excelente! I know just the place."

Chapter 6

Burgers and Brujas

Father Lopez took me to a place called Blake's Lotaburger. Its color scheme was red and white. The mascot resembled a younger, clean-shaven Uncle Sam, decked out in a top hat, blazer, and bow tie. Of course, they were all red, white, and blue. It was very patriotic for a burger joint. Father Lopez walked up to the counter and, without even glancing at the menu posted overhead, recited his order like he'd been doing it all his life. "Lotta Double patty, green chili, and cheese, with a cherry coke please."

I had never heard of anybody asking for green chili on a burger before, but I figured when in Rome… "Make that two and put it on my tab," I said. I took some cash from my wallet and tossed it on the counter.

Father Lopez smiled. "Why thank you, Mr. Jones, I mean Gideon," he said, quickly correcting himself. "I didn't know they liked green chili on their burgers in California." He pronounced California by rolling the R like a native Spanish speaker would.

"Well, they don't actually, but I've always been a bit culinarily adventurous. I like to sample the local cuisine when I travel."

Father Lopez's smile broadened. "Well, you are in for a treat! A Lotta green chili burger is delicious and hearty fare indeed."

In no time at all we were sitting in a corner, munching on our burgers with gusto. Whoever decided to jazz up burgers with green chili was a genius, but it wasn't for the faint of heart. Not only was it flavorful, it was definitely *spicy* stuff! The green chili in New Mexico packed quite a punch! The Anaheim green chilies in California were weak and bland in comparison.

For a while we sat in silence, ravenously tearing into our meal as if we were famished. It would be more accurate to say *I* did. The good Father showed much more restraint and decorum. He ate his meal at a slower pace. When he saw me licking my fingers, Father Lopez paused in his repast. "I notice you have been keeping an eye on the door in-between bites. Are we being watched?"

Father Lopez had his back to the door while I chose the seat that afforded a clear view of whoever walked in. It was an old habit. "Sorry, Father. I guess I can be a bit paranoid."

"No need to apologize. It's a prudent precaution in your line of work, I am sure."

I nodded my head in agreement. "Right you are Padre, right you are. To answer your question, no I don't think we were followed. We don't have the place to ourselves, but the other patrons seem to be absorbed in their own conversations. No one is within earshot as long as we keep our voices down."

"Very well then. I shall begin. The abductions started two weeks ago. All the victims are children between the ages of nine and eleven. They were taken in the dead of night and each of the kidnappings happened near the banks of the Rio Grande."

I took out a little steno pad and started jotting down notes. "What made you think there was occult involvement?"

"At one of the sites, the parents of the child found one of these."

Father Lopez reached down into a large leather satchel he had brought with him. It opened at the top with a split handle design. It looked like a medical bag doctors carried back in the days when they still made house calls. From it, he produced a wad of cloth that looked like a crumpled-up handkerchief. He gingerly unfolded it, taking care not to touch whatever was inside the makeshift wrapping. When he finished, it revealed one of the ugliest little things I'd ever seen. It wasn't much bigger than a deck of cards and it kind of resembled a voodoo doll; if that doll was black, bloated, misshapen, and all covered with muck and crud.

"Well, it sure is ugly, but just what am I looking at here, Padre?"

"It is a Nadir fetish used by the brujas of the Pueblo Indians."

"Brujas?"

"Bruja means 'witch' and New Mexico has a long history of witchcraft. We even had our own version of the Salem Witch trials. In the 1750s, there was a witchcraft outbreak and a rash of demonic possessions at Abiquiu, New Mexico."

"What can you tell me about these witches, Father?"

Father Lopez paused for a moment as if contemplating something. "Ordinarily I would preface this with a brief lecture about keeping an open mind and a warning not to be too quick to dismiss things outright because they sound like silly superstition. Working with the Order of Saint George, you know firsthand that evil does exist, and it can do more than corrupt the hearts of men. It can..." Father Lopez paused for a moment, unsure just how much he could or should reveal.

I decided to help him out. "It can take physical form. When it does, it's the stuff of nightmares. I understand your hesitation, Father. People who haven't witnessed monsters or magic firsthand will write you off as a crackpot if you say the wrong thing in front of them, but there's no need to tiptoe around the topic with me. I've seen dark magic and I've fought demons. I want to be ready for what I'll be facing. Please continue with the unedited version."

Father Lopez nodded his head. "Yes, of course. You should be prepared for what you will be facing. What is there to tell you about brujas? Well for starters, brujas are full of hate; a frightening and powerful hatred that corrupts and consumes their souls. In fact, it is often said they take up the craft for revenge. In the old days, there were even schools women would seek out to learn witchcraft from advanced practitioners. Brujas were feared, for they could curse people. The victims of these curses would suddenly and inexplicably fall ill and die or meet with an untimely and fatal accident. People would even hire brujas as a sort of supernatural assassin. It is whispered in some places that, if you know where to look, you can still find and hire them.

"In addition to their ability to curse people, brujas have many other dangerous spells and deadly divinations at their disposal. They concoct and brew all manner of potions and elixirs. It is also said they possess unnatural strength and speed. They can shapeshift, taking the forms of owls, large vicious dogs, or sometimes wolves. Brujas can even fly, but not on a broomstick or staff as the witches of Europe were said to do. Here in New Mexico for a witch to take flight, they transform themselves into balls of energy or fire. To gain these powers, they make pacts with demons. These pacts usually involve some sort of human sacrifice." Father Lopez gestured towards the grotesque little Nadir fetish. "Where these are found, the sacrifices were usually children."

Upon hearing this, my blood began to boil. In my world, the innocent should be protected, not preyed upon. *Especially* children! Father Lopez must have seen the change in my demeanor.

"I see you are morally outraged. That is good. Anger is not necessarily a bad thing if controlled, focused, and used to fuel our actions for good works. Then it becomes like the righteous rage of angels. This tells me Father Dominic sent the right man." With that, Father Lopez leaned over and opened the large leather bag by his side. "Father Dominic sent this for you."

I leaned over and peered inside. It was a sight for sore eyes! On top of several boxes of ammunition was a Colt 1911 .45 caliber pistol with several spare magazines and glass vials I knew contained holy water. It was a supernatural hunting kit.

"Father Dominic said to tell you the boxes are filled with consecrated thumpers… Whatever that means."

I felt a predatory smile creep across my face as I answered. "It means the bullets have more gunpowder than normal, giving them some added punch. They also have a hardened steel core instead of soft lead, essentially making them armor piercing. Last but not least, they've been blessed and made holy by the Order of Saint George, making them demon killers."

Father Lopez's eyes widened in surprise. "You have... killed demons before Mr. Jones? I mean Gideon."

"Yes, I have, Father. In the spiritual realm, prayer and faith are your best weapons. But if demons ever take *physical* form, they make themselves subject to the laws of physics and can be harmed all the way up to dead. If you have the right tools that is," I said, gesturing to the ammo.

"Speaking of tools, I have more for you in the trunk of my car."

I grabbed the big leather satchel and followed Father Lopez to the parking lot. We walked down a row of cars, stopping at a cream-colored 1977 Mercury Monarch. He popped open the trunk. Inside was a large olive-drab duffle bag. The Father unzipped it with flair, revealing a Marlin 1895 lever-action rifle and boxes of .45/70 cartridges. Although not as concealable as a pistol, the Marlin packed a much bigger wallop. When dealing with supernatural baddies, that was a definite bonus. I felt like a kid at Christmas!

"I take it by the smile on your face this is a welcome addition to your arsenal."

"Don't get me wrong. I don't look forward to slugging it out with demons, but if I have to, this will help even the odds."

"Is there anything else I can do to help?"

I nodded. "A list of the parents of the missing children along with addresses and phone numbers would be nice."

"Of course." Father Lopez handed me a folded piece of paper. "If you need anything else," he handed me a business card, "please don't hesitate to give me a call."

"Thank you, Father Lopez."

The good Padre's expression hardened and there was steel in his voice. "You can thank me by bringing back those children."

I understood where he was coming from and nodded my head knowingly. When I spoke, there was steel in my voice as well. "I will, Father. Rest assured, I'll also make this bruja and her demon buddies pay."

Chapter 7

Visions

Isabella glanced at her alarm clock and winced. It was already 12:20, after midnight and she *still* couldn't fall asleep. She sighed, flung the bedcovers aside, and hopped out of bed. She didn't bother to turn on the lights. Having laid awake for over an hour now, her eyes had long since grown accustomed to the darkness. There was no need to temporarily blind herself by switching them on now. Besides, she could see surprisingly well at night and found the doorknob to her bedroom with no difficulty whatsoever.

She padded silently down the hardwood floor in the hallway, clad only in a pair of tube socks and an oversized t-shirt, on her way to the kitchen. What she needed was surely there. Most nights, she just couldn't seem to quiet her overactive mind. She would toss and turn, getting very little sleep. Since she'd started having the nightmares, however, it was much harder now to even *fall* asleep let alone *stay* asleep for any length of time. They seemed so real and they were so disturbing. Truly, she dreaded falling asleep, but she had to go to work in the morning. It wouldn't do for her to stumble around only half awake like some sort of zombie. She would just have to make herself something to remedy that. It was part of her craft, after all, being a curandera.

There was even less light in this part of the house, nowhere near any windows. Isabella could tell she was standing on Saltillo tile now instead of wood flooring, even with socks on, so she made a right turn into the kitchen. She ignored the light switch. Moonlight shone through the window above the sink, illuminating this room much better than the pitch-black hallway. Isabella strode confidently across the room, her long black hair shimmering in the moonlight, cascading all the way down to her derriere. Her bearing was more befitting a regal queen, resplendent in an elegant gown, than a humble curandera clad in tube socks and a t-shirt. She stopped short of marching into the cabinets and opened a drawer by the stove where she found the box of matches.

Isabella took the matches to the kitchen table where she kept the oil lamp; preferring its gentle glow, which could be turned up or down slowly by adjusting the length of the wick, as opposed to the harsh glare of electric lights. Once the lamp was lit, she went to the pantry to get what was needed for her cure. After gathering supplies, she steeped some chamomile tea as a base for her brew. Slowly, she added more ingredients: sage, extra dried chamomile, bee balm, mint, rosemary, lady's slipper, California poppy, and yarrow. Isabella then went to a different cupboard where she kept her essential oils and grabbed a vial of lavender oil. She applied it to her upper lip, temples, and forehead, massaging it in slowly. The old natural remedies were a dying art. Her grandmother, a curandera herself, taught her to use them to great effect. Now, Isabella carried on the tradition.

Before long, she was sipping her anti-insomnia tonic from a large coffee mug at the kitchen table. Isabella clutched a rosary normally kept on a set of hooks mounted to the wall where she kept her keys. The necklace had a series of beads and a crucifix. Making the sign of the cross, she kissed the crucifix and recited the Lord's Prayer. Moving on to the first set of ten beads, she recited a

Hail Mary prayer for each bead and finished the set of ten with a Glory Be prayer. The prayers helped calm her restless mind. Soon her concoction took effect. Isabella found herself yawning, her eyelids suddenly very heavy. Her mind calm and her spirit centered, she returned the rosary to its hook, turned off the lamp, and went back to the bedroom where she climbed into bed and promptly fell fast asleep.

It was the same as before. Isabella found herself in a dark place that stunk of human feces and urine. There was a group of children huddled in the corner and a huge, vicious dog chained to a stake driven into the ground some fifteen feet away. The massive canine looked like a pit bull-rottweiler mix. It was very agitated, barking and growling, ferociously straining to free itself and maul the frightened kids. The poor youths were terror-stricken. This time, there was a new child, a young boy. He was clutching his ankle and crying.

"Please! It hurts! It hurts really bad! I think it's broken. I won't tell anyone, just let me go. It hurts, I want my mommy! PLEASE!"

Isabella wanted to rush over to the boy, take him in her arms, and comfort him. Unfortunately, in the dream, she was rooted in place, unable to move. She could only watch the poor child suffer. To Isabella, it was torture being powerless to help in any way while innocent children were in pain and misery. She tried to turn away and spare herself any further anguish from witnessing the awful plight of the poor little ones but was unable to even do that.

This time, something happened that was different from the previous nightmares. She heard a man's voice. His words were slightly slurred. Was this guy drunk? More importantly, he sounded vaguely familiar to Isabella. She couldn't quite remember who it was, and she could only see shadows and silhouettes from where she was frozen.

"Callate cabrón! That little shit is going to get us caught!" The man's voice had a thick, unmistakable Hispanic accent; a Norteño to be more precise.

A woman answered him, but her accent was different. Isabella wasn't certain, but thought the woman sounded like one of the Pueblo Indians.

"Let them cry. We are miles from the town. No one will hear them. Iss cheetz ay yah melika wattsida."

Isabella didn't know those last words, but the cadence of the language was distinct, confirming Isabella's suspicions that the woman was Pueblo Indian.

"Listen, I don't even know why you had me come all the way out here! I told you I didn't want to know what you were going to do with those kids. I don't want to get mixed up in this shit!"

"Oh, but you need the money. Times are hard, que no?"

"Yeah, well not as hard as they would be in jail!"

The woman's tone changed, and it made Isabella's blood run cold.

"Believe me, melika wattsida, there are worse things that could happen to you than being locked in a cage. *Much* worse."

Apparently, the woman's tone had the same effect on the man as it did Isabella. When he spoke again, all traces of belligerence were gone. "Listen, I don't want to cause no trouble. Just give me the rest of the money and I'll get out of your hair."

"Not just yet, melika. I still need one more child."

"What!?! One more! Are you crazy!?! The cops are already looking over my shoulder and word is some gringo private eye is snooping around now too, down in Santa Fe. I can't risk it!"

"I'll quadruple your price."

"I don't know… Quadruple?"

"Think about it. That's enough money to disappear into a bottle for the rest of your life, if you want, melika."

"Why do you keep calling me 'melika'? What the hell does that mean? You're not calling me asshole or something in Pueblo, are you?"

"Don't worry melika, I mean Bruce."

BRUCE! That's who it is, Isabella thought to herself.

"Someone's here!" the woman shouted.

"What!?! I told you to shut those brats up!"

"No! Not this plane, but in the spirit realm!"

"Spirit realm? What are you talking about, loca?"

The woman ignored Bruce and emerged from the shadows, marching straight towards Isabella. This was new. In the previous nightmares, Isabella was invisible. As she emerged from the shadows into the dim light, Isabella could tell the woman was definitely Pueblo; dark-skinned with long black hair streaked with bits of grey. Like the dog, the woman seemed furious. Almost rabid.

"Who are you!? What are you doing here!?"

Isabella tried to run but she was still rooted in place.

"Answer me!" The woman leapt towards Isabella like a mountain lion pouncing upon unsuspecting prey and slapped her savagely across the face.

Isabella sat up in bed, drenched in a cold sweat. That was no mere nightmare! It was just too *real*. Her face was actually stinging where she got slapped! Isabella gingerly touched her face and instantly regretted it, wincing in pain. That couldn't be! She jumped out of bed and rushed to the bathroom. She turned on the light and stared into the mirror. It took a bit for her eyes to adjust to the light but there was no denying it. Plain as day, there was a big angry red mark in the shape of a hand on her face.

Chapter 8

Mister Creepy

I spent three whole days interviewing the parents of the missing children. It was one of the least desirable aspects of my job. The poor people were a real mess; outraged, traumatized, hysterical, or in such misery and anguish they were essentially in a state of shock. I really hated seeing them go through that sort of pain. I'd rather move a steaming pile of shit with my bare hands or get hit repeatedly in the balls. Most everyone has an Achilles heel, something that hits them extra hard. I'm a tough guy, but I'm no exception. I have a few. Seeing a woman cry, good people being taken advantage of, or a parent grieving over the loss of a child just tears me up inside. If anything the distraught parents said could point me in the direction of the kids, it would be worth it.

The last names on the list were in a town about twenty-six miles north of Santa Fe called Española. It was a small town. That fact made me a bit hopeful. In small towns, people tend to notice things out of the ordinary. Unfortunately, the interview with the parents and their neighbors didn't turn up anything useful. It was after 6:30 pm and getting dark as I scratched the last name off my list. I dejectedly shambled towards my rental car, head hung in defeat. As I opened the car door and prepared to get in, something in the corner of my eye caught my attention. I glanced up and saw a man watching me from the shadows across the street. He gave off a creepy vibe. Once he realized he'd been spotted, he bolted;

literally turned and ran in the opposite direction, sprinting for all he was worth.

I immediately gave chase, not really knowing why other than my gut told me I should. Why was he spying? Right outside the house of one of the missing children no less! Turning around and running once spotted? Very suspect behavior, that. Those were the actions of someone who was up to no good and most likely a scumbag to boot.

This particular scumbag was very fleet of foot. Unfortunately for him, part of my exercise regime was running the hills of San Francisco. We're not talking a brisk jog. I RAN! A nasty encounter with some ninjas last year convinced me to up the intensity of my workouts, especially cardio. Mr. Creepy wasn't going to get away so easily.

Turns out all that physical conditioning paid off. I was slowly but surely closing the distance between us, as if I'd pulled out a fishing rod, hooked him, and was slowly reeling him in. Mr. Creepy seemed to sense this. Just before I could reach out and grab him, the man made a sharp left into someone's yard. I skidded past him, unable to adjust to my evasive maneuver quickly enough.

He scaled a six-foot wall into the backyard of the property like a squirrel on amphetamines. I was up and over it as well, although not quite as quick or nimbly as Mr. Creepy. Incorporating some sort of obstacle course into my workout might be a good idea. As we tore through the backyard, I tripped on something in the dark and stumbled right into some hanging laundry left to dry on a clothesline, momentarily entangled by some bedsheets in the process. A big dog started barking raucously. The back porch light came on and I saw the silhouette of a man who appeared to be holding some sort of rifle. With a thick New Mexico accent, he bellowed.

"Who's there?! You cabrónes better get the hell outta my yard or I'll fuckin' blow you away!"

I heard the unmistakable sound of a shotgun being racked. Mr. Creepy took that as his cue to scale the back wall out of the property, which was taller than the wall in the front yard by at least a foot. The threat of being shot was an excellent motivator and he made it up and over with no difficulty. Good idea. I was in the process of making my exit, with both arms and one leg over the wall. One leg still dangled on the other side when I heard the blast of the shotgun. Luckily, the booming noise wasn't immediately followed by excruciating pain. He missed. I certainly didn't want to give him another chance.

Fueled by a rush of adrenaline, I swung my other leg over and dropped down to the other side of the wall. I tucked chin to chest and rounded my back into a judo forward roll, hopefully minimizing the chances of injuring myself in the fall. It worked. I got to my feet unharmed; scared shitless, but otherwise unscathed. I landed amidst some bushes. This side of the wall was apparently where the little housing development ended. All around me was a tangle of thick brambles and scraggly trees. I wasn't sure which direction Mr. Creepy headed, so I paused a moment and listened. I was rewarded with the sounds of someone hastily and noisily making their way through the brush. I took off like a shot in that direction. Was that a silhouette up ahead? Almost there! Better turn up the speed!

It probably wasn't the smartest thing to run pell-mell like that in the dark, especially in that kind of terrain. The odds of twisting an ankle or worse were fairly high. Mr. Creepy was the closest thing I had to a lead. Losing him was not an option, so I pressed on despite the risk. A low-hanging tree branch scratched my face. After that, I ran by reflex, arms in front of me bent at the elbows, forearms facing out like a boxer's guard. Instead of warding off punches, it was protecting my face from getting all scratched up. Branches and brambles were probably doing a number on my blazer though, damnit!

I couldn't see worth a damn and stumbled. Another judo roll was necessary to avoid a face plant or twisted ankle as I fell over a protruding root. I lost sight of Mr. Creepy again. Slowing my pace to a jog, I took time to look around. There was a full moon out and it gave off a surprising amount of light, but the trees and brush were so thick. It made spotting him nearly impossible. I stopped and listened again.

I didn't hear Mr. Creepy crashing through the underbrush. He couldn't have been beyond earshot, though. With the speed I poured on, the guy couldn't have been too far ahead of me. Maybe he was doing the same thing; keeping quiet and trying to figure out how close I was. If I stayed patient and kept silent long enough, Mr. Creepy would probably think he had lost me and head off again at a slower pace. It would be impossible to escape then. So, I stayed put and didn't make a sound.

Chapter 9

Payback

As I stood silently, waiting for Mr. Creepy to make a sound, the temperature dropped rather suddenly. I could see the fog of my breath as I exhaled. That's when I noticed nothing else was making any noise either. It was more than just Mr. Creepy and me being quiet. The night *itself* was unnaturally still. There were no animal noises, not even insects. The hair on the back of my neck stood up. As far as I knew, Española wasn't far enough north to be in bear or mountain lion territory, but I could *feel* something out there in the night watching like a predator; waiting in ambush, ready to pounce. I'm not a guy who jumps at shadows. As a private eye, I've been in more than my fair share of tight spots and dangerous situations. As a result, I don't scare easy.

Last year, though, I had a run-in with the supernatural; demons to be more precise. That is a whole new level of scary. In fact, the word scary doesn't do it justice. When you're literally running for your life from gruesome, gargantuan monsters with massive claws and huge, razor-sharp teeth because they want to *eat* you, well it's a bloodcurdling and horrifying experience. One that leaves an impression. It awakens something primal deep within you. A part most of mankind has long forgotten, a part that remembers what it's like to be hunted, to be prey. That primal awareness was letting me know I was in danger. Kind of like a sixth sense. The unnatural, eerie silence seemed to validate my dread. It was as if Mother Nature herself was holding her breath, terrified.

I reached inside my blazer and drew the Colt 1911 from my shoulder rig. Taking care not to make any noise, I gingerly moved some low-hanging tree branches aside with my left hand while keeping the pistol at the ready with my right.

The parting branches revealed a shockingly frightful monstrosity. The ghastly creature was easily over seven feet tall and was ungracefully thin, rawboned like it didn't have enough flesh for its frame. What skin it did have seemed to be stretched so tight, it was starting to tear in places, revealing disgusting wounds that oozed a rancid mixture of blood and pus. The thing was so pale, it was cadaverous. It was mostly bald but had patches of long, stringy, black hair that still clung to its scalp in unsightly clumps. Its face was gaunt, and its eye sockets were dark and sunken in. The thing had unnaturally long arms that hung past its knees, with disproportionally large hands and long fingers ending in wicked claws that resembled talons.

As if its hideous appearance wasn't bad enough, it exuded a nauseating odor like rotting meat, so strong I wanted to retch. Although I was careful not to make a sound, as soon as I moved the branches aside, it spun around to face me. Curling back its lips in a bestial snarl, it revealed long, needle-like teeth. Then, the creature stretched out its arms as if to seize me in a bear hug and started shambling forward while emitting a deafening wail, shrill and piercing.

I immediately squeezed off four shots in rapid succession. How many of them hit home I had no idea, but at least one did. The creature clutched its abdomen and its already ear-splitting cry somehow managed to get even louder. The gunshot, however, didn't have the effect I hoped for. Instead of running off, or at least giving some sort of pause and being wary I was armed, the creature seemed incensed that I dared attack her. I knew it was female. My eyes burned as I noticed she had nasty, sagging old lady boobies that somehow managed to make her look even more hideous.

The gruesome hag came running at me with her arms outstretched, talons ready to rend and tear. I stood my ground and fired off another shot. Blood sprayed and pus erupted from her trapezius muscle near her neck, but she didn't even slow down. It was time to change tactics. This time I aimed for... absolutely nothing! I tucked tail and ran like hell! I thought I was pretty darn quick when I ran down Mr. Creepy. Turns out, I run a lot faster scared than mad. Fueled by adrenaline, I tore through bushes and brambles, ducked low hanging branches, and leapt over fallen logs, agile as a deer. The awful, unsettling wail of the hag let me know she was hot on my heels.

One moment I was running blindly for all I was worth and the next I was falling head over heels as I tumbled down the steep bank of a dry gulch. I instinctively tucked into a judo roll, which probably saved me from injuring myself somehow. I laid on my back for a moment, dazed. The horrendous wailing had stopped. All I could hear was my own labored breathing coming in pants and gasps, sounding alarmingly loud in the unnaturally quiet night.

I did my best to stifle panicked panting but apparently, that wasn't good enough. The hideous head of the hag peeked over the rim of the dry gulch with her pallid skin and clumps of stringy black hair. Her lips curled back in a predatory smile, revealing her long, needle-like teeth.

Training religiously with a handgun at the range was a sound practice, considering my line of work. As a result, I was a damn good shot... with stationary targets. My run-in with ninjas last year brought home the fact that hitting a moving target is much, MUCH harder than hitting a stationary paper target. Especially someone actively trying not to get shot! Those ninjas were intentionally changing direction at unpredictable intervals, dive rolling, and somersaulting about.

So, I decided to up my game and joined IPSC, the International Practical Shooting Confederation, a shooting sport association based on the concept of practical shooting. Their competitions require you to shoot on the move and around different obstacles. Kind of like if a shooting range and an obstacle course had a baby. Father Dominic and some of the Order of Saint George worked with me as well, incorporating dive rolls and moving targets into my training regime. Shooting while you're physically exhausted is much different than being nice and relaxed down at the range, so the Order made sure I had practice doing that as well.

As a result of said training, I never relinquished my death grip on my pistol even as I tumbled head over assets down the gulch. Firing from a prone position was also something I'd been practicing. When that hag peeked her ugly head over the rim of the gulch, I was ready for her. "Wipe that smile off your face, bitch!" I said as I squeezed off a well-aimed shot. I was rewarded with a geyser of blood and pus spraying out of where her eyeball had been an instant earlier.

The hag put her hands up to her face, covering the wound, shrieking in pain now instead of anger. I fired off another shot, the loud rapport of the .45 caliber pistol drowning out the wails of the creature. I saw the back of her hand explode as the armor-piercing round tore through it. The penetrating power of those augmented bullets was amazing. It most likely didn't stop there.

Wanting to make sure I put the monster down for good, I squeezed the trigger again. No bang! Out of bullets! I quickly ejected the spent magazine and slammed home a new one. Then I racked the slide back, chambering a round. I practiced that a lot too. The entire procedure probably took less than 2 seconds, but it was long enough for the hag to retreat.

"Not so tough when you're not dealing with little kids, are you?" I yelled. "Come on! What are you waiting for? I'm still here! Come on you ugly bitch, I dare you! I double-dog dare you! COME ON!!!"

But the creature ignored my challenge and disappeared into the night. I picked myself up off the ground and, after a moment, holstered the gun. "Yeah, that's what I thought. Ugly ass bitch."

I climbed out of the gulch and tried to find my way back to the housing development and the rental car.

Chapter 10

That Bastard Bruce

As I trudged along, the euphoria of having doled out a little payback to that creature, probably summoned by the bruja to abduct children, wore off when I realized I'd probably never find Mr. Creepy now. The only lead in this case was lost. It was a long walk back to the housing development. When I finally found my rental car, I was thoroughly dejected. I was so absorbed in my own little world of self-degradation that I didn't realize I was being watched.

"Did you catch Bruce?"

I nearly jumped out of my skin, dropping my car keys as I whirled around. My hand was already inside my blazer, on the hilt of the .45, when I saw a young boy around the age of 11 emerge from the shadows.

"Did you," he asked again.

"Jesus, kid! You can't go sneaking up on people like that. You could get hurt," I said, removing my hand from the pistol.

The boy ignored the admonishment and repeated his question. "Did you catch Bruce?"

I sized the kid up before answering him. He was a normal enough looking kid in blue jeans, sneakers, and a t-shirt. He had a skateboard tucked under his arm and long curly hair that resembled a lion's mane.

"Who's Bruce, kid?"

"The guy you were chasing earlier. Did you catch him?"

Interesting. I answered the question with one of my own. "Why are you so eager to know if I caught the guy? He owe you money or something?"

The kid eyed me up and down. "You're looking for the missing kids, right?"

"Yeah, as a matter of fact, I am. You think this guy Bruce had something to do with it?"

The boy shrugged his shoulders. "Everyone knows Bruce is a lying, cheating, barf bag who'll do anything for money. My older cousin said he overheard him talking to some Indian lady who was asking for the address of little kids. He saw Bruce give her a piece of paper. She gave him an envelope in return."

"Did you or your cousin tell anyone about this?"

"My cousin told the cops. They told him they'd look into it, but Bruce is still roaming the streets."

"This Bruce fella, he have a last name?"

"Ortiz. Bruce Ortiz."

"You know where he lives or where I might find him?"

"I don't know his address, but he hangs out at Red's a lot."

"What is Red's?"

"It's a bar down on the main strip in town. It's not hard to find."

"Thanks, kid. What's your name?"

"David."

I extended my hand. "David, my name is Gideon Jones. I'm a private investigator and I'm going to find those kids. I appreciate your help."

David took my hand and we shook. He had a good, strong grip for a kid.

"Mr. Jones, will you do me a favor?"

"Sure, kid. Call me Gideon."

"Mr. Gideon, my friend Blake is one of the kids who went missing. If Bruce had anything to do with it, kick his ass for me!"

This kid was alright! "David, if I find out Bruce had anything to do with those kidnappings, I'll do more than kick his ass. I'll beat him within an inch of his life."

David smiled a fierce grin for a kid. "I like you, Mr. Gideon."

Chapter 11

Champagne and Cognac

The next day, I went out in search of Bruce's hangout: Red's. It wasn't hard to find. The bar was on the main strip in town, just like the kid said it would be. I waited until after dark and the parking lot started to fill up before going inside. Red's was a dimly lit place. It smelled of old beer that had seeped into the dark red carpet, night after night for years, and become a permanent fixture. There was a long bar that ran the entire length of the room with several tables scattered about. A small dance floor was situated near a corner that had been cleared out for a band. Four men were set up playing a cumbia. Maybe it was salsa. I wasn't quite sure. It was definitely Latin and rhythmic. Whatever it was, I liked it! The singer was a short, olive-skinned man with a decent voice. Another Hispanic was on the drums, there was one on guitar, and a bass player rounded out the band.

It wasn't a classy establishment, but it at least had more of a good-natured, party atmosphere than the biker bar I'd last been in. I ordered a beer at the bar so as not to arouse suspicion and chose a table on the opposite side of the room from where the dance floor was. It was away from any lights and shrouded in shadows. I sat down and took in the scene. It was a Friday night and people were looking to have a good time. The dance floor wasn't crowded, but it wasn't empty either. Ladies seemed to be outnumbered by gents roughly three to one. Clearly, they enjoyed the attention they got. Fascinating stuff, but I was looking for Mr.

Creepy, or Bruce the Barfbag, as my new friend David dubbed him. *Bruce the Barfbag*, I said to myself, chuckling. I liked that kid.

After almost an hour of no Bruce, I went up to the bar to order another Coors. I wasn't particularly fond of Coors but blending in was necessary. If the bartender, or anyone else, noticed I wasn't drinking, I would stand out like a sore thumb. Besides, I was no stranger to having a few drinks now and then. I knew my own tolerance for alcohol. I was in no danger of becoming intoxicated or even slightly buzzed, at the rate of one beer an hour. Red's didn't have the same selection of brews the Mighty Mug boasted. It was Coors, Miller, or Budweiser. Coors seemed to be a local favorite and when in Rome...

The bartender had just handed me a Coors Banquet when *she* walked into the room. She had way too much class for a dive like this, but she walked in anyway. As she did, all eyes were on her and who could blame any of us? The woman was a knockout! She was wearing a black dress that was form-fitting and very flattering but stopped short of being trashy. It was sexy but still had a touch of class. She had on high heels, just high enough to give you ideas, but could still pass as functional. She wore her long, black hair down. It was dark as midnight, yet still caught the light and shimmered as it cascaded past her shoulders all the way down to her behind but stopped just short of covering it up. Thank God, because to cover up a backside like that would be a crime! Accentuated by her narrow waist and supported by long shapely legs, it was a thing of beauty that would have caught and held your attention if not for the fact that this woman was indeed buxom. She had great big full and firm-looking breasts that drew in every man's gaze like metal to a magnet. Yet even they didn't steal the show because this woman had the face of a goddess. She was strikingly beautiful. Fair skin, cool as cream, brought out dark smoldering eyes with lusciously long lashes. Her lips reminded me of a valentine; red, shiny, plump, and inviting.

Maybe I just had magic on my mind with all this witch business, but she wasn't simply good-looking. She was *hauntingly* beautiful. The longer I stared, the more I fell under her spell. For me, that really said something. I'd been burned one too many times to fall for a pretty face, or even a gorgeous face with a killer body, rare as that combo may be. I'd been there, done that, and had the scars to prove it. Her name was Nia Lockhart, Dr. Nia Lockhart, and she was the total package: personality, brains, and beauty. Beauty with a capital B! She was jaw-droppingly, stop a clock beautiful. The kind of beautiful that inspires poets. She possessed the kind of beauty a man would kill or die for. Not to take away from the angel who just walked into Red's. She was definitely the stuff of legend and every bit as beautiful as Nia (no small feat). It was just a different 'flavor' of beautiful. The mysterious woman who just walked in was like an especially magnificent glass of champagne sparkling in the moonlight, where Nia was like a glass of cognac on fire! Both drinks are quite tasty, but vastly different flavors indeed. Dr. Nia Lockhart is not only a gorgeous redhead but also a professor of anthropology at San Francisco State University. She hired me last year on the case involving an ancient artifact, ninja assassins, and demons. We wound up getting involved after I solved the case and found the artifact.

The problem was, she witnessed the ninjas firsthand but never saw the demons. As a result, she thought I was a bit wacko; a lovable wacko, but a couple cards short of a full deck nonetheless. I couldn't even blame her, really. Demons are something most people must see to believe. That case was the beginning of a new chapter in my life. The Order of Saint George started sending work my way, but it was always something with a supernatural element to it. These cases paid well but trying to explain them to Nia only cemented the fact I was off the deep end in her mind. Word somehow got out that if you had a problem or were in the kind of trouble you couldn't turn to the police for without being labeled as crazy, Gideon Jones would take the case.

There's much more work of that variety out there than I would've thought. The added income was nice, but it also meant the beginning of the end for Nia and me. There's no real future with a woman who thinks you're a bit mad. The thing is, I'm not crazy. The fact she would think I was off my rocker instead of entertaining the possibility that maybe, just maybe, I'd seen something she had not, didn't sit well. Just because she hadn't witnessed these things didn't mean they didn't exist, or that they were figments of my imagination, or that I was a nut bag. It just meant she hadn't seen them for herself, nothing more.

When the woman you love won't give you the benefit of the doubt, that hurts. It hurt more than I thought it would. Hope had been rising in me like a great big hallelujah because I had finally found the proverbial "One"! Suddenly, it was shattered and replaced with a gutshot! It's an overwhelming blow that delivers a devastating kind of pain; the kind that leaves a wicked scar and hardens the heart. The pain was so intense, I thought I was done. Not done with women. Don't get me wrong. I wasn't about to switch teams. I've got nothing against gays. Really, I've never understood all the contempt and anger directed towards them. I just don't see how a man can look at another man's hairy ass and find love. That's certainly no reason to *hate* them. I'm more of a live and let live kind of guy. Besides, more gays out there meant less competition! Things were different now though. I wasn't switching teams, but I was out of the game. Once you get your heart broken, you shut down and are none too eager to open up again.

Once bitten twice shy, as they say. I was more than a bit bummed, albeit with good reason. I was no longer one of the happy shiny people with sunny dispositions. Life kicks you in the nuts often enough, you stay guarded. I wasn't quite as depressed as Eeyore from Winnie the Pooh, but I had less spring in my step than before. There just didn't seem to be much to smile about these days. Then suddenly, BAM! One look at the angel who just walked in and I was suddenly as chipper as a squirrel munching on coffee beans! Out of the game? Says who? Put me in coach! Gideon Jones is ready to play!

Apparently, I wasn't the only one champing at the bit to meet this mysterious angel. Almost immediately they swooped in. Guys offered to buy her drinks and asked her to dance. I didn't rush in. Being a private eye, it's more my style to watch quietly and observe. Not that I lacked backbone, but I was sure a looker like her was used to being the center of attention. Rushing in like the rest of those over-eager horn dogs would do me no good. I would need to distinguish myself from the rest of the pack if I wanted a real shot at catching her eye. Patience was a virtue.

I watched as they pestered her when she was at the bar ordering a drink. Not a Coors, I noticed, but a dark liquid in a glass with ice. Probably a rum and Coke. She went to a table and sat down, but they pestered her there as well. I amused myself by watching the patrons of Red's failed attempts to pick this new woman up. They circled like X-wing fighters from Star Wars preparing for their attack run on the Death Star. They would dive bomb in, but the Force was not strong with any of them. Every Luke wannabe was shot down and sent limping away, trailing smoke.

I shook my head in disdain. These schmucks were like school on Sunday. No class! Every guy was eyeing her with lust in their eyes. The women were eyeing her as well, but with something bordering on murderous rage as they were no longer receiving any attention from the men. As I continued to watch it dawned on me. The men were leering at her lasciviously like lecherous wolves eyeing a wounded deer. They were regarding her more as a piece of meat than the sublime angel she obviously was. If I simply approached her in a different manner, say as a *human being,* I would stand out. I decided now was as good a time as any and got up from the table. It was time to show these schmucks how it was done. I took my time, remembering a true Jedi can feel the Force flowing through him. This is Red Five, I'm going in! Another horn dog was giving her some sort of pick-up line while blatantly staring at her tits. She gave him a withering look, like he was a side dish she hadn't ordered. He got the hint and left.

As I walked up, I was careful not to ogle her wares as the guy before me had done. I know full well that classy women don't care for such things, even when it's evident they spent a lot of time and effort preparing their wares for ogling. It's contradictory but the world is full of mysteries. Women are chief among them. The trick is to make eye contact no matter how appealing the boobies may be.

Chapter 12

All Good Things...

As Isabella took another sip of her Jack and Coke, she saw the shadow of yet another guy trying to pick her up fall across her table. Really?! This was a real pain in the ass, but she was determined. After her last nightmare, she was convinced these night terrors weren't dreams at all but a vision showing her those missing children on the news. She knew this had to be some new manifestation of her gift. Her grandmother also had the gift. She had taught her about it and how to use it.

Isabella descended from a long line of curanderas and mediums; healers who also had the ability to communicate with spirits. Her grandmother's gift was the ability to see and speak with those who had passed on. According to grandma, not only the dead but other spirits as well; sometimes angels or even demons. When she was older and had gone blind as a result of diabetes, she would jokingly tell Isabella, "Don't you worry mija. I may be blind, but I can still 'see'," referring to her gift. When Isabella showed signs of the gift as well, her grandmother taught her how to deal with the startling and often frightening ability. She gradually learned how to harness, control, and make use of it. Isabella now had her own yerberia, a store where she sold herbal remedies, did tarot card readings, and sometimes performed seances.

Now she had apparently developed some sort of limited clairvoyance as well. She heard it referred to as 'remote viewing'; the ability to see or acquire information about a distant location without using your physical senses or any other obvious means. Her grandmother never claimed to have *that* ability, but Isabella was more open-minded than most due to her upbringing. Instead of panicking and seeking out psychiatric help, Isabella took it upon herself to look for and rescue the children in her visions.

The last vision had finally given her a clue. Bruce Ortiz. He was a local bad-tempered drunk who was always involved in whatever shady dealings he thought would turn him a quick buck regardless of the legalities. He was known to be decidedly lacking any sort of moral compass. The consensus was that he was not only bad news, but a real no-class asshole too.

After doing a little snooping around, she found out Bruce hung out at Red's. Perhaps she could get him drunk enough to tell her where the missing children were. It was a great plan, but now, every damn cholo and pachuco (the local flavor of low life) in the damn place kept coming over and hitting on her.

"I don't need another drink and I don't want to dance. I'm waiting for somebody," Isabella said, not trying to mask the annoyance in her tone.

"Do you mind if I ask you a few questions until they show up?"

A polite response and not a lewd pick-up line? That was unexpected. Isabella looked up from her drink. The guy was definitely not from around here. He was taller than your average cholito and of lighter complexion. He had two, maybe three days' worth of stubble, but he was able to pull off the look. Combined with his broad shoulders and narrow waist, it made him appear rugged and masculine, not sloppy and ill-kept. He wore a pair of jeans and a sports jacket. Not a bad look, but not something the locals were wearing. What was a guy like this doing at Red's? This wasn't a popular tourist hang-out at all... Well, he was cute and well-mannered. Maybe she would give him a chance.

"What kind of questions?"

"Nothing personal, scouts honor," he said, making the Boy Scout salute. "Is it ok if I sit down?" he asked, gesturing towards the empty chair and smiling good-naturedly.

Again, with good manners and referencing the Boy Scouts no less! Letting him sit would stop the cholitos from bothering her, at least. "Ok, but don't get any ideas."

"I assure you my intentions are honorable, miss. By the way, my name is Gideon, Gideon Jones," he said. He smiled a very charming smile, extended his arm, and presented his hand for a handshake.

Ah, Jones! So he *was* a gringo. But he had nice manners. She took his offered hand and gave it a nice, firm shake.

"Isabella Maestas. Pleased to meet you, Mr. Jones."

"Please call me Gideon."

"Ok, Gideon. What brings you to Red's? You aren't from around here."

He arched an eyebrow at the comment. "Is it that obvious?" he asked.

She shrugged in response. "Don't take this the wrong way. You may think you have on casual attire, but nobody in Española wears a blazer unless they are going to church, a job interview, or a funeral."

He nodded his head, ceding her point. "I thought this wasn't a bad choice for a Friday night out on the town."

"For parts of Albuquerque or Santa Fe, maybe. Here, even with the jeans, you're a bit overdressed."

"Well, it's been a while since I've been accused of being well dressed so I'll take that as a compliment. Speaking of which, aren't you a bit too classy for Red's yourself?"

Isabella smiled a bit at the compliment, despite herself. This guy was good. "A girl should always err on the side of classy."

"I couldn't agree more. If there's one thing this world could use a bit more of, it's classy women." Gideon raised his beer bottle. "To classy. May it never go out of style."

Isabella's smile widened just a bit and she clinked her glass with his bottle. "To classy," she said as they both took a small sip from their drinks. "So, Gideon. Española isn't exactly known for its nightlife. What brings you to Red's?"

I gave her my best Mr. Nice Guy smile and decided to go with the truth, but a vague, edited version. "You got me. It's work-related. I was hoping to run into someone I haven't been able to get a hold of. Apparently, he frequents this establishment. I won't bore you with shop talk. Besides, you seem a bit overdressed for this place as well. If Española isn't known for its nightlife, what brings you to Red's?"

"I was hoping to run into someone too, but it looks like it's not going to happen."

The band started a new song and I started moving to the rhythm despite myself, doing a little chair dancing. Isabella noticed and asked, "You like this song?"

"I'll admit I don't understand the words, but yeah I like it. A good song can speak to you, even if it's in a different language."

Isabella nodded her head in agreement. Hopefully, that was a good sign. Her body language opened up, ever so slightly.

I smiled. This was my chance. "You want to dance?"

Isabella balked a bit at the request. "I don't know…"

"Come on, life is too short to waste good songs. Let's dance!" With that, I stood, took her by the hand, and led her to the dance floor.

Nia loved to dance and insisted we take classes. The two of us had a great time. I guess I missed it more than I realized. Although I'm far from professional, I got pretty damn good. As we stepped onto the dance floor, I channeled my inner Fred Astaire and Gene Kelly and let the music move me.

Isabella was obviously no stranger to the dance floor. She danced nimbly, hips swaying with the music. For a time, it was just the two of us, lost in the dance. It was magical. Nothing else in the world existed; just us moving in time with the music. One of life's rare gifts presented itself and we immersed ourselves in it fully.

But all good things come to an end. As the song finished, I noticed Bruce entering the bar.

Chapter 13

Contested Captive

Unfortunately, the dance floor was a bit more conspicuous than the corner I'd originally been sitting at. Bruce spotted me almost immediately. The suspicious man quickly turned to leave. I rushed after him. Glancing back over my shoulder, I hurriedly said to Isabella, "Sorry, that was the guy I was hoping to run into. I gotta go. Thanks for the dance." I sprinted towards the door, hot on Bruce's heels.

In the parking lot, I saw Bruce in front of a black 1970 Chevy Impala. He was at the door fumbling with his keys. Pouring on the speed, I dove forward, sliding across the hood of the car to catch Bruce in a flying tackle. The two of us tumbled to the ground, but Bruce managed to squirm free and scrambled to his feet. He took off running again.

Isabella rushed out of Red's, emerging just in time to see Gideon tackle Bruce to the ground. *Damn it,* she thought to herself, *work-related, hmm? Bruce probably owes him money. Knowing Bruce, this guy could even be a bounty hunter or something more sinister.* It didn't matter though. Regardless of who he was, she couldn't have this guy catch Bruce. Scum bag or not, Bruce was her only chance at finding the missing children in her visions. Isabella started to run after them but the heels she wore were hardly conducive to catching running fugitives. She quickly slipped out of them and hurriedly dug in her purse, where she kept a pair of leather moccasins for when her feet got tired at work. *That's much better,* she thought. After hastily donning her new footwear, she raced after the pair.

Bruce tore off down an alley behind Red's with the gringo in hot pursuit. In a desperate attempt slow this incessant hunter, he knocked over a trash can, spilling its malodorous contents in the process. The guy easily leapt over the obstacle, not even slowing his pace. A slow learner, Bruce tried the tactic again. This time he knocked over a stack of wood shipping pallets. These too, however, proved to be of little hindrance and the detective hurdled them as well, seemingly effortlessly.

Things looked bad for Bruce as he skidded around the corner. Dead end! He had nowhere to run. The PI turned the corner a split second later. Seeing the same thing, he slowed his pace to a walk but continued to stalk forward ominously. "End of the line, Bruce."

Bruce backpedaled a few paces, both of his arms raised to shoulder height with his palms facing out in the universal back-off sign. "What the hell do you from me?!" he asked in a raised voice, his eyes wide in panic.

"It doesn't matter because you're coming with me," said a strong but distinctly feminine voice.

Both men turned to see Isabella turn the corner with a relaxed stride and the confident demeanor of a teacher who had just interrupted two schoolboys from engaging in fisticuffs.

"*This* is the guy you were waiting for?!" I asked incredulously.

"Listen, you don't understand what's going on here," Isabella said.

She was clearly trying to placate me. I was having none of it. "You're right, so why don't you enlighten me," I said with more than a trace of annoyance in my voice.

Before Isabella could reply, Bruce took advantage of the distraction. He cheap shotted me while my back was turned, punching me just behind and below the ear. He ran, pushing his way past Isabella as he barreled back down the alley. The punch staggered me, but I didn't go down. After mumbling a few insults under my breath (true gentlemen don't curse in front of a lady) I staggered down the alley after him. I quickly turned up the speed until I was sprinting just as hard.

The head start he gained from punching me almost paid off. Almost. Bruce was nearly out of the alley when I channeled the Olympian inside me. Not breaking my stride, I crouched down and snatched up the lid from the spilled over garbage can. I hurled it at him like a skilled discus thrower going for gold. It went sailing through the air and struck Bruce on his ankle, causing him to stumble and fall.

I was on him in an instant. "So, you like to hit guys when their backs are turned, do ya? Well take this!" I slammed Bruce with a mean right cross to the jaw. As I pulled my hand back for another punch there was a resounding CRACK, followed almost instantaneously by a stinging sensation in my wrist. Much to my surprise, I found my arm held fast. I looked back over my shoulder to see Isabella brandishing a black bullwhip. The end of it was tangled around my wrist, preventing me from raining any more blows down on Bruce.

I was completely caught off guard. Where the heck had she been hiding that?! Then it dawned on me. She was using it as a belt earlier. It was black and blended with her outfit perfectly. I had no idea it was actually a concealed weapon and not a mere fashion accessory.

"I'm sorry Gideon, but I can't let you interfere. There's too much at stake."

Annoyed, I grabbed hold of the bullwhip with my free hand. "No, it's YOU who doesn't understand!"

I yanked hard, intending to pull the whip out of her hands. Isabella retained her hold, but I tugged with such force it pulled her off her feet. I didn't intend for that to happen and felt downright horrible. The remorse was fleeting, however. Isabella did not fall into a crumpled heap. Instead, she used the momentum to transition into a forward dive roll and came up at my feet while simultaneously delivering a palm strike under my jaw, knocking me off *my* feet and sending me flying backwards.

Instinctively, I tucked my chin to my chest while rounding my back and slapping the ground with my hands. Absorbing most of the impact, I fell into a textbook judo backwards breakfall. Using the momentum, I transitioned into a backwards roll and came to my feet, none the worse for wear.

I smiled despite myself. This woman gave the term 'knockout' a whole new meaning. "My, my. Aren't we just full of surprises?"

Isabella arched an eyebrow at the remark like Spock from Star Trek, keeping her cool and showing nothing but a calm, relaxed demeanor. On the inside, however, she was alarmed. This guy was no mere brawler. The way he took and recovered from that hit showed martial arts training. He was good, way too good for her to easily dispatch. She didn't have *time* for this! She had to catch Bruce before he got away. As if on cue, Bruce picked himself up off the ground, rubbing his jaw where Gideon punched him, and ran off. With an expert tug, Isabella uncoiled the whip from Gideon's wrist and, whirling around, unleashed it towards Bruce. CRACK! It entangled the fleeing man's ankle. Isabella yanked savagely on the whip and Bruce fell forward, face first.

In an instant, Isabella was looming over Bruce. Her visage was beautiful yet terrible to behold, like a fierce and mighty Valkyrie from Norse mythology. "**YOU** are coming with me!"

From behind her, Gideon said, "I beg to differ."

Isabella glanced behind her. "And *YOU* need to **BACK OFF!**" she shouted, whirling around with a spinning back fist that should have caught Gideon right in the temple. Her quick glance backward was a targeting glance, and her attack was perfectly executed.

I'm no slouch when it comes to physical altercations. It wasn't an easy feat to earn those fourth-degree black belts, you know! After that run-in with ninjas last year, I decided to take my fight game up a notch. For the past eleven months, I've been training with Master Onosai of the Hikari, a warrior monk whose Kung Fu skills eclipsed even Bruce Lee's. I was ready for her attack and blocked the strike with my elbow. I'm sure this resulted in a very unpleasant sensation for Isabella. Capitalizing on the painful distraction, I countered with a judo foot sweep called de ashi barai. The attacker cups his foot much like one would cup their hand to drink water, then sweeps it across at a ninety-degree angle at ground level catching their opponent in the ankle and taking their balance. Think of the attacker's foot as an ice cream scoop and the ball of the victim's ankle like a ball of ice cream. Then imagine the person scooping the ice cream is a deranged hockey player on steroids.

The foot sweep did the trick and Isabella went down, but she tucked her head and went smoothly into a sideways roll and was back on her feet almost instantaneously. Although I could have used several other, much more devastating techniques, Isabella was clearly not happy being on the business end of de ashi barai. She expressed her displeasure by launching a kick aimed at my head.

Instead of backing up to avoid the kick or attempting a block, I moved forward, too close for the kick to have any real effect. At such a close range, instead of kicking me in the head with the ball of her foot as she intended, Isabella kicked my shoulder with her inner thigh. Not a very effective blow. I just had to lift upwards, hyperextending the leg and ruining Isabella's balance, causing her to fall once more. Although Isabella used proper body mechanics to avoid injury in the little tumble, she was now livid.

She came up throwing more kicks in rapid succession, like a boxer would throw combination punches. Not high kicks, but first a low kick aimed at my shins, followed up with a side thrust kick aimed at my groin, and then a spinning back kick aimed at my gut. I was able to avoid all three kicks, but only by the narrowest of margins.

I grinned like the Cheshire Cat and it made Isabella furious. She launched another kick to my crown jewels, but I could tell it was a feint to lower my guard. Isabella fired off a left-right combo to my face. I didn't let my guard down at all. Instead, I stepped toward her, but off the line of attack at a forty-five-degree angle, narrowly avoiding the punches. This put me at close quarters with my attacker. Thanks to Isabella's extended right arm, which she intended to punch my face with, I was now in an excellent position to counter. So, I smoothly transitioned into another judo throw, Osoto Gari.

While my left arm pulled Isabella forward, I simultaneously pushed with my right palm on her shoulder. This push-pull movement caused Isabella's spine to twist further, ruining her balance and setting her up for the piece de resistance of Osoto Gari; a sweeping of the leg, or leg reap, as they referred to it in judo class. I couldn't help but think of a line from a movie that came out two years earlier, *The Karate Kid*. In my head, I could hear one of the members from the Cobra Kai dojo yelling, "Sweep the leg, Johnny!"

I kept hold of Isabella and rode her down to the ground, controlling her descent, greatly lessening the impact of the fall. I was deliberately avoiding the more dangerous techniques in my arsenal. This was a risky venture. Isabella was obviously holding nothing back and was too good not to take seriously. If this continued, someone was going to get hurt and that was the last thing I wanted. We had to come to some kind of truce and fast.

I was on top of Isabella, pinning her to the ground, but she struggled mightily. The situation didn't lend itself at all, but I tried for a calming tone of voice as I said, "Woah, relax. Take it easy. I don't want to fight." The brief conversation was interrupted, however, by red and blue flashing lights.

Chapter 14

Disturbing the Peace

"Hold it right there!" the police officer commanded in a booming voice, amplified through the bullhorn he was using. His partner was already out of the vehicle gun drawn and trained on the assailant advancing forward. "Get off her right now and keep your hands where I can see them!"

I complied with the police officer's orders. "This isn't what it looks like! Officers, I can explain."

"Save it for the judge. Up against the wall. Assume the position!"

"Listen, you're making a mistake here," I pleaded. I slowly stood from where I'd pinned Isabella to the ground, arms raised above my head.

Meanwhile, Isabella spotted Bruce. He had snuck away while she fought with Gideon and was now in the parking lot. Taking advantage of the police's sudden appearance, he quietly slipped into his car.

"He's getting away!" she yelled, springing up from the ground like a cat that accidentally stepped onto a hot plate, and made a run for Bruce.

The other policeman stepped in front of Isabella, barring the way to Bruce. He grabbed hold of her when she attempted to move past him. "Hold on, there! Just settle down and wait a minute, miss. We're going to need you to testify."

"Let go of me! Let go!" Isabella screamed, struggling. "He's going to get away!"

"He's not going anywhere, miss. You're safe now."

"You don't understand! Let me go!"

Isabella had been haunted by the images of the poor children, night after night; huddled in terror, not knowing why they were torn away from their families, wondering just what they had done to deserve their awful plight. They sobbed helplessly, only wanting to be back home again in the arms of their loved ones. She heard them cry desperately for mommy and daddy, for someone, for *anyone* to come and save them. Isabella *could* save them, but she needed Bruce to show her where they were. Now he was getting away! She needed to break free and get to him. She needed the cop to let her go. The police officer did not let go, no matter how franticly Isabella struggled. Suddenly something snapped. Her reaction was swift and visceral. She savagely elbowed the policeman in the gut. The officer grunted but didn't relinquish his hold of her. So, Isabella reached lower, found the police officer's testicles, and squeezed. This did the trick and the officer let go. Isabella made a break for it, but the other officer had seen the struggle and was already headed in their direction. He managed to grab one of Isabella's arms by the wrist, clamping down in a vice-like grip.

Isabella spun around and punched the policeman in the face, not once, but twice in rapid succession. Both hits landed squarely on the officer's nose. He released his hold on Isabella, instinctively cupping his hands over his now bloody nose. The other cop, clutching his groin with one hand, drew his service revolver with the other. "Freeze or I'll shoot!"

Isabella ignored him and continued sprinting towards Bruce as he fumbled with his keys, trying to open the car door. The officer fired a shot into the air. Since she had her back to him, she thought he was actually shooting at her. Knowing she couldn't help the children if she died, she immediately skidded to a halt, raising her hands high above her head. "Ok, ok! Don't shoot!"

I tried to take advantage of the distraction and moved a few paces to my left, like a baseball player attempting to steal base. I was in the process of turning to make a run for it when the officer with the bloody nose said in a nasally voice, "Hold it right there!"

The police officer had his revolver drawn. I turned to see it trained on me, not pointed up in the air. To accentuate his point, he thumbed the hammer back with an ominous click. That froze me right in my tracks. Like Isabella, I surrendered, raising my hands high above my head. "Ok, you got me. Don't shoot."

A little over an hour later, both of us were processed and locked up in adjoining cells. It was the Rio Ariba County Sheriff's department that received the call. The mostly rural, sparsely populated county did not have a very large budget, and thus only had two jail cells.

I could tell Isabella was pissed with a capital P. For the first twenty minutes of being locked up, she paced back and forth in her cell, yelling something in Spanish very loud and very fast. Although I didn't speak the language, I was sure they weren't compliments. Damn but this filly has fire! I admire that in a woman. Whatever she was after Bruce for, she wanted him bad; bad enough to risk tangling with the cops. The two of us probably wanted Bruce for vastly different reasons but maybe we could pool our resources. Hopefully, there's some truth to the old saying, 'the enemy of my enemy is my friend'. I decided to extend an olive branch.

I decided that while Isabella was in the midst of screaming obscenities probably wasn't the best time to strike up a conversation. I sat quietly and bided my time. Eventually, Isabella ran out of steam, stopped hurling insults, and slumped down onto the little cot that served as a sorry excuse for a bed in her tiny jail cell. She sat there, looking thoroughly dejected. After we sat in silence for a good twenty-five minutes, I decided to risk a little light-hearted conversation. I was sitting on my bunk, which was on the far side of my cell. I didn't want to have to raise my voice, so I walked over to the other side where the two cells shared a wall of iron bars. In what I hoped was a quiet but friendly tone, I tried to strike up a conversation.

"So, you're not only a good dancer but a hell of a fighter too." Resounding silence was my only answer but I figured it was better than the yelling she was doing earlier. I decided to press on. "Nice kicks, powerful and fast. I was originally thinking Tae Kwon Do, but you strike with your hands skillfully as well. That's not something a typical Tae Kwon Do practitioner can do." I paused for a moment, but still only silence. Undeterred, I pressed doggedly on. "Then I was thinking a kickboxer because they employ the best of both worlds, dynamic kicks *and* punches. But you can take a fall and that's not something a kickboxer trains to do." I got no reaction at all.

"Come on, throw me a bone! What's it gonna hurt to tell me?" Silence was still my only answer. Even though I'd hit a dead end, I decided to pay Isabella a compliment anyway. She had totally earned my respect. "Well, whatever the style you're good, damn good. I've been training for fifteen years, so I know the kind of hard work and dedication it takes to develop the skills you have. My hats off to you and your teacher." Still no answer. I'm not a big fan of wasting my time, so I turned to go back to my little bunk for a rest.

After a long pause, Isabella answered. "Tang Soo Do, boxing, and Aikido."

I went back to the bars, all ears, as she continued.

"My dad was a boxer, a good one too. He won the golden gloves when he was eighteen and even turned pro for a while before he met my mom and settled down. Her brother, my uncle Al Martinez, is a fifth-degree black belt in Tang Soo Do. He has his own dojo. I've trained with the two of them since I was a little girl, almost as long as I can remember. For the past five years, I've also been training in Aikido with Sensei Clark who is a sixth-degree black belt."

That made sense to me. "That's a good combination of disciplines. Boxing with its punches, Tang Soo Do with its kicks, and Aikido with its throws and joint locks. I can see now why you're such a well-rounded fighter."

"Not that good, apparently. I didn't even slow you down," Isabella exclaimed. "You're something else. What do you train in?"

"Thank you for the compliment but don't sell yourself short. Believe me when I say, you are quite a handful! I train in more than one style as well. Mainly Shorin Ryu Karate and Judo, but more recently Shaolin Kung Fu as well."

"That must come in handy as an enforcer. I assume that's why you're after Bruce, since you said it was work-related. Who does he owe money to?"

I smiled. Here I was thinking of ways to smoothly transition into why Isabella was after Bruce and she just comes flat out and asks me directly why *I'm* after Bruce. Straight to the point. What a nice change of pace. I like this woman's style! "I'm a private investigator. I'm on the case to find some missing kids and I have reason to believe Bruce may know their whereabouts."

Isabella leapt up from her bunk and ran to the wall of bars the two cells shared where I was standing. "You think Bruce knows where the children are too?!"

Not what I was expecting. "Wait *you're* looking for the missing children, too?!"

"Yes, and that pedazo de mierda was going to take me to them!"

I didn't understand the Spanish part, but I think I got the gist. "He agreed to show you where the kids were?"

"Well not exactly. I could have convinced him."

"And how exactly were you going to do that?"

Isabella's eyes narrowed to slits and there was venom in her voice when she answered. "Oh, I have my ways."

I thought back to the bullwhip. "I believe you. Isabella, why are you looking for the missing children? I've done my homework. You're not related to any of the kids and you don't strike me as a fellow PI."

"Can't I just be a concerned citizen?"

"A concerned citizen doesn't tangle with the cops like you did. I see this is personal, but I can't figure out why." I got worried when Isabella's body language suddenly changed.

In an instant, she went from excited to guarded. "You wouldn't believe me if I told you."

My instincts were telling me to tread lightly. I lowered my voice to a relaxed tone, like a psychologist trying to get a patient to confide in them. "You'd be surprised what I've seen in my line of work. The good, the bad, and the ugly. I've seen it all."

"You still wouldn't believe me."

I recalled my run-ins with the supernatural and shook my head. "I actually think it's *you* who wouldn't believe. I've seen things that defy explanation." I paused, thinking of Nia. "Isabella, listen. I know what it's like to have seen things that are out there and then try to share them, only to have people write you off as crazy. I am the last person on God's green Earth who will judge you for saying something hard to believe. Trust me."

I saw Isabella's posture shift, just a bit. The expression on her face softened and changed from one of defiance to one of contemplation. I decided to go for broke. "Come on. Kids' lives are at stake here."

"What if I told you that I'd seen the children in visions I've been having; that they've been taken and are being held by a bruja, or witch?"

I could tell she was expecting me to think she was crazy. I had to be just as honest. "I would tell you that I was hired by the Order of Saint George, an ancient and secret sect of the Catholic Church whose mandate is to protect the laity from witchcraft and demonic attack."

"Really?"

"Truly. Please tell me about these visions of yours. Don't leave out any details, no matter how small or seemingly insignificant."

Chapter 15

Kindred Spirits

We talked all night long, each fascinated with what the other had to say. I was thrilled that Isabella seemed genuinely interested and not skeptical. Daylight was now shining through the window. What? When did that happen? A bit later, a deputy interrupted our conversation. "Jones, you made bail."

I looked up to see the deputy Isabella punched earlier with tape over his nose and two black eyes. He may have been delivering good news, but he wasn't happy about it. We both got the hairy eyeball as he unlocked and opened my jail cell.

Father Lopez was standing behind him. "Good morning Gideon. I would have been here sooner, but I don't check the parish answering machine for messages until after morning mass."

Though the priest seemed less than thrilled, I smiled good-naturedly. "No worries, Father."

The good Father gave me the Catholic version of the hairy eyeball. It was remarkably similar to the common version of the hairy eyeball but somehow also managed to convey, 'God is watching, you know'.

"You seem to be in good spirits, despite your incarceration. Did you make some progress on the case?"

I stood up from my spot on the floor of the jail cell. "As a matter of fact, I have. Did you bring the manila envelope?"

In answer, Father Lopez held the aforementioned envelope in the air.

I turned to the deputy. "Then she made bail too," I said, gesturing towards Isabella. I reached inside and pulled out what was left of the twelve-hundred-dollar retainer. From it, I reimbursed Father Lopez for my bail and, good to my word, paid the deputy for Isabella's bail as well. I made a mental note to have the Order wire me some more cash for operating expenses. I have to itemize everything, and I'm not too excited to explain this to Father Dom. I think I'll call it Isabella's 'consultation fee'. That sounds much better than bail money for disturbing the peace.

Father Lopez gave the two of us a ride back to Red's, so we could pick up our cars; my rented Buick Skylark and Isabella's green 1981 Jeep Wrangler. After Isabella got out, Father Lopez pulled me close and whispered. "Are you sure you can trust her?"

"She's on our side, Padre. I saw her fight to try and get to those kids."

"Looks can be deceiving. Don't be too quick to trust her. She's a curandera. They dabble in sorcery, blurring the line between good and evil," the priest warned.

"Wait a minute. I thought curanderas fight brujas?"

"Where did you hear that? From her?"

"Well..."

Father Lopez sighed. "Just because brujas and curanderas are *rivals* doesn't mean that curanderas are *good*."

"Listen Father, she's our best shot at finding the missing children."

"I'm just saying be careful."

"I will, Father." With that, I raced after Isabella. Just because the good Padre had taken a vow of celibacy was no reason for him to go cock blocking someone who hadn't!

Isabella was waiting for me at her Jeep and flashed a smile that made me weak in the knees. "Thanks for paying my bail. You didn't have to do that, you know."

I returned her smile with interest. "Well, I'm old school. I believe if you get into a fistfight with a girl, the gentlemanly thing to do is pay her bail."

Isabella laughed. "Ah, a class act."

"Well, I'm sure you must be bushed. Before you get some sleep, here's my number," I said, handing her my business card. "You can reach me 24/7. I got one of those newfangled pagers last year and have it on or near me at all times."

Isabella smiled and took the card. "Thanks, but there's no way I could sleep now. I think I'll just head to work. I have to open shop in a couple of hours anyway."

"Without eating breakfast? It's the most important meal of the day," I said jokingly. "Come on. It's my treat."

Her protest seemed halfhearted, and she smiled while she said it. "Are you sure? You don't have to do this out of guilt, you know."

"I'm sure," I answered, also smiling. "I'm not guilty just old school, remember? You pick the locale though. I'm new around here."

"Ok, I know just the place. Follow me," Isabella said, climbing into her Jeep.

I watched her, unabashedly admiring her figure. I couldn't help thinking, *oh, but today is a good day!*

Isabella drove back to Santa Fe and took me to a little place called the Pink Adobe. It was right across the street from the San Miguel Mission, where I first met Father Lopez. I approved. It felt very 'New Mexican' in ambiance, with its old Pueblo Indian style architecture and Santa Fe style décor. To me, it was very exotic and seemed to perfectly compliment this dark-haired beauty I was with. The food was amazing. We had a traditional breakfast of fried eggs and hash browns with a Santa Fe twist. They were smothered in New Mexico chili. Spicy stuff, but so delicious!

I listened to Isabella talk about the medicinal properties of certain native plants. She explained how osha could not only be used as a rattlesnake repellent but burned as an incense to promote healing and bring good luck. Suddenly she stopped and looked at me dubiously. "You sure I'm not boring you?"

"No, I'm listening. Please continue," I said through a mouthful of eggs and chili. Isabella had my full attention. In truth, she could've been telling me she was from the moons of Saturn and I'd still be all ears.

"Well, I need to get to my shop anyway. Saturdays are when I make most of my money."

"I have some errands to do myself," I said. "If I'm lucky I just might be able to get our mutual friend Bruce back in my sights."

Isabella was immediately bristling with animosity. "I want a piece of him."

I forced myself not to smile. *Damn, this woman is sexy when she's angry,* I thought to myself. I quickly made a mental note to be mindful of my facial expressions. Grinning impishly at a woman when she was angry was not a wise course of action.

"Don't worry. You'll get your pound of flesh," I said, trying to placate her. "We're in this together. I need you to make this whole thing work anyway, believe me. I'll stop by your shop and fill you in on all the details. Which reminds me, when are you off work and where is your yerbee… yerbeereeah… thingy?"

"Yerberia," Isabella corrected. "And I want two pounds of flesh."

This time I didn't restrain myself and smiled openly. "Isabella you are my kind of woman."

Chapter 16

The Day Shift

After Isabella left, I went to a phone booth, grabbed the phone book, and thumbed through the white pages until I got to the O's. As I made my way through the listings, I was delighted to find only two entries for Bruce Ortiz in the book. Yes! It could be ridiculously easy to find people sometimes. I jotted down the two addresses in my little steno notepad. Then, I turned to the yellow pages and located the nearest RadioShack.

After picking up six walkie-talkies and a bunch of batteries at the local RadioShack, I drove back to Española. I located the two addresses listed in the white pages as the residence of Bruce Ortiz. One of the two was the home of the Bruce I was looking for; or as I now preferred to call him, Bruce the Barfbag. After driving past both houses, but not seeing Bruce conveniently sitting out on the front porch or doing yard work at either location, I drove to the neighborhood where I'd first met my new friend David. It wasn't far from one of the houses. After driving around for a short time, I found the boy riding bikes with three of his friends. I stopped the car, grabbed my duffle bag, got out, and called David over. David pedaled his bike over to me while his friends stayed back. They watched with great interest.

"Hey kid! How you doing?"

"I'm ok. What's up?"

"I'm still on the case and wondered if you and your friends would be willing to help out."

"Really?! You serious?" David asked, obviously excited at the prospect.

"Serious as a heart attack, kid."

David called his friends over. "Hey guys! Come here! This is the private eye I was telling you about!"

The boys, who had been hanging back at the opposite side of the street, now crossed over.

"Hello boys. My name is Gideon Jones. I've been hired to find the missing kids and I could use a little help."

"Hi," they answered in unison, albeit somewhat sheepishly.

David did the introductions, first pointing to a big lad who dwarfed the others in size. They were all still astride their bikes, so I couldn't be entirely sure, but he looked about five-foot-seven. The rest of his companions looked closer to five-foot-one. The boy had brown eyes and brown hair parted to the side and wore a blue T-shirt. He still had a youthful appearance and didn't seem older than the other boys, just bigger. "This is Joey." David said.

"Good to meet you Joey," I said, smiling. I offered the kid my hand.

Joey shook it and answered, "Nice to meet you, sir."

Exhibiting good manners. I immediately liked him. Who said kids were ill-mannered nowadays? "You can call me Gideon, Joey."

David next pointed to a boy with olive complexion and slicked-back coal-black hair. "This is Donnie."

I offered my hand. "Good to meet you, Donnie."

The boy shook my hand. "Good to meet you sir, I mean Gideon."

Lastly, David pointed to a skinny youth with dirty blond hair and glasses. "This is Dennis."

"Good to meet you, Dennis."

Dennis shook my hand and, learning from his friends' mistakes, answered, "Good to meet you Gideon."

"Well, now that we've all been properly introduced, let me tell you boys why I've come here." I paused a moment for effect, but I knew the boys were all ears. Even so, I squatted down and motioned for them to come closer. Lowering my voice, not wanting anyone else to get wind of my little conspiracy, I continued. "I need some help on this case and David has already given me some info. That paid off, so I know you guys are trustworthy." I turned to David. "Thanks for the tip about Red's. You were right."

David puffed out his chest in pride and the other boys eyed him, wondering just what this tip was. I took out my steno notepad and pointed to the address closest to them. "You guys know where this street is?"

Joey answered. "Yeah, it's about a mile that way," he said, pointing to the east.

"Good," I said. "I assume you all know who Bruce the Barfbag is."

They nodded their heads knowingly in unison. Dennis tried to stifle a giggle.

"I have reason to believe Bruce knows the whereabouts of the missing kids, including your friend Blake." I already had their attention, but I could tell the boys were now fully committed. They were all in.

David spoke up. Although he was the only boy talking, I could tell by the expressions of the others that he spoke for all of them when he asked, "How can we help?"

"Well, Bruce gave me the slip, but I think I've narrowed down his hiding spot to two places. The problem is, I can't be at both places at once and I don't want him to get away from me again. That's where you boys come in. I need you to keep an eye on this address, here," I said, pointing to my steno pad, "while I stake out the other place. Now, I don't want you to hang out right in front of the house. That will draw attention to yourselves. Just ride past it on your bikes now and then. Pretend like you're racing each other or playing some sort of game. That way, if anyone sees you, they won't think anything of it. Kids ride their bikes and play around all the time, right?"

The boys nodded their heads. Again acting as the group spokesman David said, "Yeah we get it."

"Good. Now you might not see anything, but if you do see Bruce, or a black Chevy Impala, or a creepy Indian lady, I want you to give me a call on one of these." I reached into my duffle bag and handed each kid a walkie-talkie. "If you do see him don't immediately take off screaming into the walkie-talkie, 'we found him!'. Instead, use the walkie-talkies the whole time. Pretend you guys are all X-wing pilots in Star Wars."

"Sweet! I love Star Wars," said Dennis.

"Me too," Donnie said.

"Focus guys. That's just our cover!" David chided the others.

"That's ok," I said. "The more you guys play and have fun the better and more believable the cover will be. If you *do* spot Bruce or the creepy Indian lady, say 'Red Leader, this is Red Five. I'm making my attack run!' I'm Red Leader. 'This is Red Five. I'm making my attack run' is the code for spotting Bruce. Anyone who hears you will think you're just playing, but I'll know better and come running. Again, 'Red Leader this is Red Five. I'm making my attack run' is our code. Got it?"

"Got it!" the boys said in unison.

"When do you boys have to be back home?"

"Dinner time," they said.

"That's perfect. I have someone who can help me out at night," I said, thinking of Isabella. "So, they'll be the night shift and you guys will be the day shift."

"Cool," said Joey.

"Yeah, cool," echoed Donnie.

I smiled. "Cool is right. You guys are my A-team and a huge help! As my way of saying thanks, you get to keep the walkie-talkies."

"Sweet!" shouted Dennis.

"That's not all," I said. I took out my wallet and handed each kid a ten-dollar bill.

"Right on!" exclaimed Joey.

"Now that's what I'm talking about!" cried Dennis.

"Hell yeah!" said Donnie.

"Dude, don't curse!" scolded Joey.

"Yeah man, show some class," added David.

"What? Like saying 'hell' is a big deal?" complained Donnie.

"No worries boys. I've heard worse," I chuckled. "You guys are really helping me out and will be putting in some work, so you deserve to get paid. Also, I don't want you boys going hungry. Around twelve-thirty I'll meet you at the next street over and drop off some McDonald's. How does that sound?"

The boys broke out into cheers.

"Ok! Now let's get to work," I said, doing my best imitation of a jazzed-up motivational speaker. Hopefully, it wasn't too corny.

It worked like a charm! The boys excitedly mounted their bikes and pedaled off as fast as they could to go keep an eye out for Bruce.

Chapter 17

Woe to the Conquered

The incessant sobbing of the captive children was an unwelcome distraction. Chumana needed to weave her spells to complete the ritual. The time for the sacrifice was quickly drawing near and she was not yet ready. Agitated, she closed her eyes and started her chant again, attempting to block out the crying of the children. She forced her breathing to become slow and measured. With practiced determination and focused will, she drowned out the distractions and replaced them with her own recollections. The spell required great emotion, more precisely, powerful hatred. Chumana knew how to evoke that in herself. The weeping children faded further and further away, as did the droning of her own incantations, as she forced herself to recall the carefully repressed memories.

Slowly, the darkness she perceived because of her closed eyes was gradually replaced by a dim light. That light grew in intensity until Chumana found herself staring into the midday sun. Except she was no longer Chumana, for it was no longer 1986 but 1756, and she had not yet taken that name for herself. She was still Chosovi. She had just come in from the fields with her children where they had been sowing the seeds for the next crop. Hopefully, her husband, Choovio, would return successful from his hunt before nightfall or there would be no meat in the stew tonight. If not, they would not go hungry by any means. There were still beans, corn, and squash for the stew. Also, they had corn flour for cakes. She was just in the mood for some meat.

There were still other chores to do before dinner was prepared. She called to the girls. Her children were all girls. Honovi was the oldest at eleven, then Ankti, who was nine, and little Mansi who was the youngest, at seven. "Come little ones! It is time to grind corn and make more flour."

"I'm not little anymore," Honovi protested.

"You are still little to me," Chosovi said, smiling. "Now do as you're told and go fetch the grindstones."

"Yes momma," Honovi said, hurrying off to get the stones.

"Momma, I want to do some weaving," said Ankti.

"Me too," said little Mansi, wanting to be included in the conversation.

"We can do that later tonight after father returns from his hunt."

"Yay!" Mansi cheered, jumping up and down, clapping her hands. Unfortunately, her little celebration was cut short by a scream.

"Momma!!" It was Honovi. She cried out and came running around the corner of their little adobe house, obviously frightened.

"What's the matter, child?" Chosovi asked.

Looking over her shoulder, Honovi pointed towards the south, where a large cloud of dust could be seen. "Spaniards!"

As if on cue, a dozen Spanish soldiers came riding on horseback and quickly encircled Chosovi's family. They were Spanish Lancers, a type of cavalryman. They were all clad in military uniforms which consisted of black knee-high riding boots, light blue riding breeches, and dark blue coats with silver buttons and red cuffs. They wore black, wide-brimmed hats with red hatbands. There were sabers dangling at their hips and muskets slung across their backs. They carried black lances with sharpened steel tips and pointed them menacingly at Chosovi and her children.

Chosovi drew her children closer to her, trying to shield them with her own body, but the lances threatened them from every direction. "Why are you here? What do you want with us?"

In answer, a sergeant unrolled a scroll and read, "Choovio and Chosovi Peña! You are hereby charged with the most heinous act of practicing witchcraft and will be taken to Santa Fe, where you will stand trial for these crimes by order of his excellency Governador y Capitan de Nuevo Mexico Francisco Antonio Marin de Valle." After reading the short edict the sergeant glanced around. "Where is your husband?"

"He is hunting. What do you mean charged with witchcraft?"

The Sergeant looked down at Chosovi from where he sat, high upon his horse, with obvious disdain. "Eyewitness accounts have placed you in the pueblo of Abiquiu worshiping the Devil."

"Abiquiu? We were only there to sell our crops and partake in the ceremonial dances. We did nothing wrong!"

"And just what are these ceremonial dances you speak of?"

"They are how we pray to God and ask him for his blessings and a bountiful harvest."

"One only prays to God in church. *You* were worshiping Satan." The Sergeant turned to his men. "She admits it. Take her. Search the house for her mate."

The soldiers dismounted, and some went into the house. They ransacked the place, needlessly smashing pottery, overturning tables, and throwing the contents of shelves onto the floor. Other soldiers roughly grabbed Chosovi and pulled her away from her children.

"Wait! Stop! Why are you doing this? We've done nothing wrong!"

The soldiers ignored her protests and, taking some rope, started to tie the hands of her children together.

"What are doing with my children?"

The Sergeant smiled. With cruel contempt in his voice, he coldly stated, "The children of witches are sold as slaves."

"No!!" Chosovi screamed, struggling to break free of her captors' clutches.

Honovi cried out, "Momma, don't let them take us!"

One of the soldiers slapped the girl viciously across the face. "Shut up, brat!"

Chosovi redoubled her efforts to escape and come to her children's aid, but two soldiers were holding her by the wrists. No matter how hard she struggled, she just wasn't strong enough to break free. Desperate, she bent at the waist and pulled with all her might with her right hand until she was able to get her face up and close to the hand of the soldier holding her. Chosovi savagely bit down for all she was worth and tore a bloody hunk of flesh out of the back of the soldier's hand.

Cursing, he released his hold on her. Using her now free right hand, Chosovi clawed the face of the other soldier who still held her left hand, raking his eyes. Yelping, he too released his hold. Now free, she immediately ran to the aid of her children. The soldier who struck her daughter Honovi now had his back to Chosovi as he tried to tie the girl's hands. It was not easy, as Honovi struggled mightily. "Be still!" he yelled and hit her again.

Chosovi stooped down as she ran toward them and snatched up one of the heavy grinding stones they used to crush and pulverize dried corn to make flour. "Leave her alone you filthy rat!"

The soldier staggered and fell to his knees as Chosovi struck him in the back of the head. Not finished, she hit him again. The soldier went down, collapsing face-first into the dirt. Still not finished with him, Chosovi prepared to hit him yet again. She probably would have hit him until his head was a bloody pulp, but the other soldiers pulled her off him.

One soldier grabbed her from behind, pinning her arms to her sides. Another soldier struck her in the face. When she turned her head in a futile attempt to avoid more blows, he simply hit her on that side. They continued to hit her repeatedly about the face and head until her cheeks were swollen, both her lips were bloody and split, her eyes were blackened, and her nose bled profusely. Then, while one of them held her from behind, they took turns punching her in the stomach until the only reason she still stood was the soldier holding her up.

Once each of the soldiers had a turn, they let go of her. Chosovi collapsed into a crumpled heap on the ground. The soldier whose hand she had bitten savagely kicked her while she was down, to the other soldiers' raucous cheers and laughter. She tried to crawl away from her assailant, but he simply delivered an especially brutal kick to her ribcage. She collapsed, no longer able to flee. The best she could do was curl up into the fetal position while he continued to kick her mercilessly. After a few minutes of this, he began to tire out but was not yet finished with Chosovi.

"Hold her down. I'm going to teach this bitch a lesson for biting my hand." Smiling wickedly, the soldier took off the belt holding his saber and handed the weapon to one of his companions. Leering at her lasciviously he began to unbutton his trousers.

Horrified, Chosovi tried to regain her feet and get away, but the other soldiers were on her in an instant, pinning her to the ground. Chosovi screamed and fought desperately to break free but there were too many of them. The other soldiers laughed as their comrade hiked up her skirt and mounted her.

"Relax, puta. You might enjoy this," the soldier with the wounded hand said mockingly as he roughly entered her.

The other soldiers did nothing to stop him, instead shouting vile encouragements as he raped her. Chosovi closed her eyes and tried to go to a far-off place in her mind. Suddenly, the loathsome pig who was on top of her abruptly stopped and the vulgar cheering ceased.

Chosovi opened her eyes to see a look of shock upon the face of the soldier who was on top of her. He stared, wide-eyed, at the bloody shaft of the arrow protruding from the center of his neck. Slowly, he slid off her, twitching like a dying cockroach.

"The witch's mate has returned!" shouted the Sergeant.

Throughout the obscene incident, he sat atop his horse, watching. It was nothing more than a diversion for his men. He drew his saber from its scabbard and urged his horse into a gallop as he prepared to ride the Indian down.

Choovio smoothly and expertly nocked another arrow and quickly took aim as the Sergeant astride his mount charged forward. Calmly taking a precious second to ensure his aim was true, he stood still as a statue as the Sergeant raced towards him, saber held high to hack him down. Choovio then released his arrow, which soared forward like a bolt of lightning and struck the sergeant in his right eye, toppling him from his horse.

Choovio sprinted forward to his family's aid, nocking another arrow as he ran. Some of the soldiers leveled their muskets and took aim at the charging Indian while others grabbed hold of their lances and rushed out to meet him.

Guessing how long he had before the soldiers fired, Choovio counted to two in his head. Not slowing down, he dove forward, sliding feet first a mere fraction of a second before the thunderous boom of the rifles. He was on his feet again in an instant. On the run, he released another arrow, which hit one of the charging lancers in the chest.

The soldiers with lances were almost upon him and Choovio didn't have time to nock another arrow. He continued to charge forward anyway, bellowing a mighty battle cry as he did. Swinging his bow like a war club, he batted aside the tip of an oncoming lance and ran up on the soldier who was wielding it.

Now in close quarters, his lance was of no use, so the soldier dropped it and began to draw his saber. Choovio got his hunting knife out faster and stabbed the soldier repeatedly in the chest. As the soldier fell, Choovio turned to face his next opponent. Suddenly, there was a searing pain in his stomach as a lance took him in the gut. Grimacing, Choovio forced himself to focus through the pain and hurled his knife at the soldier who skewered him, catching the man in the throat. The soldier released his hold on the lance and fell to the ground, dying.

The pain was terrible but Choovio withdrew the bloody lance from his belly. No sooner had he done so, two more soldiers impaled him upon their lances, stabbing him in the midsection. They drove him to the ground, pinning him to the earth. Choovio continued to struggle despite the dreadful wounds but was held fast by the lancers who put all their weight behind their weapons. Suddenly, another soldier loomed over him with his saber held high and lopped off Choovio's head.

After dispatching Choovio, the soldiers burned down their house. They tied Chosovi and her daughters together and marched them fifty miles south to Santa Fe where she was to stand trial, leaving Choovio to rot in the sun.

Chapter 18

Shaping of the Snake

The so-called trial was a mockery. The soldiers told bold-faced lies about how, after politely asking Chosovi's family to accompany them to Santa Fe, she and Choovio attacked them using witchcraft. Chosovi pleaded her case but was pronounced guilty. She was sentenced to be publicly flogged and then hung. Her children would be sold into slavery.

The following day, Chosovi was taken to the Santa Fe Plaza. It was an immense courtyard in the center of a presidio surrounded by a large defensive wall that enclosed several residences: a soldier's barracks, a chapel, and the Governor's Palace. The plaza served as the commercial, social, and political center of Santa Fe since 1610 when it was established by Don Pedro de Peralta. It was the perfect place to publicly flog a witch.

Chosovi faced a tall pole in the center of the plaza where a large crowd had gathered to watch the event. Her hands were stretched high above her head and tied to a large iron ring, attached so far up the pole it forced Chosovi to stand on the tips of her toes. After a government official read from a piece of parchment decrying her crimes as a witch, her shirt was ripped off, leaving her naked from the waist up and exposing her back. Then, to the oohs and ahhs of the crowd, a soldier uncoiled a whip and began flogging her.

With each terrible crack, the leather bit deep into her tender flesh, leaving dreadful lacerations. They whipped her over and over as she cried out in pain. Chosovi begged for mercy, but none was given. Soon, her poor back was crisscrossed with bloody wounds, but they still didn't stop. They continued and whipped her again and again, each new lash tearing off chunks of flesh. The savage and brutal flogging continued until she was an appalling sight to behold. Her entire back was one big, dreadful wound with ribbons of bloody flesh dangling off her.

When they finally cut her from the ring, Chosovi no longer had the strength to stand. She collapsed, barely conscious. They simply let her lie there in the dirt, unrestrained. They knew she was unable to even stand back up, let alone try to escape. The government official once more read from his piece of parchment. "If the witch lives, she will be hanged. While the gallows are prepared, we have another treat for the good people of Santa Fe!"

A band of Apaches, ten in number, boldly strutted to the center of the plaza with Chosovi's children in tow. "In an act of mercy, his Excellency has decreed the children of the witch shall not be put to death but instead shall be sold as slaves! Here to conduct the auction is the Apache brave, Ka-e-te-nay!" The government official gestured grandly towards the Apache warrior, then rolled up his piece of parchment and left all further proceedings to the Apache.

Without further ado, Ka-e-te-nay roughly grabbed little Mansi, whose hands were still tied, and presented her to the crowd. "How much for the little Pueblo girl!?" There was silence from the crowd. "Come now! She may be young, but she can still work!"

Still, no offers from the crowd. "Let's start with fifty dollars then!" There were murmurings of interest but still no offers. "People, this one has many years of work in her and at fifty dollars is a bargain!" The people talked amongst themselves in hushed tones, but no offers were made. "Really? No offers? There is not one among you willing to part with fifty dollars for this young girl?! You people surprise me!"

Ka-e-te-nay pulled Mansi in close to him. Her back was touching him, but she still faced the crowd. The petite girl was dwarfed by the big Apache, her little head only coming up to his stomach. He brandished a massive hunting knife with a huge blade, as long as his own forearm, for the crowd to see. The murmurings ceased, and the crowd grew quiet. Everyone watched wide-eyed, wondering just what the Apache was up to. Once he was sure he had the crowd's undivided attention, Ka-e-te-nay slowly drew the blade across the tiny girl's throat, cutting open her jugular and spewing blood everywhere. There were shocked gasps from the crowd and screams of dismay and horror at the despicable act.

Unconcerned, he let the girl's corpse fall to the ground and grabbed her older sister, Ankti. Presenting her to the crowd as he had Mansi, he pressed the bloody blade of his massive knife to her throat and bellowed, "How much for *this* girl, then? Do I hear fifty dollars?!"

The crowd erupted forth with bids of fifty dollars. The big Apache smiled. "Fifty dollars! Do I hear fifty-five?"

"Fifty-five!" a woman from the crowd shouted.

"Fifty-five!" Ka-e-te-nay echoed. "Do I hear sixty?"

"Sixty!" a man in the back cried.

"Sixty!" Ka-e-te-nay hollered with glee. "Do I hear sixty-five!?!"

Chosovi had been lying unnoticed, like a discarded piece of filth, face first in the dirt some fifteen feet away. Totally spent and unable to move, slipping in and out of consciousness, she had just come around.   To her horror, all she could see was her precious little Mansi, dead in a pool of her own blood, and Ankti with a knife to her throat.

She didn't know where she found the strength, but Chosovi pulled herself to her feet and, wailing a terrible cry, charged forward. Arms outstretched, she was intent on tearing Ka-e-te-nay to shreds with her bare hands. One of the other Apache warriors clubbed her in the back of the head with the butt of his rifle and all went black.

Chosovi awoke later that night in a shallow grave on the outskirts of town. It was maybe eighteen inches deep. They barely bothered to cover her with dirt. When she came to in total darkness, panicked and suffocating, she was able to burrow her way out. Chosovi wandered in a daze until she made her way to la Peña Blanca, the White Plain, where it was rumored a coven of witches practiced their dark arts in secret.

The tales were true. The witches found her crawling on her hands and knees, no longer able to walk. Chosovi was half-naked, bruised and bloody, covered in dirt, and on death's door. They took pity on her and took her in. They cleaned her up and slowly nursed her back to health. Upon learning her tale, the witches sought out

Chosovi's remaining daughters for her. Heartbreakingly, thinking both their parents were dead and no one was coming to save them, both young girls had taken their own lives in despair. Upon learning this, Chosovi sank into a deep pit of sorrow. All she loved in this world had been taken from her. Her grief was beyond measure. For a time, she did nothing but mourn and meditate on her loss. But Chosovi had not *lost* all she loved. No! It was *taken* from her! Soon, her sorrow turned to hatred; a staggeringly powerful, all-consuming hatred. Chosovi begged the witches to teach her their craft so she might take her revenge.

And they did. Chosovi learned how to brew potions and poisons, how to cast curses, weave spells, commune with spirits, and even conjure forth demons. In time she became powerful. One by one, she started to hunt down the Apache and Spaniards who took her family from her. She cast terrible curses upon them, ending their wretched lives.

With each life she took, she noticed it did nothing to slacken her rancor and malice. She could take a hundred lives for each of her beloved family members and would still not come close to culminating her vengeance. Chosovi decided then that it was not enough to simply *kill* her enemies. Death was not a fitting punishment. Death was too final, too swift, too *good* for them. They should be made to *suffer;* a terrible, lasting suffering so great they would pray for death as a release from their pain.

She captured the remaining Apaches and Spaniards and subjected them to terrible torture. Chosovi found her victims would eventually snap. Sanity lost, they no longer register *anything,* including pain. That simply would not do. Then Chosovi had an epiphany; a disturbing, dreadful epiphany. She decided to take her tormentors' *children,* not her tormentors themselves. By hurting the ones they loved, by stealing away the ones they held dear and snuffing out their short, innocent lives; only then would they begin to know the pain she herself endured.

Soon Chosovi found even *this* torment was not enough. So, she wracked her brain. After days of deliberation, Chosovi decided one generation of children would not suffice to atone for the loss of her loved ones. She would spare some of the children, but only so they might propagate, allowing her to prey upon the offending Apache and Spaniard entire family lines. Chosovi would haunt and torment them, generation after generation. To do this terrible thing, she made pacts with demons. In return for the blood of innocent children, they would enable her to shed her skin like a snake and extend her life. The witch found this to be fitting, for after her family was taken from her, she ceased to exist as Chosovi. When she clawed her way out of that shallow grave, she was reborn. And so, she left the name of Chosovi behind and took a new name: Chumana, which meant 'snake woman'. Like a snake, she shed her old self and took on a new form. Deadly as a serpent, she would hunt down her prey and continue to exact her revenge. Chumana would bathe in a sea of blood.

Since the Spaniards wanted her to be a witch so badly, Chumana embraced that destiny. She became a horrifyingly powerful practitioner of the dark arts. In falsely accusing and condemning her, in committing such terrible atrocities against her and her family, the sanctimonious fools had unknowingly engineered their own hell. She would now visit such horrors upon them as only a wicked witch could, preying upon them and their children for all time.

Chapter 19

Dark Rites

Chumana sat cross-legged on the basement floor in the middle of the spell circle, amidst the intricate patterns. Basements were rare in northern New Mexico, especially in rural areas. Unlike out east, there was no shortage of space. If you needed a place for your washer and dryer or to store things, there was no need to dig down. You simply built a laundry room or a shed. Chumana, however, required privacy for much of her spell craft, so she had one built in her house. It was used for far more nefarious purposes than storage space.

Chumana had painstakingly drawn out the miniature ley lines, or energy paths, with white sand; intersecting and connecting in specific patterns in order to elicit the desired effect. At different points along the rim and inside of the circle, large candles were burning, dribbling down hot wax that pooled at their base and intermingled with the sand. In addition to the candles, human bones were strewn across the circle; the remains of several of Chumana's victims. They were mainly finger bones, but there was the occasional forearm, shin bone, and two human skulls.

Eyes closed, she murmured her incantations over and over as she relived the awful memories of her distant past with terrible clarity, tapping into the hatred they evoked in her. Slowly, Chumana focused and channeled that odium, using it as fuel for her spell. Drawing forth the ichor from her old wounds, the witch repurposed it as poison for her future victims.

Slowly, the white sand began to glow a pale green, dimly at first. Gradually it grew brighter and brighter as Chumana's chanting grew in volume until she was loudly singing a primal song, old as death itself. The glowing green patterns of sand began pulsing in time with the wild canticle.

Chumana began to rock back and forth and sway, weaving her arms about in a kind of dance as she sang, though she remained seated and careful not to disturb the sand. Suddenly, her back arched greatly. With her head titled back and her arms raised high, a great booming voice that was clearly not her own, or even human for that matter, thundered forth from her open mouth. It continued the chant, impossibly loud, with such deep, reverberating bass that the house seemed to shake. As it did, the soft, flickering yellow light of the candles turned bright green, and the small flames grew in size and brightness. Suddenly, the candles became more like torches, shooting forth geysers of green flame several feet into the air.

The colossal voice lowered in pitch but slowly increased in volume. Upon reaching its crescendo, even though it was indoors, a great gust of wind swept through the room, scattering the sand and snuffing out the candles. For a tense moment, Chumana sat silent in the darkness but then burst into maniacal laughter, cackling like an old hag. The empty eye sockets of the two skulls were now glowing with green light.

Chumana leapt up from where she was sitting, taking one skull in each hand, and went to the back of the large room where a shrine of sorts had been set up. There was a small table that sat in the center of a circle drawn on the floor in chalk. Along the outer edges of the circle were runes, in an ancient language, long forgotten by most of the world.

Upon the table was a very old white dress of the early eighteenth-century Spanish colonial style, lashed to the table by thorny vines. Next to the dress was a large wooden bowl filled with muddy water. It was here that Chumana kept the spirt of Cha'kwaina, the one who cries, or as the Spaniards called her La Llorona, bound to this plane of existence to do her bidding.

As Chumana approached, a pale translucent apparition of a young woman with long black hair flew up from the table. As soon as it did, long black thorny tendrils shot out and ensnared her, wrapping around her arms and legs like thorny tentacles. She was dragged back down. The specter struggled mightily. As she did, her countenance changed from one of a panicked woman to an enraged, spine-chilling creature whose visage was terrifying to behold. It had pale, glowing eyes, and her hair fanned out like a corona.

"Release me, witch!" La Llorona commanded in an unearthly voice that managed to boom like a thunderclap, yet still have a strange repetitive quality, like soundwaves being reflected from the bottom of a deep well.

In answer, Chumana tilted back her head and laughed. La Llorona howled in fury, redoubling her efforts to escape. The thorny vines were stretched taut, visibly shaking as she struggled to break free.

Suddenly, they snapped with an audible CRACK! La Llorona flew at Chumana, arms outstretched, hands poised, ready to rip and destroy. She traveled mere inches before colliding with an invisible barrier. The chalk circle and ancient runes now glowed red. This only served to enrage La Llorona further. She slashed at the invisible partition with her long fingernails. A shower of sparks erupted forth, but the magical enclosure held fast.

When that failed, La Llorona pounded on the invisible barrier, hammering out blows of incredible force. Each sounded like a mighty sledgehammer striking a massive boulder. As she beat upon the wall like an enraged mountain gorilla, the glowing red circle and ancient runes shimmered, now a brighter shade of red, as if expending a great amount of energy to keep her restrained.

Suddenly, La Llorona stopped pummeling the invisible barrier. After locking eyes with Chumana in a blood-chilling stare, she opened her mouth impossibly wide and started screeching like a gargantuan bird of prey. Her shrill cry was impossibly loud and seemingly without end. As it continued, ear-splitting second after ear-splitting second, the glowing red circle glowed brighter still. It blazed like a beacon and radiated heat like a blast furnace. This sonic attack inflicted an even greater toll than her mighty blows.

As the circle and runes continued to shine bright red, the once invisible barrier took on a faint red hue. La Llorona continued her harsh wail. A predatory smile of triumph crept across her face. As if on cue, a dark red crack appeared upon the light red surface of the magical barrier. Quickly it began to spread, like a red spiderweb.

Instead of looking concerned, Chumana merely seemed impressed. In response to this development, she placed one of the skulls upon her chest, holding it over her heart with her left hand. As soon as she did so, the entire skull glowed bright green. The ghostly light spread, encircling Chumana in an eerie halo of pale green light.

La Llorona, sensing something was about to happen, tilted her head back and balled up her fists. Bellowing even louder, her shrill cry intensified. The cracks in the magical barrier spread faster, widening as they did. As this happened, Chumana closed her eyes and stretched out her right arm, holding the other skull, and pointed it like a macabre weapon trained upon La Llorona.

Suddenly the barrier shattered and La Llorona flew at Chumana. Twin beams of pale light shot forth from the eye sockets of the outstretched skull and struck the apparition. She recoiled and shrieked, in pain now instead of anger. Chumana opened her eyes, which were now glowing green as well, and began uttering a spell. As she did La Llorona fell to the floor, writhing in agony.

Chumana advanced forward. She shouted her spell, pouring out her own pain, misery, hatred, and utter contempt upon the spirit, focused by the beams of green light lancing out from the skull. La Llorona thrashed about on the floor at Chumana's feet, tearing her dress to shreds and pulling out her own hair, in agonizing pain. As the apparition spasmed on the floor before her, Chumana focused her terrible will and began to twist the ghost, reshaping it into a mirror image of her own tormented soul.

La Llorona's cries turned to weeping. Where a once eerie but beautiful ghost of a woman had been, there was now a grotesque and horrific *thing*. The ghastly creature was now easily over seven and a half feet tall. Its elongated arms hung past its knees and ended in wicked-looking claws that resembled talons. The thing was lanky, almost to the point of being skeletal, ungracefully thin, and rawboned as if it didn't have enough flesh for its new frame. What skin it did have was cadaverously pale, unnaturally white like an insect that had crawled out from under a rock. That pallid skin was stretched tight, like a shirt several sizes too small. It was so tight, it was cracked and torn in places, hanging off its frame in long bloody ribbons. Its jaw was almost unhinged from its face and its cheeks were gaunt and corpse-like. The eye sockets were dark and sunken in, like they were hollow. It was mostly bald, but had patches of long, stringy black hair that clung to its scalp in unsightly clumps. Its disgusting wounds oozed a rancid mixture of blood and pus, emitting an overpowering and vile stench of rotting meat.

Keeping the skull trained on La Llorona, pinning her to the ground with its twin green beams, Chumana took the other skull from her chest and pointed it towards the table. Twin beams shot out from it as well, striking the shrine and encapsulating it in that eerie green light. The limp and lifeless vines glowed green and started to slither like thorny serpents. They throbbed and pulsated, expanding, revitalized by Chumana's spell. Suddenly, they shot out again, entangling La Llorona once more.

Chumana moved, her arms together, stretched out in front of her. She placed the two skulls side by side. As she did so, the vines dragged La Llorona back to the table like a tentacled leviathan from murky depths. Soon the ghost lay strapped to the table, held fast by the thorny vines, like some sort of grotesque victim upon a sacrificial altar.

Keeping the two skulls trained on her, Chumana spoke to the spirit. "Sleep now Cha'kwaina. Cease your struggling, conserve your strength. I need you to bring me another child tonight. The little children, the descendants of the Spanish soldiers, they cry out. I think they must want company. Bring me the Apache boy, named Donnie, who is the descendant of Ka-e-te-nay. Do this last thing for me and I shall release you."

Still holding the skulls before her, Chumana closed her eyes and murmured a new spell. As she recited the ancient words of power, La Llorona ceased her struggles and started to shrink in size, from roughly seven and a half feet tall with her elongated limbs, to the size and proportions of a normal woman. Chumana continued chanting. Slowly, La Llorona began to sink into the folds of the dress, as if the material was absorbing her into it like a sponge until she faded from sight. With the spell complete, one could only see the white dress lashed to the table next to the bowl of muddy water.

Chapter 20

New Adversaries

Bruce hated going to see the Indian woman. She was nothing but bad news and gave him the creeps. It all started out just fine. At first, he thanked his lucky stars for finding the creepy lady that fateful day at Red's. She paid him large sums of cash just for giving her the addresses of certain children. No strings attached! Bruce had never made an easier buck! When those kids started going missing though? Of course it made Bruce nervous. He didn't care what she did with those addresses, so long as it didn't blow back on *him*. Now people were paying attention and that changed things entirely.

To make matters worse, in the middle of all this heat, she had him go see her late at night. Instead of Red's, he had to go all the way to her place out in the boonies. She wanted the address of one more kid. He didn't want to do it, of course. Those missing kids were big news now, being featured on TV. The police could be watching, and a meddlesome private eye was snooping around. Easy money was one thing but doing time was something else. This time, the crazy bitch offered *way* more money but threatened to rat him out, or worse, if he didn't deliver. The 'or worse' part was what really scared him.

Bruce knew this skank was trouble. If she was capable of kidnapping, murder wasn't so far a stretch. When the loca freaked out and started talking about the spirit world it was just too much. Craziness, Bruce would have written off, especially when she ran to where those kids were at and started yelling at someone who wasn't there. But when the Pueblo woman jumped and didn't land? He wasn't even drunk! She just hovered in the air like she was fighting with something Bruce couldn't see. *That* was some freaky shit. *Especially* when she slapped at thin air. It made a loud smacking sound like she had walloped a side of beef. Then, finally, she dropped to the ground.

This Pueblo lady was a devil worshiper or something and Bruce didn't want her putting a hex on him. His grandparents used to talk of such things. A devil-worshiping bruja would put a curse on you. Then, you'd suddenly fall sick with doctors unable to find a cure or even a reason why. Or worse! They could make your pecker shrivel up and fall off! It was bad enough to have such a little prick, but to have no chorizo at all and just little huevitos? Now that would be a cruel punishment indeed!

Bruce was a coward at heart anyway, but this Pueblo woman had him scared shitless. So, when that out-of-town private eye and the hot woman who owned the yerberia jumped him at Red's he knew he'd better warn her. If she thought Bruce ratted her out, she might curse him or worse. Even though she gave him the heebie-jeebies, he drove out to her place and knocked on the door, nervous as a long-tailed cat in a room full of rocking chairs.

After pounding for what seemed like half an hour, Chumana opened the door, eyeing him with a scornful gaze. "Why have you come, melika wattsida? I did not summon you," the Pueblo woman said with obvious disdain in her voice.

Bruce did not care for her tone of voice or the 'I did not summon you' comment, but wisely chose to ignore both. "Believe me I don't want to be here, but I've got some important news. Let me in."

Chumana eyed him suspiciously for a moment. "What news do you bring, melika wattsida?"

"The kind that should be shared behind closed doors," Bruce said, looking nervously about, hoping no one was watching.

Chumana rolled her eyes. "We are miles from town, wattsida. There is no need to act like a frightened deer."

"I got good reason to be nervous. Just let me in, ok?"

"You had better not be wasting my time, wattsida," Chumana sighed begrudgingly as she opened the door. She motioned for Bruce to sit on a threadbare couch and seated herself in an old wooden rocking chair opposite him. "So, tell me. What is the important news you bring?"

Bruce immediately started rattling off the previous night's events. He told her how Gideon and Isabella chased him into the alley behind Red's but then started fighting each other, so he was able to escape.

As she listened to Bruce's tale, Chumana's irritation was replaced with great interest, especially when he described Isabella. "This woman used a whip, you say?"

"Yeah. Weird huh?"

"Did she have black hair?"

"Yeah."

"And a fair complexion but was not Anglo?"

"No, she's no gringa. She owns the yerberia in Santa Fe."

"Is she a curandera?"

"I don't know. Maybe? Shouldn't we be more concerned about the private eye?"

Chumana ignored Bruce's question and stood up from her rocking chair. "You have done well to tell me of this, Bruce. Do not worry about this curandera or the Anglo investigator. I will deal with them. You lure the Apache boy, Donnie, to the river tonight as we discussed earlier."

"Are you sure? Maybe we should lay low for a while. We don't want to bring the police down on us."

Chumana fixed Bruce with a frightful gaze and made no attempt to hide the irritation in her voice when she replied. "There will be no police to worry about. I said I would deal with this curandera and melika investigator and I will! Now do as your told, wattsida, and lure the Apache boy to the river tonight!"

Bruce got up from the couch, afraid of angering Chumana any further, and quickly made a beeline for the door. "Ok, ok. I'll lure the kid to the river."

There was unnatural bass in her voice and Bruce swore the room grew darker and dropped several degrees in temperature when Cumana spoke next.

"Do not fail me in this Bruce, or I promise you will regret it!"

Petrified, Bruce bolted.

Chumana watched with satisfaction as Bruce ran to his car like a frightened deer and drove off. Her thoughts returned to the new development. She'd had run-ins with a black-haired curandera who brandished a whip before. The woman was a thorn in Chumana's side, thwarting her plans several times and lifting curses off many of her intended victims; a powerful practitioner for someone who had lived but one lifetime. Although she was a worthy adversary, Chumana eventually bested her, casting a curse upon the curandera that caused her to go blind.

And now, just as her plans were poised for culmination, someone who could travel in the spiritual plane of existence shows up where the children are being held? Then her lackey has a run-in with a whip-wielding curandera? Suspect timing, that. But her battles with the curandera had been *decades* ago. It could not be her old adversary. No, this woman of whom Bruce spoke could not even be her old foe's child, for even she would be too old now. There were just too many similarities for this new curandera to not somehow be related. It must be her granddaughter, Chumana decided. Yes, that made sense. She must have taught the arts to her grandchild.

No matter. She had defeated the matriarch, so she could deal with this young pup as well. Chumana closed and locked the door. Taking a deep breath in preparation for what was to come, she turned and went to her bedroom. Once there, she drew the curtains and opened the window. After this was done, she stripped off her clothes. Standing naked, she began her spell, uttering words of transformation. The bruja felt the metamorphosis begin. It was a quick but unpleasant process. Others would call it agonizing but Chumana made friends with pain long ago. Still, she fell to her knees as the spasms wracked her body. Clenching her teeth, she endured the discomfort. Sweating profusely, her breathing became labored and her vision narrowed. For an instant, everything went black.

Sight returned to her, much sharper than before. The agony was gone as quickly as it had arrived. Sitting atop a pile of clothes, where a woman had been standing moments earlier, was a great grey owl. Chumana spread her wings and flew out the window. She quickly gained altitude, circling higher and higher. After getting her bearings, the great owl headed south towards Santa Fe. Chumana would seek out the yerberia and pay this new curandera a visit.

Chapter 21

McDonald's & Meditation

Using the walkie-talkies, I took the boys' lunch order. On my way back from Mcdonald's, I munched on some French fries. Listening to Kenny Loggins' new song "Danger Zone", I mulled some things over in my head as I drove. The boys were helping by keeping an eye on the other house, but maybe I was relying too much on mundane approaches to finding the missing kids. Something my two mentors in the realm of the supernatural, Father Dominic and Master Onosai, were always telling me was to keep an open mind and continually strive to broaden my horizons. Maybe I wasn't using all the assets I had at my disposal.

Isabella told me she had somehow been transported to a different place and saw the children in real-time when she had her visions. I believe her because *I* had been transported to a different place and time when I witnessed some hair-raising things via a magic scroll from Master Onosai. Isabella said she'd essentially been along for the ride and hadn't actively sought the children out. Rather, when she fell asleep, she was somehow taken there. It was almost as if the kids, or maybe something else entirely, were desperately trying to get her attention and show her what was happening.

Perhaps there was a way to be more proactive and use these visions of hers to track the children down. Father Dominic and the Order of Saint George were an excellent source of information on the supernatural, but he was on a different assignment somewhere in Europe. I knew if he was on assignment, he had his hands full. Master Onosai, on the other hand, just might be able to help.

Father Dominic and the Order of Saint George have been helping me improve my skillset when it comes to firearms training. Master Onosai has been helping me improve in my hand-to-hand and martial arts skills. In addition to combat, Master Onosai had also been teaching me how to meditate.

In the 60s and '70s, western culture began to get much greater exposure to eastern philosophies and concepts, including meditation. Now, in the 80s, a vast number of people still thought of meditation as hippie mumbo jumbo and mysticism. With my martial arts background and run-ins with the supernatural, I'm much more open-minded than your average Joe.

With Master Onosai as my guide, I learned how to develop my awareness, concentration, focus, and clarity through meditation. Because of this additional training, I could see parallels between Isabella's visions, remote viewing, and some heightened states of awareness in meditation. If anyone could find a way to help Isabella use her visions to help track down the missing children, I was sure it was Master Onosai.

I pulled up to the pre-arranged meeting spot, which was one street over from where the boys had been casing the house Bruce might be in. I passed out burgers, fries, and sodas, much to the boys' delight. Then, I had my little crew gather round. They all sat on the curb happily munching away.

"Thanks, Gideon," David said through a mouthful of food.

"Yeah, thanks a lot. I love McDonald's!" said Donnie.

"Their fries are the best!" Joey chimed in.

"Truer words have never been spoken," Dennis agreed.

"I wish they gave out something like the paper crowns you can get at Burger King, though." Joey added.

At this, Donnie broke into song, with the Burger King jingle. "Hold the pickles, hold the lettuce. Special orders won't upset us. All we ask is that you let us..."

The other boys all joined in with a resounding chorus of, "Serve it your way!" The group burst out laughing.

David spoke up. "Hey! Gideon brought McDonald's, not Burger King!"

"True," Donnie said, nodding sagely.

"Well then..." Joey said with a big smile on his face. He started singing the famous Mcdonald's jingle. "Two all-beef patties..."

The rest of the boys joined in quickly, all singing along. "...special sauce, lettuce, cheese, pickles, onions on a sesame seed bun!" They all chuckled heartily, then resumed their meal with delight. Being boys, they soon started goofing off in-between bites.

I smiled and thought, *ahh to be young again.* Then I remembered that thirty was far from old. Back to the business at hand. "You boys enjoy. You've earned it. But listen up, there's been a development."

The boys were all ears and stopped their playful banter. Nothing could be heard but the sound of their chewing.

"I'm going to have to head south and will be out of walkie-talkie range. If you see Bruce or that spooky Indian lady, I want you to give me a call." I handed each of the boys my business card. "That's my pager number, so I'll get it even if I'm not near a phone. Speaking of phones there's a payphone down at the end of the next street over. You guys know where it is?"

"Yeah," the boys all answered in unison.

"Good, but you'll need quarters for that so…" I reached into my duffle bag and gave each boy a roll of quarters. "I know you'll have some left over, so you can use the rest down at the arcade."

The boys burst into cheers then David led them all in a new song. "Gideon's great! Better than chocolate cake!"

The other boys joined in. "Gideon's great! Better than chocolate cake!"

I said my farewells to the boys and drove over to the phone booth I'd told them about. I dialed Master Onosai's number, singing, "Gideon's great! Better than chocolate cake!" to myself as I did.

Master Onosai picked up after the third ring. I stopped my singing and relayed to Master Onosai how I was on a case searching for children kidnapped by a witch and that an ally had been having visions that sounded like what Father Dominic called 'remote viewing'. I told him how similar it seemed to what I'd experienced when I used the magic scroll to witness the attack on the Kanagawa Monastery by the Kage clan when they tried to steal the Horn of Ryujin.

Master Onosai reacted as if I'd just told him about the weather in New Mexico, not witches and visions. "How can I be of help in this matter, Chosen One?"

Master Onosai referred to me as Chosen One because of an ancient prophecy. It foretold of someone who had a tattoo of an eagle and a dragon, just like I had. This person would save the Horn of Ryujin from falling into evil hands, thus preventing great suffering. I did exactly that. Although I can't argue fitting the bill, it still felt weird being called Chosen One.

"Well Master Onosai, although Isabella can see the children as if she were there herself in these visions, she doesn't know exactly where *there* is. She says when she falls asleep, she just finds herself there, almost as if someone is trying to show her the plight of the children and summons her there. I was hoping you might be able to give us a way to use these visions of hers more proactively. Let *her* be the one behind the wheel, so to speak, so we can use the visions to give us directions to this location. Then, we can find the place on our own and rescue the kids. You showed me meditative techniques to expand my focus from the narrow-minded range of attention that focuses on our physical bodies to a more open focus of the world around us. Can we use a similar method for her to be aware of the journey and how she got there?"

"Very good, Chosen One! You have taken the first steps into a larger world, where one progresses past the mechanics of using a tool and begins to think what he can now create with this tool. The answer to your question is yes. There are techniques like lucid dreaming. This is when, during a dream, the dreamer is aware they are dreaming, thus able to have control of their actions in the dream. Sometimes, to a certain extent, they can control the dream environment as well. Let me tell you how this can be done."

Chapter 22

Bad Eggs

As I drove south to Santa Fe, it seemed all the radio stations were conspiring together to only play songs that made me think of Isabella. First, it was "Venus" by Bananarama, then "Take Me Home Tonight" by Eddie Money, followed by "Why Can't This Be Love" by Van Halen. I gave up trying to change radio stations, thinking perhaps the universe was trying to tell me something. I settled on "Stuck with You" by Huey Lewis and the News and sang along in good spirits as I drove to Isabella's yerberia. "Yes, it's true. I am happy to be stuck with you."

Isabella's shop was downtown. Parking was hard to come by, so I had a bit of a hike before I made it to her shop. I didn't mind. I used the opportunity to take in the sights. All the buildings were of the distinctive Pueblo Indian style with flat roofs, vigas, and brown stucco walls. It gave the feeling you had stepped back in time. There were even Indians, sitting cross-legged on the sidewalks, selling silver and turquoise jewelry. Definitely not something you saw in downtown San Francisco.

Close to the plaza, there was a small park with grass, trees, benches, and an obelisk war monument. The stores in this area were more high-end, catering to a wealthy clientele. There were several art galleries bordering on ostentatious. As you moved farther out the stores weren't nearly as pretentious. There were more restaurants and touristy shops selling t-shirts and knickknacks. As I made my way to that area, I started to get the feeling I was being watched.

Over the years I've learned not to ignore 'gut' feelings like that. I paused to look at the wares of one of the stores through a big plate glass window. A passerby would think I was window shopping, but I was really using the window's reflection in a clandestine manner to see if anyone was following me.

If people just ambled by, odds were, I was being paranoid. If someone suddenly stopped in their tracks to look at their watch or abruptly stooped down to tie their shoe, it was probably a ploy to stay behind me and follow unnoticed. That kind of move would be obvious to a seasoned private investigator like me. I'd immediately spot the guy following me or, to use PI lingo, 'flush my tail out into the open'.

Oddly enough, I didn't see anyone. I pressed on, but still couldn't shake the feeling I was being tracked. As I continued walking there were no more windows handy to use as convenient mirrors. After a few blocks, I used another tactic. I don't smoke, but I keep a pack of cigarettes and a zippo lighter in the inside pocket of my trench coat for just such an occasion.

Taking a cigarette from the pack, I placed it between my lips. In a hopefully unforeseen move, I rapidly turned around one hundred and eighty degrees, cupping my hand over the cigarette as I brought up the lighter, as if shielding it from the wind.

Again, anyone following me would have to do something contrived to slow their pace enough to remain behind me. This sneaky PI tactic didn't turn up anyone either. Eventually, I made it to Isabella's yerberia. As I opened the door to the shop, I paused in the doorway and looked over my shoulder in one last-ditch effort to catch the person following me. All I saw was a big grey owl perched on a telephone pole across the street. It appeared to be watching me with great interest but really, it was only an owl. I shrugged my shoulders and went inside. Maybe I was just being paranoid with all this witch business.

Once inside, I took in the scene. Isabella's yerberia reminded me of the Chinese medicine shops my friend Jimmy Chen would frequent in Chinatown, if the proprietors converted to Catholicism. The pungent scent of exotic herbs mixed with burning incense filled the shop with a distinct and pleasant aroma. There were shelves and display cases everywhere containing all sorts of glass jars and plastic baggies of varying sizes filled with a multitude of dried herbs and powders. There were bottles of different gels and lotions, as well as little vials of various essential and scented oils, and incense sticks along with decorative incense holders for sale.

The décor was very Catholic, with all sorts of pictures and little wooden carvings and figurines of Jesus, the Virgin Mary, various saints, and angels on display. Besides this being an apparent design theme, there were many religious items for sale as well. Where other stores showcased postcards in small turnstile displays, Isabella filled hers with Catholic prayer cards and bookmarks. There were also devotional medals and rosaries for sale, along with tiny vials of holy water. There was even a section of shelves filled with religious candles. The wax for the candles had been poured into glass tubes about eight or nine inches tall and almost as wide around as a drinking glass. Instead of being clear, they had pictures of Jesus, the Virgin Mary, or saints on them.

Isabella was speaking Spanish with a female customer who looked to be about eight months pregnant. I assumed they were probably discussing the herbal equivalents of prenatal vitamins or some such thing. Not wanting to bother her while she was with a customer, I busied myself with looking at different herbal teas. Being a PI at heart, I casually observed from the sidelines.

The woman seemed agitated and concerned about something. She spoke very rapidly, but it was all in Spanish. I had no idea what she was saying. Isabella seemed unfazed by the woman's tone and whatever she was saying and merely nodded in response. After a bit, Isabella stepped from behind the counter and escorted the lady to a little waiting room of sorts set up in the corner of the shop. She helped the pregnant woman into a large, overstuffed chair and had her put her feet up on an ottoman. After her customer was comfortable, Isabella stepped through a beaded curtain to a back room and could be heard rummaging through things.

Isabella returned with an armful of supplies, which she placed on a side table near the chair. First, Isabella took a vial of what I recognized to be holy water, thanks to my tutelage under Father Dominic. She wetted her fingertips and then made the sign of the cross on her forehead and the forehead of the pregnant woman. Taking the vial, she sprinkled more holy water on the woman's stomach. Isabella took what looked to be a small bundle of dried sage and brushed the lady with it while she mumbled something in Spanish. I assumed prayers since she'd just been using holy water. She started from the woman's head and worked her way down to the woman's feet, like she was sweeping something off her, focusing mainly on the pregnant woman's stomach. When she finished with this brushing or sweeping,

Isabella took the sage and lit it on fire with a lighter. After letting the little bundle burn for a few seconds, she blew it out and waved it over the woman. Smoke wafted over her while she closed her eyes and recited what sounded like more prayers in Spanish.

Isabella took the end of the burnt sagebrush and ground it into a bowl. She took a small vial of oil, poured about a quarter of it into the bowl, and mixed it together with her fingers. Isabella instructed the pregnant lady to lift her shirt. Once the woman's very pregnant belly was exposed, Isabella rubbed the mixture of ash and oil on her stomach while reciting more prayers in Spanish. She dried her hands on a towel, then picked up a crucifix and an egg from the table. She presented the crucifix to the woman, who kissed it. Holding the egg in one hand and the crucifix in the other, Isabella seemed to pray over the egg.

After a few minutes of this, Isabella put the crucifix down and began to rub the egg all over the pregnant lady's stomach, again reciting prayers in Spanish. This was all very strange to me. Frankly, I would have written it off as superstitious mumbo jumbo, except for the odd feeling I got as Isabella performed the rites. Subtle, but still perceivable, it was similar to the hum you hear sometimes when you walk under big power lines, or the 'bad vibe' you get from playing with an Ouija board that makes the hairs on the back of your neck stand up. I could actually *feel* a tingling sensation and was getting goosebumps.

After several minutes of this 'egg treatment', Isabella placed the egg in the bowl with the oil and sage. She took the vial of holy water and sprinkled it on the woman's stomach, reciting some final prayers. This ended their session. The woman pulled her shirt back down, rummaged through her purse, and handed

Isabella twenty-five dollars. She exited the shop in a much better mood, smiling and waving as she left.

Isabella motioned for me to come closer after the lady departed. Grinning, I sauntered over to where she was cleaning up after the procedure.

"So that must have looked strange. Did I scare you off?" she asked jokingly.

"On the contrary. It was nice to see you in action," I replied.

Isabella smiled at my response. "Really? You didn't think that was crazy?"

I paused for a moment before answering. "Well, I'll admit it's not something you see every day, at least not in my neighborhood. It's been a few years since my Spanish class back in high school, so pretty much everything you guys were saying might as well have been in ancient Babylonian. Since I couldn't understand what was being said, I'm not about to write it off as nuts. Because hey, I don't really *know* just what went down. I'd just be guessing, and not even educated guesses. Also, I can't really explain it, but I definitely *felt* something. One of my teachers, Master Onosai, says the *wise* seek to understand that which they do not know while *fools* will pass judgment upon that which they do not comprehend. I try not to make a fool of myself whenever possible."

Isabella looked impressed. "That's a good policy. It sounds like this Master Onosai is a smart guy."

"He *is* pretty sharp and wise beyond his years. There are some techniques of his I'd like to share with you. First, though, could you fill me in on just what happened with the egg? I'm dying to know!"

Isabella seemed delighted I took a genuine interest in her work and, despite my lack of experience, proceeded with an open mind.

"It's called a limpia, which is a curandisimo ritual of spiritual cleansing used to break and lift curses. The pregnant woman felt she was a victim of brujeria, or witchcraft. Her husband, the unborn child's father, used to be with another woman before he married her. This ex of his has resented the pregnant lady ever since. In fact, she harbored such bitter jealousy that she hired a bruja to put a hex, or curse, on her to sabotage the pregnancy. If the pregnant woman is right in her assumption that she is a victim of a hex, the limpia ritual I just performed transferred the curse from the baby to the egg. Even if she's just being paranoid and it's all in her head, the limpia alleviated her fears at least. There will be no undue stress to burden her. Either way, I performed a service and helped her out."

Isabella's explanation captivated me, and I told her so. "This is all very fascinating stuff. Tell me, is there a way to know if the curse was real or just imagined?"

"Actually, yes. An ordinary egg that has never been refrigerated, like this one from my aunt's chicken coop, will take a little over a week before it goes bad. You can't tell by looking at them, but when you crack them open to cook, they smell bad and you know to throw them out. If the egg has absorbed a curse it will rot in as little as nine or ten minutes! They shrivel up, turn black, and give off a horrible smell right through the shell!"

I grimaced, making an exaggerated expression of disgust as I envisioned the putrid egg. "Yuck! That sounds nasty!"

Isabella laughed. "They smell worse than they sound." The two of us laughed at the joke then Isabella resumed the conversation. "Ok, I satisfied your curiosity. Now it's time for you to return the favor. What's this technique of Master Onosai's you were going to share with me?"

I relayed everything Master Onosai told me about the special meditation techniques. They would allow Isabella to be aware of the journey, from her bedroom when she fell asleep, to where the children were being held captive by the bruja. We made plans to use the strategy that very night to find the missing kids.

As we conspired to put our plan into action, my pager went off. I looked down and saw it was David and his friends. "I'm sorry but I have to go. Some informants of mine just spotted Bruce."

Isabella hurriedly jotted something down on a piece of paper. After locking eyes with me for a moment, she handed it to me. "Go but meet me at this address." She pointed to the paper. "As soon as you're done. One way or another we'll find the missing children."

"My thoughts exactly," I said, quickly taking the piece of paper from her. I turned and ran out the door.

Chumana sat and watched the Anglo private investigator run out of the yerberia from her perch across the street. She remained atop the telephone pole, still as a statue, and patiently waited for Isabella to leave her shop. As soon as the young woman closed for the night, she took off from high above and followed the curandera home unnoticed.

Chapter 23

Dealing with the Devil

I sprinted back to my rental car, thankful for my daily workout regime. The vehicle was several blocks away. I made record time but was panting heavily, almost completely out of breath, by the time I got there. The hills in San Francisco were steep and I was used to running six miles, not five and a half blocks! Of course, I ran at sea level, not seven thousand feet. The dramatic difference in elevation was devastating. It was a good thing I'd managed to run Bruce down inside half a mile, because after a full out run for three-quarters of a mile, the air in Santa Fe was just too thin. I had to slow down.

Luckily, driving didn't require any great cardiovascular endurance. I climbed into the car and put the pedal down. My tires squealed as I raced out of the parking lot and into the street where I maneuvered through slower-moving traffic. I weaved in and out, passing other cars at breakneck speeds, slippery as an eel.

The Buick Skylark didn't have the same oomph as the Grey Ghost, my souped-up 1979 Chevy Nova back home. With its racing suspension, upgraded exhaust system, and high flow headers, the Grey Ghost had a hell of a lot of added torque and horsepower. The Skylark got the job done though. When I cleared the city limits, I got the Buick up to one hundred and fifteen miles per hour in the stretch between Santa Fe and Española. Even though I was really eating up miles at that speed, I wanted to go even faster. I didn't want Bruce getting away this time and I couldn't stand the thought that Dave and his friends might be in danger.

Bruce pulled into his driveway, shaken up after his meeting with Chumana. He was convinced now that the Indian woman was some sort of bruja. The way she said, 'Do not fail me or you will regret it.' It wasn't normal! It was *waaay* too deep. A human being just doesn't make sounds like that. He was sure if he didn't deliver the Apache boy, she would make good on her threat.

When he saw some boys riding bikes in the street by his house, and noticed the Apache kid was one of them, he was more than a little relieved. His elation quickly turned to dread. After seeing him pull into the driveway, the boys radioed on their walkie-talkies and slowly started riding off in the other direction. It seemed they were taking their little game elsewhere. Jumping out of the car, Bruce tried his best to put on the airs of a good upstanding citizen. Smiling, he called the boys over, hoping to tempt them with what would have worked on him. "Hey boys! How would you like to make a quick buck?" He fanned out some twenty-dollar bills and held them out for the boys to see.

The boys had never seen so much money and stopped in their tracks. The man smiled, but even to the kids it looked forced. Ever the group leader, David spoke up. "Doing what," he asked warily. The suspicion and distrust were obvious in both his tone and body language.

Thinking on the fly, Bruce made something up. "Don't worry. It's nothing like hard labor. A friend of mine was going to deliver a package to me tonight but I can't be there. I need you guys to pick it up for me, that's all."

"Why can't he just leave it on the doorstep," David asked.

Bruce was starting to get annoyed with the boy's questions but bit his tongue and played nice. "It's too important for that. I can't risk leaving it out unattended. That's why I need you boys to pick it up for me. I'm willing to *pay*!" he said, emphasizing the word pay while gesturing with the twenty-dollar bills.

"How much money," Donnie asked, wide-eyed, gazing at the twenties and giving in to temptation.

"One hundred dollars," Bruce proudly announced, sure this would win the kids over.

"Apiece," asked Dennis.

"Hell no! There's four of you!" Bruce complained.

"Then it's only twenty-five dollars apiece, which isn't *that* much," Joey chimed in.

"Ok then. TWO hundred dollars," Bruce counteroffered.

"Better... but, I still don't know," said Joey.

"Yeah. If you can manage two hundred why not three," added Dennis.

"Three hundred? That's too much," Bruce protested.

"I guess you'll just have to find someone else to get your package, then," Donnie said.

"Yeah. Come on, guys. Let's go," Joey said as he turned his bike around and started to pedal off.

The other boys followed suit.

"Wait! Don't go! I'll give you three hundred. Just get me the package *tonight*."

The boys stopped, all smiles.

"Looks like we have ourselves a deal, mister," Donnie said, smiling. "Now pay up."

"Hold on. I need the package first! There's no such thing as something for nothing. Not a penny until I have the package in my hands."

"Ok. Just half up front then," Donnie countered.

"If I give you that much, you'll just take off and I'll never get my package."

"We need some sort of show of good faith here," Dennis said.

"Ok. I'll give you each twenty now and another three hundred when I get the package, so you guys get three hundred and eighty total. That's my FINAL offer."

"It's a deal," said Donnie.

Bruce started walking over, grinning like he was the big bad wolf and had just cornered little red riding hood.

Suddenly David chimed in. "No deal!"

"Come on kid! That's a lot of money," Bruce complained.

David ignored Bruce and instead talked to the boys. "This barf bag is probably behind Blake's kidnapping. For all we know, he's setting us up. Even if he isn't, we don't make deals with scum like him!"

Bruce was visibly flustered. Panicking, he tried to salvage the deal. "Hey, if your friend doesn't want in, fine. That just means more money for the rest of you."

"Guys don't listen to him," David shouted.

Angry now, Bruce started to advance on David. "Listen, you little shit! Let your friends make up their own minds!"

When David saw Bruce coming towards him, he took a slingshot out from his back pocket and loaded the little leather patch with a marble. He stretched the rubber tubing all the way back to his face, taking a second to aim before he released it. David let the marble fly and his aim was true. The marble struck Bruce right in the middle of his forehead.

"Mierda!" Bruce exclaimed as he staggered backwards, his hand on his forehead. The blow from the slingshot hurt a *lot*. Taking his hand away, he saw the marble struck him so hard it broke the skin. There was blood on his hand! "Hijo de puta! You're gonna pay for that, you little shit!"

Enraged, Bruce ran towards David who immediately hopped on his bike and took off, pedaling for all he was worth. The other boys took off as well, but Bruce singled out David. He sprinted towards him, spewing forth obscenities in Spanish as he ran at the boy. Bruce managed to grab the back of David's t-shirt and nearly pulled him off the bike.

David had a death grip on the handlebars and managed to stay on the bike, even though his t-shirt ripped from the force of Bruce's attempt to pull him down. The sound of tearing fabric spurred him onward as he pumped his legs even faster, pedaling away on his bike. Glancing over his shoulder, David saw he was leaving his pursuer in the distance. He decided to risk a show of defiance. Still holding on to the handlebars with his left hand, he released his grip with his right and stretched out his arm. He extended his middle finger, giving Bruce 'the bird'.

"Chingate cabrón!" Bruce yelled returning the gesture. Knowing he couldn't run the boy down on foot, Bruce hopped into his car and continued the chase.

The 1970 Chevy Impala quickly caught up to David. Eleven-year-old boys know shortcuts that most don't, however, and David quickly swerved down a narrow alley where the big Chevy couldn't follow.

Cursing, Bruce slammed the car into reverse. His tires squealed in protest as he did. He knew where the little shit lived, so he would just get there first. He stomped down on the accelerator and the Chevy tore off down the street towards David's house.

As David emerged from the alley, he saw Bruce's big black Chevy Impala swerve around the corner at the end of the street. He wasn't sure he'd make it to his house in time. He heard Joey's voice come through the little speaker on his walkie-talkie. "David quick! Come to my house!"

Just then, he saw Joey round the corner on the opposite end of the street, pedaling his bike like the Devil himself was hot on his heels. Joey's house was closer, and David tore off in that direction.

Bruce saw David heading for his friend's house at the opposite end of the street and gunned the engine of his Impala. It lurched forward, quickly gaining on the boys. Despite their best efforts, pedal power proved to be no match for a 454 cubic inch turbo jet V8 engine with 390 horsepower. Despite their head start, he cut them off, pulling up onto the sidewalk in front of Joey's front yard.

Bruce leapt out of his car as the two boys circled around the big Impala, dumping their bikes on the front lawn. They made a mad dash for the front door. He got there first.

"Where do you two think you're going," he asked threateningly.

"Help!" Joey yelled at the top of his lungs.

"Ain't nobody gonna get here on time. You little shits are gonna pay!"

"Oh yeah, well Gideon Jones will be here any second," David shouted defiantly.

"Help!" Joey yelled again.

"Who the hell is Gideon Jones," Bruce asked insolently.

"He's a badass private eye, and he's going to kick your ass," David boldly proclaimed.

"Help!" Joey yelled, not nearly as bold.

"You think I'm afraid of some gringo PI?" Bruce puffed out his chest, full of bravado.

"You'd better be. He'll gut punch you so hard you'll poop your kidneys out," David warned.

"Help!" Joey yelled again.

"I ain't afraid of no pinche gringo chota wanna be," Bruce boasted arrogantly.

"But are you afraid of *this*," asked a distinctly feminine voice from behind him.

Bruce spun around to see a young teenage girl with short brown hair and glasses pointing a .38 caliber Smith & Wesson Special right at him.

Bruce immediately put both his hands up in the universal 'I surrender' posture and started backpedaling. "Don't shoot," he said meekly, all his former bravado vanishing in an instant.

The girl kept the revolver pointed right at him and advanced forward. "You leave my little brother and his friend alone and get the hell out of our yard!" she commanded with steel in her voice.

"Blow him away, Karissa!" Joey cheered.

"Yeah Karissa! Blow him away!" David echoed.

"No! Don't shoot! I'm leaving. I won't bother you guys ever again," Bruce pleaded. He ran to his car, clambering in as fast as he could, and sped off.

"Aww, you should have blown him away," Joey complained.

"Shut up, Joey. What the hell were you two doing hanging around Bruce Ortiz? Everyone knows he's bad news. How about thanking me for just saving you," Karissa said, scolding her little brother.

"Sorry. Thanks! We were minding our own business, riding our bikes, when Bruce came up and offered us money to pick up a package for him. We turned him down. When he wouldn't take no for an answer, David shot him in the face with his slingshot!"

Karissa burst out laughing. "Good for you, David."

Bruce was in a foul mood as he pulled into his driveway. He slammed the car door as hard as he could and cursed his luck in Spanish. The Apache boy, Donnie, rode up on his bike.

"I'll take you up on your offer, but I want sixty dollars up front and three hundred and forty more when I deliver the package."

Bruce smiled wolfishly. "Smart move, kid. All you have to do is go down to the river tonight after dark. I'll show you where."

Chapter 24

Uninvited

Isabella followed Gideon to the door, not believing she'd just handed him her home address on that piece of paper. She watched him run down the street, trench coat flapping behind him like a superhero's cape. The song "Holding Out for a Hero" by Bonnie Tyler came to mind and she started singing as she went about closing up shop. "Where have all the good men gone and where are all the gods? Where's the streetwise Hercules to fight the rising odds? Isn't there a white knight upon a fiery steed?"

At this point, Isabella stopped singing and took out Gideon's business card to examine it more closely. The company logo was a chess piece, the one in the shape of a horse, called the knight, wearing a fedora under the words *White Knight Detective Agency*. Hmmm… coincidence or a sign, she asked herself.

After a moment, she decided it was a good sign. She wasn't sure of exactly what just yet, but that was ok. Good was good enough. There was no need to rush into things and define it any further than that, although it had been a while since she'd been in a romantic relationship. Sure, Gideon was tall with rugged good looks, polite, charming, and happened to share her love of the martial arts. He even seemed genuinely interested in what she did for a living and not just the size of her breasts. *That is no reason to go all weak in the knees*, she told herself. She was perfectly content to be single. Isabella pocketed the business card and resumed her singing.

"Late at night I toss, and I turn, and I dream of what I need!" Blushing, Isabella stopped singing again. It was a silly song anyway. She sniffed at the air, detecting a foul odor. Grimacing, she quickly took the bowl with the egg, which had shriveled up and turned black, outside and threw it in the dumpster. Upon returning to the shop, she lit some more incense, finished cleaning up, and locked all the doors.

Once outside, Isabella hopped into her green Jeep and started heading southeast towards Glorieta, a little community outside of Santa Fe where rent was much cheaper. It was nestled in the woods, which for Isabella was a bonus. The privacy was wonderful, and she could harvest some of the herbs needed for her craft out there. She drove along in good spirits, completely unaware of the big grey owl following high above.

When she got home, Isabella took a bottle of sweet Lambrusco red wine from the fridge and poured herself a big glass. Then, she turned on some soft music and plopped down in her comfy, overstuffed couch. She put her feet up on a nearby ottoman and enjoyed the view of the setting sun through her living room window.

The Sangre de Cristo Mountains, the southernmost subrange of the Rocky Mountains which run from southern Colorado to northern New Mexico, ended at Glorieta Pass, just southeast of Santa Fe and practically right outside Isabella's front doorstep. Sangre de Cristo is Spanish for Blood of Christ. The mountains were named for the striking reddish hues observed during sunrise and sunset.

Drinking wine while watching the sunset was one of Isabella's favorite guilty pleasures. She lounged on the couch until her glass was empty and the room had grown dark. With a sigh, she got up, turned on the lights, and started rummaging through the fridge in search of leftovers she could reheat for dinner.

Meanwhile, Chumana landed among the trees, just outside the young curandera's yard. As soon as night fell, under cover of darkness, she changed back into a woman. There was a chill on the night air and the witch could see the steam of her own breath as she stood beside a pine tree, naked and shivering. She learned long ago to ignore such minor inconveniences. Closing her eyes, she focused her will and began to murmur a spell.

She repeated her chant over and over. As she did, the curls of steam from her breath began to thicken and gather into dense tendrils of mist that sank to the ground and hung low, slithering there like misty serpents in the night. They gathered until the ground was covered in a blanket of fog. As Chumana continued chanting, fog erupted forth from her mouth like a geyser. Billows of fog rolled out until thick clouds of fog hung in the air. Confident she was now obscured from view, the witch boldly marched up to the young curandera's house.

Inside, Isabella put a Tupperware container of beans and red chili into the microwave and set the timer for two minutes. A mere fifteen seconds into the countdown, the power went out and everything went black. Lamenting her luck, Isabella carefully felt her way along the kitchen counter in the dark until she reached the end. She groped around for the handle of the drawer where she kept one of those new, big Maglite flashlights that used four D cell batteries.

Isabella had placed it there for just such an occasion, hoping the huge aluminum flashlight would be easy to find in the dark. As it turned out, she was right. She found the handle to the drawer, opened it, and started feeling around. The massive Maglite was easy to distinguish by touch alone. Upon finding it, Isabella ventured out the side entrance of the house to find the circuit breaker box. Hopefully, power would be restored with the simple flip of a switch.

Outside, Isabella was momentarily taken aback. Fog was not a common occurrence in Santa Fe or the surrounding areas, especially so thick as it was now. In fact, she couldn't recall *ever* seeing fog like this. She hoped Gideon wouldn't have any problems finding her place.

It will be even harder to find if the lights are out, she thought to herself as she went to the side of the house. She found the circuit breaker box and lifted the lid. While Isabella searched for the tripped switch, Chumana slipped silently past her in the thick fog and crept into the house, completely undetected.

Isabella found the tripped breaker fairly quickly. After flipping the switch, she was rewarded with light spilling out into the night from the half-open door. Turning off the Maglite, Isabella went back inside, her thoughts on dinner. She was shocked to see a naked woman, thin and deeply tanned, with long black hair streaked with grey, about five feet two inches tall, standing in the middle of her kitchen.

Chapter 25

Cat/Dog Fight

"Who the hell are you and what in the world are you doing naked in my house!?" Isabella demanded.

"I am here to ensure you no longer intrude in affairs that do not concern you, *curandera*," Chumana replied, putting emphasis and inflection on the word 'curandera' as if it was the vilest insult.

"I don't know what you're talking about, loca. You better get the hell out of my house before I call the cops," Isabella said, pointing to the door.

Chumana eyed Isabella with obvious disdain. "Do not lie to me, curandera! I saw you when you traveled through the spirit realm to spy on me!"

Upon hearing Chumana refer to the spirit realm, realization dawned on Isabella. "*You!* You are the bruja who has the children!" Isabella cried, the righteous rage of angels welling up inside her. She drew back the big flashlight like a club and took an aggressive step towards the witch.

Chumana seemed unfazed by Isabella's threatening advance and merely smiled. "Yes, and you have meddled in my affairs for the last time." With that, the bruja waved a hand in front of her as if swatting at a fly.

Isabella flew backwards, struck by an invisible force hard enough to knock her off her feet. Her martial arts training served her well. By reflex, she tucked her chin and rounded her back into the backwards breakfall she had done so many times in her Aikido classes. Releasing her hold of the Maglite, she slapped the floor with both her hands to minimize the impact.

Isabella was on her feet again in an instant. She charged the witch, not intimidated but livid she'd been struck by this phantasmal force. In answer, Chumana quickly raised both her hands above her head and immediately brought them back down again. Isabella collapsed, mid-stride, as if gravity had increased tenfold.

Keeping her hands down, like she was pressing on something, Chumana suddenly swept her arms sideways as if she were knocking the contents of a table onto the floor. Isabella went sliding across the kitchen floor, crashing violently into the wall. The witch repeated the gesture again and again. Each time, Isabella slid across the floor, from one side of the room to the other, smashing into the wall with powerful force.

These telekinetic attacks took their toll. Isabella lay stunned on the floor, panting and unable to regain her feet as she saw stars swimming before her eyes. Chumana did not let up. With another sweeping gesture, she levitated Isabella off the ground, bringing her all the way up to the ceiling, where she stayed hovering in midair for a moment, struggling futilely like a worm on a hook. The witch brought her crashing back down to the floor with a painful thud.

Isabella let out a moan as she lay spent upon the floor. "Ooooh, mierda."

Chumana laughed at her adversary's plight.

"Go ahead and laugh. I'll make you pay for that, perra," Isabella hissed through clenched teeth.

With another wave of her hand, Chumana sent Isabella sailing across the room to bang into the wall again. This time she kept the curandera pinned up against it, about a foot off the ground. Kicking her feet franticly, Isabella tried in vain to break free. The witch stood several feet away with one arm outstretched, her fingers splayed apart as if she were physically pinning Isabella herself instead of using a spell. She addressed her opponent.

"It is now time for you to die, curandera." Chumana began to curl in and clench her fingers like squeezing an imaginary ball.

As she did, Isabella began to choke and gasp as she flailed about, still pinned to the wall. She clawed desperately at the air trying to somehow pry away the invisible arm that was strangling her.

"Die," Chumana hissed with extreme malevolence in her voice as she kept her arm outstretched and her fingers clenching.

Isabella, still pinned to the wall, face bright red as she fought for air, reached to her left. Desperately groping about until her fingers encountered the knife block there, she withdrew a large butcher knife. "You first," she gasped as she threw the knife at Chumana.

The butcher knife tumbled end over end as it sailed through the air. Striking home, it buried itself deep in the witch's shoulder. Having a knife plunged into her effectively broke Chumana's concentration and Isabella dropped to the floor.

As Isabella sat there, gasping to regain her breath, she saw the witch start to pull the knife out. She sprang up, crying out in anger as she charged forward, and tackled Chumana to the ground. Isabella slammed the witch with a wicked right cross and then another. "Die!? We'll see who dies!" she yelled, hitting her again. "I'm going to beat you to death, bitch!!" With that, Isabella mounted her and began to rain down blows upon the pinned witch.

Chumana squirmed and bucked wildly but Isabella stayed on top, pummeling her with blow after blow. The bruja struggled mightily, much stronger than a woman her size should be. In fact, she was stronger than any man Isabella had sparred with in her training. Despite Chumana's greater strength, Isabella's superior skill allowed her to remain on top of Chumana, in a dominant position, as she repeatedly punched her. Although she couldn't escape, Chumana managed to turn around so Isabella could no longer punch her in the face. After Chumana did this, Isabella grabbed a fistful of her long hair and pounded her head onto the tiled kitchen floor.

Chumana began to convulse and spasm, growling like an animal. Undeterred, Isabella slammed her head into the floor again. Suddenly, Isabella heard loud popping and snapping sounds. As Chumana's convulsions continued, she began to sweat profusely.

In response to this new development, Isabella tried to beat the witch's head onto the floor harder but found she couldn't. Chumana's neck and shoulders had somehow grown more powerful and Isabella couldn't force the witch's head down anymore. *Fine,* Isabella thought to herself. Giving up trying to bang her head down, she slammed her elbow into the base of Chumana's neck instead.

Chumana growled, but not the imitation growl of a human mimicking an animal. It was the guttural sound of an enraged beast. Isabella looked down in horror as coarse black fur began to sprout from Chumana's skin at an impossible rate, growing several inches in a mere second. Isabella suddenly found herself no longer atop a woman, but astride a massive, snarling black dog!

This new form was larger and even more powerful. It bucked Isabella off. Teeth bared, it leapt at Isabella, toppling her to the ground. Lunging forward, the beast was ready to tear out her throat. At the last instant, Isabella grabbed the Maglite, thrusting it in front of her. The huge dog chomped down onto its hard aluminum handle instead of Isabella's tender flesh.

With its massive paws, the huge dog pinned Isabella to the ground. Shaking its head back and forth violently, it tore the flashlight from her grasp, sending it flying across the room. Then, the colossal dog lunged for her throat again. This time, Isabella was forced to place her own arm in front of her throat.

The great black witch-dog bit down, sinking its teeth deep into Isabella's forearm. Isabella cried out in pain and screamed anew as the monster shook its head back and forth, damaging her injured arm even more. She saw the handle of the butcher knife still protruding from the witch-dog's shoulder.

Isabella withdrew the knife and slashed it across the dog's face. Yelping, the giant dog released its hold on her arm and backed away. Quickly, Isabella regained her feet. Locking eyes with the snarling beast, she said, "Oh no, bitch. I'm not through with you."

Leaping forward, Isabella tackled the beast and stabbed the big butcher knife into its side. The great black dog yelped in pain and tried to scramble free, but she clung tightly to the huge beast.

"You aren't going anywhere, perra! It's YOU who's going to die!!" Isabella screamed. She stabbed the witch-dog in the side again. She withdrew the butcher knife so she could plunge it down a third time. The witch-dog began yipping, yowling, and growling in a strange manner. It sounded like the creature was trying to talk with a mouth not shaped for human speech.

"Beg all you want, but I'm going to carve you up into little pieces!" Isabella hollered.

Suddenly, she was no longer grappling with a great black dog. One instant she had her arms wrapped around its massive torso, and the next, a huge owl was in its place, screeching and beating its wings wildly.

Big as the owl was, it was much smaller than the massive dog. The sudden change in size had Isabella mostly holding thin air, which momentarily loosened her grip on Chumana. Taking advantage, the witch squirmed free and flew out the still-open door.

"Me cago en tu puta madre! Hija de la grand puta!" Isabella yelled. In addition to hurling insults, she flung the butcher knife at the fleeing owl, missing only by the narrowest of margins.

Chapter 26

The Best Laid Plans

I forced myself to slow from one hundred and fifteen to fifty-five miles per hour when I reached Española city limits. Anxious, as I was worried about the kids, it seemed like I was crawling along at a snail's pace even though I was moving much faster than the traffic in town. Weaving my way through the slower-moving cars, I barely registered the honks and angry hand gestures I provoked.

As I reached Bruce's neighborhood, I slowed down further to twenty-five miles per hour. Bruce had no idea what kind of car I drove and probably wouldn't recognize me. Speeding through a residential area would only draw attention to myself. Difficult as it was, I composed myself. Although I was a bundle of nerves on the inside, you never would have guessed as I drove past Bruce's place. I looked calm and relaxed, possibly even bored to the casual observer. As I rolled past Bruce's house there was no black Impala sitting in the driveway. On a hunch, I drove to Dave's neighborhood.

As I pulled onto David's street, I saw Bruce's car speeding away. I was about to give chase when I noticed David and his friend Joey standing on the front lawn of one of the houses with a teenage girl. Was that a pistol in her hands?!

I pulled up, rolling down my window. "Are you boys ok," I asked, concerned. "I'm a friend, miss," I quickly added, as the girl start to raise the .38 special.

"It's all right Karissa. We know him. This is Gideon Jones. He's a private investigator looking for the missing kids," David told Karissa.

She quickly lowered the pistol. "Sorry, Mr. Jones. It's just, that the boys were in a bit of trouble," Karissa said apologetically.

"What happened?" I asked.

Joey excitedly chimed in. "You just missed it, Gideon! Bruce tried to hire us to pick up a package for him. We refused, but he wouldn't take no for an answer, so David shot him in the face with a slingshot!"

I just barely stifled a laugh. "You did what?"

Joey continued enthusiastically. "Yeah! Pow! Right in the forehead with a marble! Bruce was *SO* mad. He chased us here, but Karissa pulled a gun on him and he took off!"

Karissa blushed. "Bruce is really bad news and he looked like he was about to hurt the boys," she said, trying to justify her actions.

"Everyone knows Bruce is a real barfbag, Karissa. I don't think you overreacted. Sounds to me like you did the right thing. In fact, that was good, quick thinking on your part. The boys were lucky you were here," I said.

Karissa smiled at the compliment.

"Yeah! He won't be coming around here again!" Joey said proudly.

"Even so, I never intended for anything like this to happen when I asked you boys to call me if you saw Bruce so..." I pulled out my wallet. "Here is some hazardous duty pay," I said, giving each boy a twenty-dollar bill.

"Wow!" said Joey.

"Thanks, Gideon!" David said.

"Yeah thanks," added Joey.

"You're welcome. You boys earned it. You've been a big help, but I want you to steer clear of Bruce. Stay as far away as possible from him now. I'll handle things from here on out, ok?"

"You got it," said Joey.

"No problem," said David.

"Good, I've got to get going now. You boys take care. It was a pleasure meeting you, Karissa." I hopped back in the car and drove away. I cruised by Bruce's house again but still no black Chevy Impala. My little gamble had backfired and scared Bruce off. Damnit!

It's time to implement plan B and put Master Onosai's techniques into action, I thought. I pulled out the address Isabella gave me earlier and flipped through my Rand McNally Road Atlas, looking for a good route.

Course mapped out, I headed south again. As I drove along, I took in the scenic view of the setting sun, noticing how it bathed the nearby mountains in a vibrant red glow. After I exited the Santa Fe city limits and got closer to Glorieta, it grew dark. Unexpectedly, I encountered a very dense fog just as I was supposed to arrive, according to the map anyway.

Hailing from San Francisco, I'm no stranger to coastal fog. I can't recall ever seeing it quite so thick. How was there even fog here? There's no nearby body of water to draw moisture from. I slowed down, easing my foot off the gas pedal. I could barely see. Suddenly something crashed into the car's windshield hard enough to nearly shatter it, leaving an intricate labyrinth of cracks across the driver's side.

I slammed on the brakes. *Oh god, did I just hit someone?* I quickly got out of the car to investigate. The biggest owl I'd ever seen was sprawled out on the road. The beast had a wingspan longer than the stripe down the middle of the road. Those are much longer than most people realize. Ten feet is the federal guideline for every street, highway, and rural road in the United States.

The huge owl appeared to be dead. There was a fair amount of blood on the road. Ordinarily, I'd feel terrible for harming a great bird like that, but... something about the creature gave me the creeps. I contemplated taking out my pistol and putting a bullet in the massive bird's head just to make sure it was dead. Suddenly, I heard a woman yelling what sounded like obscenities in Spanish.

"Isabella?! Is that you?" I called out, walking towards the sound of her voice.

"Gideon?!" Isabella answered as she came running out to meet me.

As it turned out, I stopped right at Isabella's driveway. Isabella came closer and it seemed like she materialized out of the mist. I was thrilled to see her, but my excitement quickly turned to concern when I saw her cradling her left arm. It was covered in blood.

"Are you alright? Isabella, what happened?"

"The bruja! She attacked me, but after I stabbed her with a butcher knife a few times she turned into an owl and flew off." She stopped for a moment and shook her head. "That sounded a lot crazier out loud."

Instead of the disbelief Isabella was expecting, I drew my .45 caliber pistol. "I hit a big owl with my car as I was pulling up!" I ran back to the car with Isabella right on my heels.

The car lights were still on, so it was easy to find even in the dense fog. When we got there, the huge owl was gone. A small pool of blood and a few feathers in the road in front of the car were all that remained.

Isabella said a few choice words in Spanish then, quickly composing herself, she turned to me. "You've got to show me those techniques of Master Onosai's. She's hurt and now is the time to go after the children."

"Why else do you think I'm here, darlin'?" I said, giving Isabella my most charming smile.

She did a quick double-take as I said it. "Wait a minute. Did you just call me darling?"

"It's a figure of speech," I reasoned.

"It's a term of endearment," Isabella countered.

"But also a figure of speech."

"Uh-huh. We'll talk about this later. For now, let's focus on finding the kids," Isabella said as she turned and walked off towards her house.

I followed, admiring her form as I did. "Oh, I'm looking forward to later."

At that, Isabella froze in her tracks. I was preparing an apology for overstepping bounds when she looked back over her shoulder and gave me a flirtatious smile. "Focus, Gideon."

"Oh, I'm focusing."

"Good," Isabella said continuing onward.

As Isabella walked, I couldn't help mutter, "It's hard for a man not to focus on a body like that."

"What did you say?"

"I said I'm focusing, I'm focusing!"

Chapter 27

The Physics of Magic

Once inside, I looked at Isabella's wound again. She had a nasty bite on her left forearm. "First things first. We need to take care of that arm. Do you have a first aid kit around here?"

"Yeah, hold on a second." Isabella walked off, returning in a moment with a first aid kit the size of a briefcase.

I helped her stand up the kitchen table, which had been knocked over in her struggle with Chumana. We set the big case down and looked through its contents. In addition to your standard Band-Aids and aspirin, it was stocked full of large sterile pads for wound dressing and bandages.

I let out a low whistle of appreciation. "You used to be a nurse or something?"

"I just adhere to the school of thought that it's better to have it and not need it than to need it and not have it."

"You're a woman after my own heart, Isabella. Those are words to live by. Before we bandage you up though, we should clean it up first."

We went to the kitchen sink and washed Isabella's arm with soap and water. When she was cleaned up, I went back to the first aid kit to rummage around. "Do you have any iodine or some other type of antiseptic?"

"Even better," Isabella said, going to a cupboard and bringing back some herbs and a mortar and pestle.

"So, what you got there?" I asked as she ground up the herbs.

"Aloe Vera, arnica, goldenrod, and yarrow. All excellent for the treatment of wounds."

Once Isabella ground the ingredients into a paste, she applied it to the pads. I took them and placed them on her forearm. She winced a little. Impressed with her pain tolerance, I wrapped her arm thoroughly with bandages.

"Ok, so start telling me about these techniques of Master Onosai," Isabella said, rummaging through her pantry.

"And what are you doing?"

"I'm making myself some ginger and turmeric tea with some cloves added for good measure."

"Also good for wounds?"

"No, for pain. They're natural pain killers."

"So, no aspirin then?"

"Actually, I'm going to take some extra-strength Tylenol and Ibuprofen. If I wash it down with ginger and turmeric tea instead of plain old water, it will work even better."

"Ok, just no alcohol. I know from experience that it can be an excellent pain killer, but you'll need a clear head for what we're about to do."

"No worries. It's just a bitter tea. No mind-numbing qualities."

While Isabella readied her tea, I explained what we were about to do. I broke it down and explained the reasons for each step in the process. For some people, having a rudimentary understanding of *why* in addition to *how* helped increase their confidence and belief in the techniques. Faith was an important key for this to work.

Isabella took her medicine and sat across the table from me. She sipped her tea and listened with rapt attention as I detailed the process and what she had to do. I explained that, essentially, people experience an overload of stimuli and information throughout the day. We have subconscious filters. These filters block trivial information so we can focus on what our brain deems important.

Not a bad practice, but one with an unintended side effect. The subconscious sees much more than people realize and stores that information for later use. Most are never aware of it, so few try to access it. Isabella raised her hand to ask a question as if she were back in school. I paused and motioned for her to ask her question.

"I'm sorry to interrupt. This is all very interesting stuff. Fascinating actually, but what does it have to do with finding the children?"

I smiled. "Excellent question. To answer it, let me give you a little magic 101. You see, my mentors in magic have explained to me that magic doesn't exist *outside* of reality. It's part of it and operates under the same set of rules. For instance, when a demon takes corporeal form, it's immediately bound by the laws of physics, not exempt from them.

"Magic is a way to manipulate energy in ways scientists aren't quite able to explain yet. But hey, they can't even fully explain gravity! They just know it exists and that the more mass you have, the greater the gravitational pull. They can't tell us *why* it works the way it does. One day they might, and one day science might be able to explain what we now call magic instead of rejecting it outright, but for now, it can't.

"Think of today. Cars are commonplace machines we utilize for transportation. One hundred and ninety years ago, they would most likely have been considered some sort of supernatural construct or the work of the devil by most people. Whether something is mundane or supernatural depends largely on one's knowledge base and perspective. But whether you consider a car to be the work of General Motors or the devil, it is bound by the laws of physics.

"Power is derived from the utilization of resources, be they physical or chemical. Resources are finite. Just like your car needs gas to run, and once it's out it can't travel anymore, a wizard or witch needs to get power for their spells from somewhere. That power is finite, and usually takes quite a toll on the user. Just like you or I would be exhausted after running a marathon, a witch or wizard would be exhausted after casting a powerful spell. They operate under the same rules of physics we do.

"When you travel from point A to point B, whether in corporeal or ethereal form, you take a route. Even though your conscious mind may not remember the journey, that doesn't mean the journey didn't take place or that your subconscious mind didn't dutifully take note of it and file it away. That's where Master Onosai's meditation techniques come in. They allow you to access that part of your subconscious mind, so you can recall the journey and retrace the route leading us to the children."

Isabella nodded her head in understanding. "Ok, I'm in. Tell me what I have to do."

I smiled. It was an uplifting change to have a beautiful woman believe me when I talked about magic instead of writing me off as a nutcase. "First we'll need to eliminate any potential distractions. Where's your phone?"

Isabella pointed to the hallway where a phone was mounted on the wall. I got up from my seat and unplugged the phone. "Any others?"

Isabella shook her head no.

"Good. Next, we'll need to remove as much sensory stimuli as possible. Do you have something we can use as a blindfold?"

Isabella nodded. She got up and went to her room, returning with a blue silk scarf. "Will this do?"

"That's perfect. Next, we'll need a comfortable place for you to sit or lie down. It's best if your back is as straight as possible and your head is supported."

"I guess that would be my bed."

"Well then, take me to your bedroom."

Chapter 28

Hot Tubs and VCRs

At first glance, Isabella's bedroom gave no indication of being a woman's room. At least, I didn't see any stereotypical feminine trappings. There were no make-up products, pieces of jewelry, floral prints, or any traces of pink to be found. Instead, there was a queen-size bed with a comfortable looking forest green quilt, a set of bookshelves, a writing desk, and a dresser with a stereo and set of speakers on top of it. A single picture hung on the wall opposite the bed. It depicted a tranquil lake scene and was the only adornment on the walls, save a coiled bullwhip that hung from a hook by the bed within arm's reach. I knew from experience that, for Isabella, whips were not merely ornamental.

I pointed to the chair in front of the desk. "Do you mind if I have a seat?"

"No, of course not. Sientate," Isabella answered.

Hopefully, that meant to sit down. As I sat, I gestured towards the bed. "Please, make yourself comfortable as well."

Isabella plopped down on the bed facing me, took a deep breath, and asked, "So how do I do this?"

"I'll do what's called guided meditation, walking you through everything step by step. These steps may not make sense, but they're designed to help you transition from your conscious mind to your subconscious. First, I need you to lie down on your back with your hands by your sides, palms facing down."

Isabella did as I instructed.

"Good. Now, without moving your head or neck at all, I want you to look up as far as you can. Like you're trying to see something just beyond your field of vision. Remember, don't move your head at all. Just use your eyes. Good. Now, keep looking up as far as you can. I actually want you to strain your eyes as much as you can."

"I can't look any further without moving my head."

"That's perfect. Now, I want you to hold your eyes there, wide open. Don't let your eyelids close even a little, not even the tiniest of fractions. Good. Keep them wide open just like that while I count to twenty. I don't want you to let your eyes drop either, not even a little. Keep them rolled back in your head as far as they will go. Good, just like that." I slowly counted to twenty. "You're doing great. Now close your eyes. Let your eyelids fall naturally, don't squeeze them shut. Perfect. How does that feel?"

"Now that I've stopped, it feels good. I had no idea how tiring it would be keeping my eyes open like that," Isabella admitted.

"Good. I want you to focus on how good it feels now that you've closed your eyes. I'm going to take your scarf and blindfold you. I don't need you to sit up or anything. Just lie still and let me do all the work."

I gently wrapped the silk scarf around her head, blindfolding her. Once it was secure, I continued with the guided meditation. "I want you to take a deep breath. Slowly inhale through your nose and exhale through your mouth."

Isabella did as she was instructed.

"Good. Again, another deep breath. In through your nose, out through your mouth. Good. Now keep breathing deep breaths just like that. With each breath, become more aware of the relaxed feeling you're experiencing in your eyes.

"Now, just as you are aware of your eyes and how good they feel, now that you aren't straining them, I want you to become aware of the rest of your body. Start at your feet and slowly work your way up to the top of your head, as if you're very slowly and gently easing yourself into a tub of hot water feet first. Visualize that very thing. You are slowly immersing yourself in a hot tub. As you gradually slip deeper into the tub you can feel the hot water's relaxing effects soothe away any aches and pains, releasing any tension. Focus on the soothing sensation the hot water has on your body. Take your time and go slow. Pay close attention to your muscles as they relax and let go of their pent-up tension. Be aware of this feeling as it travels all the way up your body, from the bottoms of your feet to the top of your head. This should take several minutes. As all that unconscious tension slips away, you're left with no distractions, just a sense of calm. Once you're done, I want you to slowly raise the pinky on your right hand to signal to me that you finished."

I stopped talking and watched Isabella pay close attention to her breathing. It slowly became deeper and more relaxed. She continued for several minutes. Now she was ready to make the transition into her subconscious. As if on cue, Isabella slowly raised her right pinkie. I smiled and continued.

"Excellent. Now, I want you to focus on the sound of my voice. I am going to count backward very slowly from thirty to one. As I do so, you will make the transition from your conscious mind to your subconscious mind. Slowly you'll sink deeper and deeper into your subconscious, just like when you drift off to sleep. But *now* when you drift off, you'll be aware and in control of your actions. You'll revisit your visions of the kidnapped children. This time, instead of being caught up in what's happening, you'll simply be watching a movie of what happened. Just like when you watch a VHS tape on your VCR, you have a remote control. You can pause, fast forward, and rewind. You can also play back at a much slower speed. Ok, here we go..."

I slowly counted down from thirty. As I did, I noticed her breathing make the subtle but perceivable shift from someone who is relaxed to someone who is asleep, or in Isabella's case, someone who had tapped into their subconscious. Perfect.

"You're now watching a movie of your last vision of the kidnapped children, at the beginning, with the barking dog. You realize this isn't the beginning. Someone fast-forwarded through the part about how you got here. So, you are going to rewind and play it back, in slow motion, the journey to this place. Pay very close attention to the details. Remember everything. Once you see this journey and know the way to the place the children are being held, you will come back to consciousness. Ok, go ahead and hit the rewind button on the remote control."

I waited with bated breath as I watched Isabella's chest rhythmically rise and fall, fervently hoping this technique, or perhaps more accurately this gamble, would work and lead us to the kidnapped kids. As the minutes dragged slowly on, I became more and more anxious. I wanted to pace back and forth but I was afraid the creaking of the chair might disturb Isabella. In fact, I was terrified of making any noise at all, fearing it could bring her back before she completed her task. Even the sound of my breathing seemed impossibly loud. The barely audible ticking of my wristwatch felt more like the deafening clang of symbols. I tried to muffle the watch by covering it with my other hand.

Underneath a thin veneer of confidence and swagger, I was just as desperate to save the children as Isabella. With each passing minute, I grew more restless. Finally, I decided I needed to employ some other meditation techniques Master Onosai taught me to remain calm and focused. I tried to force my heart rate to slow and my breathing to remain steady and even. Through dogged determination and focus of will, I regained some semblance of normalcy. Suddenly, Isabella gasped loudly, as if she had been holding her breath the whole time. She abruptly sat up, tearing the blindfold from her face as she did.

"What happened? What did you see?" I asked, not trying to mask the intense concern in my voice.

"It worked! I know where the children are."

Chapter 29

Necessary Evil

Anita sat quietly on her back porch, slowly pitching back and forth in her rocking chair, crocheting. Her deft fingers nimbly employed the metal hooks. Over and over again, they repeated the process of creating fabric by interlocking loops of yarn. Slowly but surely the afghan began to take shape. Advanced in years now, Anita would spend her evenings working on little craft projects like this. She was no big fan of television, preferring the quiet solitude of her back porch where she could enjoy the mild autumn evenings before they grew too cold. Suddenly, her concentration was broken as she spotted a giant ball of light soaring through the night sky.

Making the sign of the cross, the old lady hurriedly snatched up her things and went inside, locking the door behind her. Most of the native New Mexicans of her generation knew great balls of light in the night sky were actually brujas, going about some evil errand. It was best not to meddle in their affairs. In fact, it was generally good for one's health and life expectancy to stay as far away as possible from witches and their wicked ways.

Chumana soared through the night sky, following the Chama River east. In the old days, transforming into a sphere of energy was the preferred mode of transportation for the more skilled practitioners of the dark arts. Although more conspicuous than traveling as an owl, it was faster. In those times there were very few who dared to meddle in the affairs of her kind.

Alas, the old days were gone. Traveling in this manner was much more likely to draw attention to herself. Chumana had no choice. The Anglo investigator broke her wing when he hit her with his car. That melika wattsida Bruce told her the private eye and the young curandera had been fighting each other, but the two were obviously partners. She had seen the big Anglo at the curandera's yerberia and again at her house. That couldn't be a coincidence.

There were too many disturbing incidents of late. Anglos nowadays tended to be clueless about magic, discounting even the possibility of its existence. The police were no exception. Yet, here was an Anglo investigator who was on her trail and discerning clues the police had missed. Now, he was working with someone who understood the dark arts.

Curse that meddling curandera! She was much tougher than Chumana had bargained on. The brat not only withstood her attacks but nearly did her in with that big butcher knife! Things were unraveling fast and she couldn't allow that. Not when she was so close! Tonight, the stars would be in the proper alignment for her to perform the ritual. Everything was perfect, or at least, it should have been. Now she was hurt and had spent much too much energy in her fight with the curandera. Although it was necessary, this spell of transportation also depleted her precious reserves of magical energy. It was a gamble to use her valuable resources in this manner, but time was of the essence. If the curandera could travel to her abode in the spirit realm what was to stop her from doing so in the physical realm? Now that she called upon her Anglo ally, the young curandera would undoubtedly strike tonight.

She *had* to be ready for them! Chumana veered left from the banks of the Chama River, the glowing sphere of energy that was now her form heading south, rapidly eating up the miles to her property in Ojito Seco. Soon, the glowing ball of energy entered through the open window the great owl had left from hours earlier. There was an immense and blinding flash of light. Where the luminous sphere had been one second earlier now lay the naked and frail-looking form of a middle-aged woman in a collapsed heap, exhausted, bleeding from several stab wounds, and cradling her broken arm.

Chumana just lay on the floor for a moment, recuperating. She lacked the strength to do much more than that. Although her body lay still her mind was racing. There were methods she could employ to speed up her healing and grant her the strength needed to perform the ritual. What if the curandera and her Anglo partner were to arrive? Even if she were at full strength, Chumana knew she could not perform such a complicated work of magic and battle enemies at the same time. She feverishly racked her brain trying to come up with an answer to her dilemma. Each possible solution had a fatal flaw, save one. She would have to contact *him*.

She would be forced to call upon Hashkeh Naabah. She loathed doing so. Her people and the Navajo were ancient enemies but, through guile and the use of blood magic, she had bound the skinwalker to her service for one task. Ideally, Chumana would rather deal with the curandera herself and prolong the girl's suffering to make her pay for the stab wounds she had inflicted. The crazed skinwalker would most likely tear her to shreds and be done with it.

Skinwalkers and witches were more often rivals than allies. Calling Hashkeh Naabah an ally was a stretch, for he would be pressed into her service. Desperate times called for desperate measures. The Navaho skinwalker would have to do. Chumana could not afford to have the curandera and her private eye interrupt the ritual.   Prolonging the girl's suffering was not paramount. The skinwalker would still mete out a gruesome end to the curandera and her partner. Chumana sighed.   The skinwalker would most likely leave behind a terrible mess for her to deal with, as if the blood sacrifice of children to the Nadir wouldn't be enough mess. A small matter in the grand scheme of things, she thought. She slowly picked herself up off the floor and, dragging her feet, shuffled out of the room to make her preparations. A wicked grin creased her face as she thought. At least her dogs would eat well tonight.

Chapter 30

Ready for Action

I watched Isabella hurriedly don a pair of hiking boots and a denim jacket. After putting on the jacket, she took some brass knuckles and placed them in one of the pockets. When this was done, she put on a thick leather belt. Leaving it unfastened, she threaded the end of the belt through the loop of a massive leather sheath. After fastening her belt, she sheathed a hunting knife so big it would have made both Rambo and the Australian guy Mick from that new *Crocodile Dundee* movie proud. I whistled and, in my best Aussie accent, said, "Now *that's* a knife."

Isabella smiled wolfishly. "Except the cold-blooded reptile *I'll* be carving up is that bruja!"

Finally! Someone got my movie references! This woman was not only strikingly beautiful but had a great sense of humor and an indomitable spirit. She was willing to face this witch head-on to save those kids. As I watched her prepare to face whatever dangers lay ahead, I realized I was getting emotionally attached to Isabella. It wasn't just her looks or the things they had in common. She had a good heart and more than that, *guts*. She was willing to put herself in harm's way to protect the innocent. Here, standing before me, was a rare gem of a woman; one who lived her life by a code similar to the one that guided me. Suddenly, I felt my stomach knot up. It took more than a big knife and a can-do attitude to tangle with the supernatural.

"As impressive as that blade may be, I think you'll need a bit more tonight."

Isabella nodded her head and went to her bedside to grab the bullwhip. I took a deep breath before I spoke, choosing my words carefully. I didn't want to sound condescending. "That whip does have better range than the knife but I'm afraid you might need something more lethal tonight."

"Oh, this whip is different than the one I used the other night in the alley behind Red's."

Isabella presented the big bullwhip for me to examine more closely. The black whip was heavier than I expected. It was made of braided strips of leather. Thickest at its handle, it gradually tapered down to a very slender tip.

"It's made of kangaroo hide; the lightest, yet strongest of leathers with a tensile strength much greater than cowhide. It's about four feet longer than the other whip so I have much better range with it. The cracker, which is the very tip of the whip, has a nasty surprise!" Isabella could see the puzzled look on my face, so she explained. "You see, the cracker is what makes the whip crack. Without it, the whip won't make much of a sound. When a whip cracks it's moving faster than the speed of sound, which is seven hundred and sixty miles per hour. That cracking sound you hear is really a sonic boom!"

Isabella could probably tell by the expression on my face that I was impressed. It was clearly one of her favorite topics, and she excitedly elaborated further. "The cracker functions to disperse the sound so the whip can be heard easier. In the old days, crackers were made of horsehair. Now it's much more common for them to be made of nylon. Neither material is very dense, nor particularly sturdy, so not the most ideal of weapons. The whip wasn't really designed to be a weapon. It's much more of an intimidating noisemaker. As a little kid, I watched movies where Zorro, and then a few years ago Indiana Jones, brandished it as a weapon. The martial artist in me wanted to see how I could adapt it into my own arsenal.

"Even though horsehair or strands of nylon might not do much to the human body ordinarily, when they are traveling close to eight hundred miles per hour, they can certainly give you a nasty laceration. No one wants to be on the business end of a whip, but it's nothing life-threatening. So, I upped the ante and knotted a couple of lug nuts into my cracker! Now I can deal out more than nasty cuts. I can deliver broken bones, including cracked skulls!

"Even the handle of my whip is no joke. Underneath the kangaroo hide is an iron bar with a weighted end, kind of like the pommel on the hilt of a sword. If someone gets inside ordinary whip range and wants to get up close and personal, I can bludgeon them with it."

As a martial artist, I could appreciate what this whip could do in the hands of a skilled practitioner. Isabella was no slouch when it came to hand-to-hand combat, but I was still afraid she really didn't know what she was getting herself into. "Isabella, I know you can take care of yourself but when it comes to practitioners of the dark arts, they play for keeps."

Isabella closed her eyes, remembering the bruja choking the life out of her with that phantasmal force and later turning into the massive black dog that tried to tear her throat out. "I know, Gideon. She's already tried to kill me tonight, but I can't get the vision of those poor children out of my head. Who knows what she'll do to them? Well I won't let her! Next time we meet I'll stab the bruja through the heart!" she said, tapping her big hunting knife for effect.

"Isabella, I don't doubt your courage or resolve. I'm just afraid you're a bit underequipped. I tangled with some sort of creature the witch conjured a couple nights ago. The thing wasn't from this world. It had to be close to eight feet tall with wicked claws and razor-sharp teeth. I shot it several times, but I don't think I killed it. I hurt it just enough that it decided I was more trouble than I was worth." I paused and held my breath. I knew full well that Isabella was more open-minded than Nia, but this pushed the limits.

Isabella made the sign of the cross. "Demonios!"

I winced. "Does that mean crazy?"

Isabella gave me a funny look. "You really don't know any Spanish, do you?"

"Very little, I'm afraid."

"Demonio means demon."

"So... you don't think I'm crazy?"

"Crazy? You're one of the few people I know who isn't walking around with their head buried in the sand!"

"Isabella, I could kiss you!"

She cocked her head. "What?"

"Well, you see..."

"Never mind. Let's focus on the task at hand." With that, Isabella walked out of her room.

"Right," I said. "Where are you going?"

"If we're dealing with demons, we'll be needing some things," Isabella called out from up ahead.

I rushed to keep up and found her in the kitchen. "What sort of things?" I asked.

Isabella took her rosary from its hook. "Holy items for starters."

I nodded in agreement. "Those can come in handy. I have one of my own," I said, showing her my blessed medal of Saint Michael.

"Oh, that's right! You work for the Order of Saint George. Are you some kind of priest?"

I shook my head vigorously. "I'm not in the Order, I just work with them sometimes. No vows of celibacy for me!"

"Good," Isabella said, smiling.

"Good?" I asked, suddenly very hopeful.

Isabella turned bright red. "Good that you don't need a rosary. I don't think I have a spare. Do you have any holy water?" she asked, changing the subject. She moved to a cabinet and opened it up, rummaging through its contents.

"As a matter of fact, I do, but you can never have too much of the stuff. If you have some, bring it along."

Isabella stuffed some bottles of holy water into the pockets of her jacket.

"Faith and holy water do help but I was actually thinking along the lines of superior firepower. Follow me."

I opened the side door Isabella led me through earlier that evening. When we stepped outside, I noticed the thick fog from earlier had lifted, revealing a bright star-filled night and a full moon. I stared up at Earth's natural satellite and frowned. Not good.

"What's the matter?" Isabella asked.

"It's during full moons that witches and wizards perform some of their most macabre rituals and deadly divinations."

"Well, we better not give her the chance then," Isabella said, slinging her whip over her shoulder and climbing into the Jeep. "We'll take my Jeep. You won't be able to drive with that busted windshield."

"Hold on a second," I said, jogging over to my car. I popped open the trunk and took out the great big green duffle bag Father Lopez gave me earlier. I lugged the cumbersome thing back over to Isabella's Jeep.

"Holy cow! What do you have in there, a spare engine for your car?"

"Better," I said, setting the colossal bag down. I unzipped it with flare, unveiling the multitude of firearms within.

"Jesus, you brought your own armory!"

I smiled at the remark. "You bet your sweet ass I did."

Isabella gave me a look that seemed to warn, 'watch your language', but I continued unperturbed. "Witches can summon forth demons and are known to have all sorts of supernatural nasties guarding their lairs. It's best if you're well-armed when you bump into any of those things. Monsters are scary and very real. They can do all sorts of nasty things, but they can be hurt too, hurt all the way up to dead. In fact, that's the Order of Saint George's specialty. All the weapons you see here in this bag are large caliber, tried and true monster killers, complete with armor-piercing rounds that have been blessed and consecrated by Order priests. As you can see, I have enough to share."

Isabella smiled; not a jovial smile but the fierce grin of a warrior about to do battle. "Well then, how about we go and blast some monsters back to hell?"

I returned her predatory smile. "I thought you'd never ask, darlin'."

Chapter 31

Works of Art and Waring with Witches

With Isabella looking over my shoulder, I started rummaging through the huge green bag, equipping myself with two shoulder rigs and a gun belt. Now I had four different Colt 1911 .45 caliber pistols: one under each arm and one on each hip. Then, I donned my trench coat and stuffed the pockets with spare magazines, vials of holy water, and a small flashlight. Lastly, almost as an afterthought, I grabbed a stiletto switchblade knife.

After outfitting myself, I reached into the bag and pulled out one of the walkie-talkies from RadioShack. I passed it over to Isabella. "Here. If we get separated, we'll still be able to communicate." I then pocketed one of the walkie-talkies for myself. Next, I handed Isabella the twin to my small flashlight. Digging through the massive duffle bag once more I withdrew a shotgun from its depths but paused in the act of handing the gun over to Isabella. "How much experience do you have with firearms?"

"My father taught me how to shoot when I was twelve. We still go out to the boonies to shoot aluminum cans and beer bottles every now and then. To be honest, it's the martial arts, not firearms, that are my passion. I mainly go for his benefit and only 3, maybe 4, times a year. I'm not especially good at it."

I shrugged my shoulders. "That's better than two-thirds of Americans and probably more than 95% of Europeans." I presented the firearm to Isabella.

"This is the Remington 1100 model 12-gauge shotgun. It's semi-auto so you don't have to use a pump-action to eject the spent shell before firing your next shot. Just pull the trigger. It has a 28-inch barrel and holds five rounds. I'll load it for you." I held up one of the shells for Isabella to see.

"These are slugs not shot, meaning the shells have one solid projectile inside instead of several smaller pellets like bird or buckshot. A shotgun slug is much bigger than the bullet from a rifle and more than twice as heavy. The sheer weight of a shotgun slug makes it extremely deadly. These, even more so. They're armor-piercing slugs, made of steel with tapered points instead of traditional slugs, which are made of lead and generally more cylindrical in shape. Basically, they're so deadly they can even kill demons. I know this from experience."

I thumbed the shells into the shotgun. "A 12-gauge can have a bit of a kick, but the Remington 1100 is gas-operated with a mechanism that noticeably reduces recoil. This one has a nice rubber recoil pad on it as well, so the kick isn't bad at all."

I reached into the bag and took out a sleek-looking black pistol. "Here's a nice backup gun for you; the Beretta M9. It's 9mm so it won't kick as much as my Colt .45 caliber 1911. Although it has a smaller projectile, the magazine holds 15 rounds. Hopefully, it will be a while before you run empty. As an added bonus, the ammunition is augmented with hard steel cores instead of much softer traditional lead bullets. Terrible news for monsters. The safety is off on both weapons so don't put your finger in the trigger well until you're ready to shoot." I handed over the Beretta and a spare magazine.

Realizing she would need more space; Isabella ran back into the house. She quickly doffed the denim jacket and grabbed a pea-green military jacket instead, placing the walkie-talkie, flashlight, and vials of holy water into big pockets. She'd always been a tomboy, so most of her clothes reflected that side of her personality. One didn't run a yerberia or gather herbs and other plants in the outfit she wore to Red's the night she met Gideon. Happy with the ample space and infinite pockets, she ran back to the car.

I very much appreciated how Isabella could go from outfits like she wore in the club to this. The fact that she looked good in anything she wore did not escape me. Isabella put the gun and magazine into a pocket. She put some spare shotgun shells in another pocket. The Remington, she held onto with both hands. I took the Marlin 1895 lever-action rifle from the big green bag, gazing at it with a reverence usually reserved for the works of a master painter or sculptor. To me, it *was* a work of art. Legendary gunsmiths like John Moses Browning, Samuel Colt, and Eliphalet Remington were not unlike the great artists Donatello, Picasso, or Da Vinci. They just used a different medium.

Isabella wore an expression that said, 'you have to be kidding me'. Just in case the look on her face was unclear, she vocalized her concerns. "Shouldn't you use a gun from *this* century?"

I chuckled, remembering my own similar reaction when Father Dominic first showed me the gun. "Don't be deceived. What you see before you, my dear, is the Marlin 1895, a 20th century version of the old west lever-action repeater rifles. This big bore beauty has a seven round capacity and is nicknamed 'the guide gun.' It has massive power and rapid cycling. It's often used to hunt dangerous game, like grizzly bears and lions. The Marlin uses big beefy .45/70 caliber cartridges, which my good friends in the Order of Saint George have upgraded with hardened steel cores. It could probably take down a Tyrannosaurus Rex or, in our case, a demon."

Isabella raised her hands in an apologetic gesture. "I'm sorry. I stand corrected."

"No need for apologies. I was unaware of the rifle's virtues until my good friend and mentor Father Dominic Lane enlightened me. The good Padre is in the Order of Saint George and taught me the finer points of warring with witches and demons. I'll share some of those lessons with you. These firearms will come in handy, but you should also know your enemy. Witches and demons hate mankind, hate them with a capital H, but all that hatred blinds them. You can use that against them in a fight.

"For instance, it's easy to taunt a demon and goad them into running straight into a trap. Witches and wizards can be a lot craftier and not so easily tricked, but they have their weaknesses too. We talked about how spells drain them and that their energy is finite. The more powerful the spell, the more energy it requires. Also, more powerful spells require a lot of concentration. When a witch is preparing one, it's the perfect time to strike because they're not focused on defense."

Isabella nodded her head, taking in the advice.

"Lastly, to quote Father Dominic, 'Never underestimate the awesome power of divine intervention. It takes faith to fight the good fight.'"

Isabella grasped the cross of the rosary which hung around her neck, bowed her head, and started praying in Spanish. I could make out 'padre dios', which I'm pretty sure means Father God, but not much else. Although I didn't understand all the words, I got the gist of what Isabella was doing. Following her cue, I grasped the medal of Saint Michael, bowed my head, and said my own silent but fervent prayer asking for God's aid in saving the children. We said 'amen' at the same time.

I took Isabella's hand in mine and looked her in the eye. Quietly, yet with resolute determination, I said, "Let's go save those kids and make that bruja *pay* for ever messing with children."

Flashing that fierce smile again, Isabella parroted my earlier statement back to me. "I thought you'd never ask, darlin'."

Sexier words have never been uttered. Suddenly, I felt an overwhelming desire to kiss Isabella. It wasn't quite the right moment yet, so I settled for saying, "Woman, where have you been my whole life?"

Isabella was momentarily taken aback, not expecting my response, but quickly recovered. Her fierce predatory smile changed into a flirtatious grin as she remembered the song playing when she was closing her yerberia. "Holding out for a hero." With that, Isabella abruptly turned on her heel and climbed into her Jeep.

I wondered just what a strong, intelligent, and independent woman like Isabella would ever need a hero for. It was official.

Women would remain one of life's chief mysteries. When I heard Isabella start up the Jeep, I found myself singing the theme to the Mighty Mouse cartoon as I jogged to the passenger side. "Here I come to save the day!"

Once we were both in the Jeep, Isabella sped from Glorieta to Santa Fe, then raced north along U.S Route 84. I'd taken the route from Santa Fe to Española a few times. As we continued northwest past the small town, it seemed like we left all traces of civilization behind. Pitch black, there were no lights to be seen anywhere, nor any sort of landmark. Master Onosai's techniques had clearly worked. Isabella seemed to be guided by an internal compass, speeding along the lonely stretch of road. Her eyes were fixed straight ahead, like a hawk intently tracking its prey.

The terrain that zipped by in the darkness somehow seemed ominous and unnerving. I busied myself with trying to determine our whereabouts on the road atlas. About half an hour northwest of Española, we came to the small town of Abiquiu. It was so tiny! I barely blinked and we passed it by. This was partly because Isabella was racing along at breakneck speeds, but it really was a downright teeny little town.

Soon after we passed Abiquiu, Isabella turned down a rural road that followed the banks of a river. Using the atlas, I guessed it was state road 162 and the river was the Chama River. After a couple miles, Isabella turned onto a bumpy dirt road heading south. I couldn't find it on my map. Calling it a road was a bit generous. Really, it was barely more than a trail. I was glad we were in Isabella's Jeep and not my rental. The Buick probably wouldn't hold up on such a byway.

I had to brace myself to avoid being thrown around the cab of the Jeep. It felt like riding a bucking bronco. After bouncing along like that for what seemed like an eternity, but was probably closer to fifteen minutes, I turned to Isabella and asked, "How much further 'til we get to the witch's lair?"

"We should be there any minute now," she answered.

I cried out in a panic. "Shit! Turn off the headlights and slow down!"

Isabella was caught off guard. "What's the matter?!"

"We don't want to announce our presence. We want to try and catch her off guard if possible."

"Oh. Sorry," she said. She killed the lights and eased off the gas until we were rolling along at a mere 5 mph.

"No worries. Go ahead and pull over. We'll continue on foot from here."

Isabella pulled off the road at the foot of a small hill and cut the ignition. We climbed out and, upon reaching the crest of the hill, were surprised by how much light the full moon provided. We could see the end of the narrow, bumpy dirt road about a quarter-mile up ahead. There was a large ranch-style house at the end of the road, sitting on about 16 acres of land. Behind the house and to the left was a stand of cottonwood trees and to the right was a small apple tree orchard. In front of the house was a big open field of tall wild grass, which the road cut right down the center of, making it seem like the house's long private driveway.

"It's a good thing we stopped when we did," I said. "The witch would have easily seen the lights of the Jeep when we crested the hill. I think we still have the element of surprise. Let's use those cotton trees for cover and circle around the house. We'll try to sneak in from behind."

"Sounds good to me," said Isabella, stooping her shoulders and crouching a bit as she took off at a slow jog through the waist-high grass. She held the shotgun close to her body.

I followed close on her heels, holding my rifle in a similar manner.

Chapter 32

Nocturnal Encounters

Although we were moving as silent as ghosts, with the chirping of crickets the only noise to be heard, I was painfully aware of how easy it would be to make out our silhouettes in the bright moonlight. I tried to make myself invisible through force of will. Just in case that didn't work, I bent over at the waist, nearly in half, as I jogged through the tall grass. We managed to cross most of the open field and were parallel to the big house, instead of in front of it. The cottonwood trees were only about twenty yards ahead. Something moved towards them through the high grass. Whatever it was, the thing couldn't be very tall. The waist-high grass concealed its form completely, but you could still tell *something* was coming. It cut a swath through the wild grass, parting the tall blades like a shark's fin through dark waters.

I touched Isabella's shoulder to get her attention and pointed to the parting grass. She raised her shotgun to fire, but I placed a hand on the barrel, lowering it before she could pull the trigger. "Wait," I hissed in a loud whisper. "Let's try to avoid shooting and do this as quietly as possible for now."

A huge snarling dog appeared, perhaps a Rottweiler mix. It had to weigh close to one hundred and forty pounds. It lunged towards us, leaping above the tall grass, teeth bared and ready to rend and tear.

I reacted instantly, twisting at the hips. With my left hand, which gripped the barrel of the rifle near the front sight, I pulled it towards me. Simultaneously, I pushed out with my right hand, which held the rifle on the upper part of the stalk, just below the receiver. I struck the dog with the butt of the rifle just behind its jaw, swatting it out of the air.

The big dog let out a surprised yelp, but I showed no mercy. Before the beast even landed, I sprinted towards it with my rifle held high above my head, ready to strike again. The dog recovered surprisingly fast and was on its feet in an instant. I brought the butt of the rifle down hard, hitting the massive dog right between the eyes. It let out another high-pitched yelp of pain as its legs gave out from under it. I hit the dog one more time for good measure and the colossal canine finally lay still.

Whether the beast was unconscious or dead, I didn't know. As soon as I delivered the final blow another enormous dog emerged from the tall grass and pounced on me, knocking me backwards. I barely had time to bring the Marlin up so the beast would chomp down on the rifle barrel instead of my throat. For an instant, I was pinned to the ground with most of the dog's substantial weight on my chest. Not a good position to be in. I immediately brought my legs in close to my body and planted both my feet near my butt, soles of my shoes firmly on the ground. I pushed up with my legs and hips, arching my back and pivoting on my left shoulder. This effectively got me out from under the mammoth dog.

Meanwhile, taking a page from my playbook, Isabella rushed in holding her shotgun by the barrel with both hands. She swung it like a baseball bat and clubbed the dog in the face with the stalk of her weapon. The blow hurt the animal, who yelped in surprise and pain, but didn't take it out of action. Forgetting me for the moment, enraged, the huge dog rushed Isabella, knocking her to the ground. Now she was on her back with the gargantuan dog biting down on the barrel of her shotgun.

I quickly looked about for my rifle. I'd lost it in the tall grass. Isabella saw me searching and cried out. "Quick! Use my whip!"

I spotted the long, braided weapon, partially uncoiled, within arm's reach. It must have slid from Isabella's shoulder when the gigantic dog knocked her down. I balked at the idea, never having used a whip before.

"Woman, you have the wrong Jones! My name is Gideon, not Indiana!"

"Hurry," she cried, desperation in her voice as the massive dog shook its head back and forth, violently trying to rip the shotgun out of her hands.

Springing into action, I grabbed the whip. The tool felt alien to me but, remembering Isabella's description of it, I had an idea. Holding the whip in the middle with both hands, I swung it mightily, bringing the iron bar handle crashing down on the dog's spine. With a yelp of pain, the beast released its hold of Isabella's shotgun. Not yet finished, I attacked again, this time reversing the direction of my swing. I caught the huge canine under its jaw with the iron handle in the bullwhip equivalent of an uppercut.

This time, the dog had enough and ran off, defeated, with its tail between its legs. "Not bad," Isabella said, accepting my hand. She helped herself up off the ground. "Not exactly what I would have done, but not bad."

"I'll admit this baby does have its appeal. You'll have to give me some lessons when all this is over," I said, handing the whip back to her.

"It's a date," Isabella said with a smile.

"Funny. I never envisioned a date with you involving whips, but as long as it doesn't include chains, I guess I'm ok with it."

"Quit being so sucio."

"Susy what?" I asked, puzzled.

Isabella shook her head. "Sucio means dirty. I'm going to have to give you Spanish lessons as well."

"Yes ma'am," I said with a smile. I softly sang the lyrics to "Hot for Teacher" by Van Halen under my breath while I searched the tall grass for my rifle.

Isabella heard me and gave me a sideways look as she chided, "Stop it." She smiled as soon as she said it.

I stooped down, having found the Marlin, and nodded to myself. A quick glance confirmed it was none the worse for wear.

"Well, that could have been a lot worse," I said, blowing some dirt off the rifle's front sight. "We're relatively unscathed and didn't make too much noise. If we're lucky, the bruja still doesn't know we're here yet."

I jogged to the cover of the cottonwood trees. I was about to whisper to Isabella but saw she wasn't following. Instead, she stood rooted in place, still as a statute.

"What's the matter?"

She gave me an incredulous look. "Can't you hear them?"

I paused and listened but didn't hear anything. Even the chirping crickets were now silent. "I don't hear anything."

"The children! They're crying, calling out to us," Isabella said as she ran towards the house.

I chased after her, grabbing her by the arm. "Isabella wait! I'm serious. I don't hear anything! This is some sort of trap!"

Suddenly, a massive shadow fell across us. I released my hold on Isabella and turned to face whatever had blotted out the light of the moon. Heedless of this new development, Isabella sprinted off towards the house, chasing after the voices only she could hear.

Chapter 33

Ancient Evil

Isabella was vaguely aware of Gideon calling after her, but she was fixated on the cries of the children. They were coming from inside the house, so she raced to the backdoor. Finding it unlocked, she flung it open and rushed inside, heedless of whatever dangers were on the other side. Getting to the children was all that mattered.

Inside, all was pitch black, but it was more than just dark. Isabella could sense a presence. She took out the flashlight Gideon had given her. With her left hand, she placed it on top of the shotgun which she cradled in her right arm. She held the small flashlight there. Wherever she shined light, the shotgun was conveniently pointing in the same direction.

Panning the light back and forth, Isabella couldn't spot any immediate threat. She cautiously stepped inside. The cries of the children stopped. Isabella repressed an urge to call out to the children and ventured further into the bruja's abode. The place gave Isabella the creeps and not just because she knew a witch lived there.

If a house is occupied, if it's *lived* in, it gives off a subtle vibe. Most people don't immediately recognize it consciously. It's like going house shopping when the realtor takes you on tours. Empty houses have a different 'feel' to them than occupied ones, and there's more to it than being unfurnished.

If a house is someone's home, it has a subtle aura about it, a kind of warmth that has nothing to do with temperature. This place, despite being furnished, felt barren and cold. It wasn't dirty or unkempt, but Isabella could detect an odd, very faint, odor. It was a dank and earthy smell, reminiscent of the grave.

The tiny hairs on her arms and the back of her neck stood up as a chill ran down her spine. Treading softly, attempting to make no sound, she made her way down the hall. There were several doors, but she heard the faint cry of the children again, coming from the opposite direction. Quickening her pace, she padded softly off in the direction of the voices calling to her, captivated by their siren song. She followed them like a moth drawn to a flame. The voices led Isabella to a lone door. Opening it, she saw a staircase leading down into a basement.

Isabella paused for a moment, searching for a light switch, then thought better of it. Gideon was right. They shouldn't announce their presence. After taking a deep breath, as if preparing herself for a plunge into icy waters, she made her way down the narrow stairwell into the darkness below. The first step produced a loud creak as the old wooden step took her weight. Isabella froze in place, ready for the bruja to come rushing out of the darkness, but nothing happened.

She realized the distant sound of the children had stopped again. In their absence, the silence was deafening. Isabella descended the stairs much more slowly, one step at a time, careful to test each wooden plank before placing her full weight on them. There would be no groans or creaks that gave away her location. Thus, she descended into the darkness below with such trepidation. It was as if she feared she was going down into the very depths of hell. With each new footfall, her apprehension grew until she was filled with dread.

Suddenly, she heard a skittering sound. Shining her flashlight in that direction revealed a huge cockroach on the wall beside her, big as a mouse. The nasty insect scurried off as soon as it was spotlighted. Isabella jumped, stifling a scream, and nearly fired her shotgun. She stopped and forced herself to slow down her breathing, which was now coming out in shallow, ragged pants. She didn't proceed again until her heart, pounding in her chest like a wild rock and roll drum solo, had regained some semblance of normalcy.

No one who knew Isabella at all would accuse her of being a coward. In fact, most people would use labels like confident, spirited, and gutsy to describe her. The fear that now gripped her was uncharacteristic to say the least.

People who knew her well would not merely say she was brave. They would also describe her as someone who had a strong sense of intuition, good instincts, and able to pick up on vibes people gave off. The people in the paranormal community, however, would give it a different label and say Isabella was a sensitive; someone who could feel the presence of spirits. Her grandmother called it 'the gift.' This gift was causing the feelings of dread within her now. Isabella was sensing the presence of a powerful and malevolent spirt.

As she continued to make her way down the staircase Isabella could feel the temperature dropping. She was able to see the fog of her own breath. Reaching the bottom of the stairs she scanned the area with her flashlight, revealing a large basement, as big as the entire house upstairs, possibly even larger. In some ways, it was like her own yerberia. The walls were lined with shelves stocked with all sorts of herbs, salves, and potions. Many of these ingredients Isabella knew to be poisonous. Unlike her shop, however, the place was teeming with animal pelts. There were a great number of bones and several jars full of organs. Isabella was taken aback when she saw many of the bones were human remains, not animals as she originally assumed, and among them were those of children.

Keeping her shotgun at the ready, Isabella crept about the place searching for any signs of the missing youths. Aside from the odd wing of bat, eye of newt, and tongue of pig, there wasn't much in the way of clues. Just a macabre assortment of pickled organs and mummified appendages; the vile ingredients used to power a witch's curses. As if the place wasn't nightmarish enough, as she surveyed the contents of the shelves, Isabella saw more roaches and other insects skittering about in the darkness. It added a whole new layer of creepy. She could feel her skin crawl, but she doggedly continued to hunt for any sign of the missing children. Suddenly she heard a woman crying. Not a loud mournful wail but rather soft pitiful sobbing. Wary of a possible trap, Isabella headed towards the sound, her finger in the trigger well of her shotgun. As she slowly stalked off in the direction of the crying her sense of foreboding increased. She noticed a lack of insects, as if even the roaches avoided this section of the basement. She crossed an open area strewn with sand and burned down candles which were little more than tiny wicks protruding from pools of wax on the floor. Scattered about were more bones.

The beam of her flashlight illuminated the figure of a woman with long black hair clad in a white dress hunched over a table, weeping. "Mi hijos," she kept bawling over and over. It was

Spanish for 'my children'. Isabella immediately assumed this must have been the mother of one of the missing children.

Raising the barrel of the shotgun high so it was no longer aimed at the woman, Isabella called out in a soothing voice as she stepped closer. "It's ok. I'm here to help."

The woman abruptly spun around, revealing a ghastly face that would haunt Isabella for the rest of her life. The woman's complexion was as pale as the white dress she wore. The expression on her face was a mask of horror, simultaneously conveying both sorrow and burning hatred. Her eyes were milky white with no pupils. They wept tears black as tar that stained her face as they rolled down her cheeks. Her mouth opened impossibly wide, twisted in a contorted and wretched grimace of agony and remorse.

Her quiet sobs transformed into a piercing wail as she lunged forward to seize Isabella in her grasp. She was stopped short, her arms held fast, bound by thick thorny vines. Long nasty barbs punctured her flesh, drawing blood as black as her tears. "Release me, curandera! Free me from the bruja's clutches," the thing wailed as it fixed its unearthly gaze upon Isabella.

Although not quite able to reach her, the frightful creature was mere inches from her face, so close that Isabella's nostrils were assaulted by the foul reek of stagnant water. She staggered backwards, reeling from the horrific visage of this inhuman thing. In her panic, Isabella tripped over something in the dark. She fell to the floor, losing her grip on both the shotgun and the flashlight. Isabella franticly scooted backwards on her rear, pushing with her legs as she dug in her pocket with one hand. She held the other in front of her, grasping the crucifix on her rosary in a feeble attempt to ward off this evil specter.   Isabella reached the far end of the basement and could go no further, trapped with her back pressed up against a wall.   The banshee-like wraith wailed, struggling to break free of its thorny restraints to get to her.   Without the flashlight shining directly upon it, Isabella could see that the thing was emanating a faint, pale blue light.   Although they were indoors on dry land, its dress and hair fanned out as if it were completely submerged under water.

"Mi hijos! I must find them! Free me, curandera! I must get to them! Mi hijos, MI HIJOS!"   The creature wailed, black tears rolling down its cheeks.

She was only feet away, but the eerie words sounded as if they echoed from the bottom of a deep well. The stench of stagnant water wafted over her. Terror-stricken, Isabella knew she was face to face with the infamous La Llorona.

Chapter 34

Skinwalker

I spun around to face whatever was casting this vast ominous shadow. To my surprise, I saw a man of average height standing approximately five-foot-nine inches tall, maybe five-foot-ten. His build was lean and athletic. He had long black hair, tangled and unkempt, falling all the way to his waist. Even with the only illumination being moonlight, I could tell the man was deeply tanned. If I had to venture a guess, I would say the stranger was a North American Indian. From what tribe, I couldn't say with any certainty, but not hailing from these parts. The man's features weren't the only thing giving me confidence in my guess. It helped that he was clad only in a loincloth and wolf pelt draped over his head and shoulders.

The strange man was grinning maniacally. Combined with his attire, this would have been unsettling on its own but the shadow he was casting was impossibly large for his frame and seemed canine in nature. This wasn't simply because the man was wearing a wolf pelt. The proportions of the shadow were all wrong to be human. Even though the man was standing perfectly still, the shadow was pacing back and forth like a caged animal.

His eyes shone bright red with no discernable pupils. It all let me know, in no uncertain terms, that this stranger was bad news. Having dealt with wizards and witches before, I wasted no time. I immediately brought the rifle up to my face, taking aim. Before I could pull the trigger, however, the strange man bolted.

Moving impossibly fast, he was practically a blur. One instant he was right in my sights, the next he was standing some thirty yards to the right among the cottonwood trees.

I quickly brought the rifle about, trying to re-acquire my target. I had the Indian in my sights again. Just as I was about to pull the trigger, the man took off with another burst of speed, disappearing into the trees. I kept the rifle to my eye, ready to fire if need be, but didn't give chase. If this tribal shaman wanted to run instead of fight, why look a gift horse in the mouth? A disturbing sound pierced the night, like a man grunting as he endured intense pain. Somehow it was a little *too* guttural and bestial.

There was a series of ghastly, wet popping noises, like bones snapping and muscles and sinew tearing, followed by a long and tormented scream. Halfway through the piercing cry of a man in terrible agony, it morphed into the deep, resonant howl of a wolf. It was different from the familiar howl of a majestic canine serenading the moon. It was a perverse monstrosity, impossibly loud, as if bellowed by a beast larger than a grizzly bear. The ghastly howl had such booming force I could feel the bass reverberating in my chest. My blood ran cold. Me! The guy who faced off against demons, suddenly felt the taste of fear at the back of my throat.

The howl ended and the night was suddenly eerily still. No trace of the normal sounds of nocturnal animals or even insects could be heard. The crunch of dry brush and snapping of twigs as something huge and heavy stomped brazenly through the trees towards me, giving no thought or effort whatsoever to mask its presence, seemed extraordinarily loud.

It burst into view. The hulking beast that stood before me looked to be at least seven feet tall and had to weigh close to five hundred pounds. Thick fur did not hide the fact that it was heavily muscled. It was an unnatural combination of both man and beast. Bipedal and standing on two legs, it had a slightly stilted stance since it had the haunches of a wolf. Although covered in fur, its upper torso was more man than wolf, being broad-shouldered and barrel-chested.   Heavily muscled humanoid arms ended in oversized hands. Strangely elongated fingers would've been more at home on a mountain gorilla except for the deadly looking claws.

Like its body, the creature's head and face were an eerie mixture of both man and wolf. It had the mane and pyramid shaped ears of a wolf but a much shorter, stunted muzzle. The brow and cheekbones of a man-made it capable of human-like expressions. I could tell by the look on the thing's face it was smiling, not a cheerful grin, but more akin to an arrogant smirk. The beast's mouth, full of large razor-sharp teeth with prominent oversized canines, made the look even more sinister. The beast stared directly at me with its blood-red eyes, standing exposed and apparently unconcerned that I was armed with a rifle. It sharply contrasted with running each time I pointed the Marlin at him when it was in human form. Just as a lion stalked its prey, the creature boldly advanced towards me, slowly and deliberately.

I couldn't help thinking this monster had seen the business end of a gun before and was none the worse for wear. I'd learned the hard way that a demon's hide was impervious to normal bullets. Perhaps it was the same for Native American Werewolves. I knew my rifle was loaded with augmented ammunition, however. That was a game-changer. Keeping the rifle pointed at the monster

I shouted a warning, bellowing it forth like the powerful kiais used in my martial arts training.

"**STOP!!** One more step and I'll blow you to hell!"

The beast paused mid-step for a moment, tilted its head back, and laughed. It was similar to a hyena but, unlike the spotted African beast with a high-pitched cackle, this was deep, booming, and full of bass.

"All right then! Let's dance!" I yelled, aiming dead center of the monster's chest before squeezing the trigger. The beast's laugh was cut short as it was slammed from the impact of the 425-grain bullet with a muzzle velocity of 2,350 feet per second. These heavy-hitting rifle cartridges were known for their bone-crushing power, able to flatten a grizzly bear. That was before the Order of Saint George augmented them with rigid steel cores instead of soft lead. The monster staggered several paces backwards but managed to keep its feet and did not fall. Enraged, it roared a mighty challenge.

Working the lever action of the Marlin, I ejected the spent shell casing and chambered another round. All the while I kept the rifle up to my face and maintained a bead on my target. In answer to the monster's deafening roar, I shouted back, "Say hello to my little friend!" in my best Al Pacino imitation, quoting the famous line from the movie *Scarface.*

I fired off another shot. Again, my aim was true. The monster staggered back several paces from the impact of the round. There was no spray of gore. This was unsettling because when I shot demons with these rounds, I drew blood.

The monster recovered then dropped down, galloping on all four limbs as it charged, covering distance at an alarming rate of speed. Keeping the rifle up to my face, I worked the lever-action again. As the monster leapt towards me, soaring through the air and cutting through the thirty feet between us in an instant, I chambered another round. The boom of the Marlin sounded an instant before the monster crashed into me with the force of a stampeding bull.

The beast may have been big, but it was still vaguely human-shaped. My martial arts training served me well. I instinctively exhaled while rounding my shoulders and tucking my chin into my chest as the monster knocked me backwards. Releasing my hold on the rifle, I grabbed big fistfuls of the beast's fur like I was grabbing hold of someone's suit jacket lapels. While I did this, I brought both my legs in close to my body and placed the soles of my shoes into the hip sockets of the monster. I pushed out with my legs and launched the beast in a judo throw called Tomoe Nage.

Using the creature's own momentum against it, I used my arms to guide the path of the beast's fall, ensuring the beast crashed down on its head. There was an audible crunch as the monster's neck snapped.

Chapter 35

Maria's Malady

The stench of stagnant water triggered a long-forgotten memory. When Isabella was a little girl, no more than five years old, she would often walk the banks of the Rio Grande with her grandmother, helping her gather plants and herbs for her trade as a curandera. On one such occasion, Isabella noticed a large pool of stagnant water with rotting vegetation, surrounded by muck and mud. Her grandmother saw her eyeing the area.

"Cuidado, mija. Don't go off and play over there. If you get stuck in the mud, La Llorona will get you!" her grandmother warned, knowing little Isabella loved to make mud pies.

"Who is La Llorona?" Isabella asked, staring up at her grandmother with big brown eyes. Her hair was braided in twin tails and tied with green ribbon.

Isabella's grandmother adored her but frowned at the question. "You don't know? Your mother should've told you this already," her grandmother said, making a t'sk sound, signifying her disapproval. "I will tell you then. La Llorona is an evil spirit, a ghost that haunts the Rio Grande and other places, looking for little children like you to steal away from their parents."

Little Isabella gasped. "Why would she do something so mean?"

Her grandmother looked at the precious girl, still so innocent. "Ah mija, not everyone is good. There are bad people and bad things out in the world too, so you need to be careful."

Little Isabella pondered this. Being surrounded by loved ones and people who cared for her all her short life made the concept hard to grasp. "But why would she do that, abuela?" she asked.

The curandera stared down at her sweet grandchild, a bit sad, not wanting to shatter the young girl's illusions that everything was sunshine and rainbows. On the other hand, it was her duty to prepare her for the cruel fact that the world could be a dangerous place.

"She wasn't always that way. People don't start out evil. They can turn bad over time, the way an apple left out slowly turns brown and yucky. It gets rotten on the inside, no longer good to eat."

"How did La Llorona turn rotten?"

"It was a long, long, time ago; hundreds of years ago in fact."

Little Isabella's eyes widened at such a big number.

Seeing she had her grandchild's full attention, she continued. "It was so long ago that she wasn't even called La Llorona. She was still using her name, Maria. She was a gorgeous young woman. One day, Maria caught the attention of a dashing young man, handsome and wealthy. This nobleman was so enthralled by her great beauty that he proposed to her.

"Maria was a peasant from a poor family. They were elated a rich nobleman would want to marry her and agreed to the proposal. Maria was very much in love with the man and bore him two children. For a time, the family was happy. But for a marriage to last, its foundation needs to be built on something stronger than looks alone. Even though Maria was very beautiful the nobleman got bored and fell out of love with her.

"He would leave to drink and chase after other women but tell Maria he was going out on business. At first, he would only go out once and a while. Eventually, he would go more often and stay gone longer, being absent for days at a time. Maria missed him terribly and was always happy to see him when he returned. Her husband didn't seem happy to see Maria. Only their children held his interest.

"Maria came to suspect her husband was cheating on her. The next time he left, she followed him and caught him in the arms of another woman. Maria confronted him but he scoffed, saying he wasn't even sorry. He didn't care about her anymore. He only loved their children, not her. Maria was furious and attacked the other woman, but her husband stopped her, defending his mistress. Maria then attacked her husband, but he was much bigger and stronger than her. She couldn't possibly hurt him. He laughed and told her to go back to their children and look after them. That was all she was good for and it was all he cared about.

"In a fit of jealous rage, Maria went home to their house by the banks of the Rio Grande, grabbed her two young children, and drowned them in the river to get back at her husband. Too late, she realized what she had done. She tried to save them, but they were already dead. Maria went mad with grief, walking the banks of the Rio Grande day and night, crying and wailing, calling out to her children. One day, she plunged into the river, drowning herself. Even after her death, her ghost haunts the banks of the Rio

Grande at night, walking back and forth, searching for her lost children, and calling out to them. People could hear Maria's ghost crying so they came to call her La Llorona, the weeping or wailing woman. Because of the foul, evil thing she did, La Llorona is cursed to haunt the river for all time, searching for her lost children but never able to find them. Her spirit is so desperate that her ghost will try to take any child she sees, mistaking them for her own. The child will never be seen again. For hundreds of years now, people have warned their children not to play by the river alone, especially at night, or La Llorona will take them!"

Isabella remembered thinking it was a sad story. Being face to face with La Llorona, she didn't need to be a sensitive to know this was a tortured soul. It was also equally obvious, however, that this was an evil and dangerous entity being held against its will. Isabella had no idea why the bruja was holding her captive but perhaps she could use it to her advantage.

"Maria, I am not your enemy."

La Llorona immediately ceased struggling against her thorny restraints. She cocked her head to the side and stared at Isabella with milky white eyes. "What did you call me?"

"Maria. That's your name."

La Llorona retreated a step, shaking her head. "Maria...? No, I am La Llorona."

Isabella took advantage of the extra space and scrambled to her feet. "Not always. Once you were Maria, a long time ago."

"Ma...ri...a..." La Llorona repeated slowly, as if trying to pronounce a new word for the first time.

"That's right. Maria. Don't you remember?"

"Maria..." La Llorona repeated, struggling to recall her past.

"You had a family! Remember?"

At Isabella's mention of her family, La Llorona buried her face in her hands and sobbed. "Mi hijos!" she wailed.

"That's right! You know the pain of losing your loved ones. Now the bruja has taken innocent children. Help me find them!"

La Llorona stopped crying and lifted her face from her hands, fixing her eerie gaze upon Isabella. "I have shown you, curandera. I came to you in your dreams."

Isabella gasped. "It was you who gave me the visions?"

La Llorona smiled, revealing ugly stained teeth. A bit of saliva dripped from the corner of her mouth, black as the tears she cried. "Yes, there are few who can perceive the spirit realm. I searched far and wide for one who could hear me, until I found you, curandera. I called to you, night after night. I feared you would not come. There is little time. The bruja will kill them tonight as a sacrifice to her Nadir overlords."

"You brought me here, but I don't see any children."

"Release me, curandera."

"Where are the children?"

"Release me!"

"Where are the children?"

"She tortures me! Please!"

Isabella drew her big hunting knife from her leather sheath and showed it to La Llorona. "If you want me to cut you free, you must tell me where the children are first."

"I will tell you after you release me."

"I will leave you here to rot unless you tell me now!"

Isabella held out her rosary, letting its crucifix dangle in front of La Llorona's face. The wraith recoiled from the holy object. "Tell me!"

"I will tell you."

"Swear to the Lord God Almighty, upon the souls of your lost children, that you will help me!"

La Llorona cowered before Isabella, shaking her head no.

"Do it," Isabella commanded.

La Llorona continued to shake her head.

"Swear it!" Isabella shouted.

Still, La Llorona remained silent.

"Swear it! Juralo!" she repeated in Spanish.

La Llorona remained stubbornly mute. Isabella paused for a moment. She closed her eyes and said a silent prayer, focusing all her desperation to find the missing children and her moral outrage at the plight of these poor innocents. Channeling all her faith in God, she bellowed forth a mighty command that could compel the strongest of foes to submit.

"JURALO!!!"

La Llorona prostrated herself on the ground at Isabella's feet. "Lo juro! Juro por Dios, juro por las almas de mis hijos!"

Upon hearing La Llorona swear to God on the souls of her children, Isabella sawed at the vines with her knife. The big blade was razor-sharp and had considerable heft. Even so, Isabella had to use all her strength to cut through the dense fibers. When she managed to slice through the last bit of the first vine, there was a sudden and massive release of energy. Isabella not only cut through the vine, but severed the magical forces contained within it. She was knocked backwards, as if struck by a very powerful, but narrowly focused gust of wind.

With the magical energy now dissipated, La Llorona tore the other vine from her wrist like tissue paper. As she levitated several inches off the ground, her dress and hair fanned out around her like a spectral peacock displaying its plumage. La Llorona tilted her head back and laughed. It was a frightening, unearthly sound that echoed as if rebounded from within a vast, cavernous expanse, much larger than the space they currently occupied.

Isabella cut the laughter short. "Remember your oath, Maria."

La Llorona fixed her gaze upon Isabella and continued to stare at her with those milky white eyes, devoid of any pupils, for an uncomfortably long time. Breaking the tense silence, she declared in her unnerving, unearthly voice, "The children are in a barn behind the house, not far, but hidden from view in the copse of trees." Having fulfilled her vow, La Llorona closed her eyes and slowly faded from sight like the last bit of morning fog retreating from the harsh rays of the sun. One moment she appeared as a solid being, the next a translucent apparition, finally disappearing entirely.

Chapter 36

Not the Size of the Dog in the Fight

I scrambled to my feet, ready for action. I relaxed when I saw the beast sprawled on the ground before me, its neck bent back at an unnatural angle, obviously broken. "That's right! That's what happens when you tangle with Gideon Jones! You dance with me, you better bring your A-game!"

Happy as an NFL player who just scored a touchdown, I did a little victory dance. It was equal parts salsa and shadow boxing. Suddenly, the beast made an unsettling sound, like a congested grizzly bear snoring, as it struggled to breathe through a ruined windpipe. I turned to see the monster place its massive hands on either side of its head. With a sickening crunch, it snapped its neck back into place.

"You've got to be kidding me!"

The skinwalker used its now fully functional neck to turn and stare at me. The monster was the stuff of nightmares; its red eyes burning with hate, black lips curled back in a snarl baring huge fangs. Honestly, I felt more exasperated than terrified. Reaching into my trench coat with both hands, I drew twin Colt 1911 .45 caliber pistols. Pointing them menacingly at the skinwalker, I stared the monster in the eye. "You should've stayed down."

I mag dumped both magazines, pulling the trigger as fast as I could. I got off sixteen rounds in under two seconds, at point-blank range, right into the monster's face.

The skinwalker was knocked back to the ground where it thrashed about, hands cupped over its face. The beast was in obvious pain, crying out with terrible half human half wolf screams. I ejected the spent magazines and slammed home news ones. "I guess your eyes weren't bulletproof."

All too soon, the beast's cries ceased. The skinwalker pulled its hands from its face, revealing two perfectly good eyes. This time, fear took over and I sprinted into the woods, running for my life.

Not to brag, but athletics always came naturally to me. My regular training focuses on increasing speed, stamina, and endurance. I incorporate wind sprints on those steep San Francisco hills. I don't just train regularly. I push myself hard, very hard. In fact, I'm downright fanatical in my training. I train as if my life depends on it. It does! On more than one occasion, I've had to literally run for my life.

Once from ninjas, who turned out to be in peak physical condition themselves, and more than once from demons who were both supernaturally strong and fast. As a result, I'm proud to say I'm faster and in better shape than most college athletes. Combine that with the fact that, when a human being is in a life-threatening situation, there are certain automatic physical responses designed to help the body survive.

These traits are a gift from our caveman ancestors who had to fight and run for their lives on a regular basis. The nervous system shifts into high gear, speeding up reflexes. Adrenaline and other hormones are produced, enabling several things to happen that stack the deck in the body's favor when it comes to survival. Eyes dilate, allowing one to take in as much light as possible, sharpening sight in the dark. Smooth muscles relax, allowing lungs to take in more oxygen than normal. The body automatically reroutes energy from non-essential systems like the immune and digestive systems. They shut down to direct more energy to muscles, giving added strength and speed.

All these adaptations allowed ancient man to make the evolutionary cut and saved my bacon on more than one occasion. This time, as I tore through the woods at near Olympic sprinter speeds, I could tell it wasn't going to be enough. The skinwalker was quickly gaining on me, ready to pounce.

Long ago, I learned to trust my instincts, so I suddenly reached out to grab a tree branch. Not slowing down, I held on for dear life, swinging abruptly off to the side as the skinwalker tore past me a fraction of a second later. Releasing my hold on the branch, I continued to sprint off in a new direction, not slowing down one bit.

My trick only bought me a little time. Soon, I could hear the skinwalker tearing through the brush behind me, gaining. Again, my instincts kicked in. I went into a judo dive roll off at a forty-five-degree angle from my current trajectory, just as the skinwalker leapt at me. I dodged the attack in the nick of time.

I came out of the roll at the base of a huge tree. Turning around, I saw the skinwalker skidding to a halt. Quickly changing direction, it barreled towards me once more. This time I held my ground. While digging in my trench coat with my back against the tree trunk, I taunted the creature.

"Come on! Show me what you got! I'm through running! Come get some!" I spread my arms wide as if preparing for an embrace, inviting the skinwalker to attack.

The skinwalker obliged, roaring a challenge. It ran at me on all fours at an alarming rate of speed. It had to be over forty miles per hour. While the beast was still over twenty feet away, it leapt through the air, covering the distance between us instantly. I executed a martial art move called yoko-nagare. It was a ninjutsu technique Master Onosai taught me. The Master was not a ninja himself. The Hikari, his monastic order, has been at war with the Kage ninja clan for centuries. They've picked up a few things from their ancient enemies over time.

One instant I stood before my adversary with arms open wide, inviting an attack, the next I swept my right leg in front of me while sinking with my left leg, all the way to the ground. I essentially dropped from sight at the last second. The momentum of the motion carried me into a roll over my right shoulder, narrowly avoiding the skinwalker. It slammed heavily into the tree instead of me. The monster stayed in a crumpled heap at its base.

Taking advantage of the moment I just bought myself, I uncorked the vial of holy water I took from my trench coat with a flick of my thumb and lobbed it. The bottle shattered upon contact, its contents spilling across the chest of the skinwalker. The beast howled in pain as the blessed liquid burned off its hair and ate its way through skin. I'd seen vials of holy water essentially melt demons into smelly puddles of disgusting goo. Skinwalkers, however, differed from demons in this respect. Although the holy water burned the creature, it didn't dissolve it completely. To my dismay, I watched the burns stop spreading and start healing before my eyes.

The skinwalker started to claw its way back up off the ground, so I threw another vial of holy water. This time I aimed for the creature's face. As it howled in pain, I sprinted off in the opposite direction, making a mental note of how many bottles I'd gone through. Only four left. I had used pretty much every weapon in my arsenal. This thing shrugged off everything I threw at it!

I was flat out of options. Even running away wasn't working, as the creature was incredibly fast. What was I going to do? I heard the skinwalker howl in rage as it recovered from the holy water. It began to tear through the forest after me. Damn! What was it Father Dominic told me about werewolves?

Chapter 37

Demonic Delicacies

Isabella crossed the open space between the bruja's house and the woods at a run, holding the shotgun close to her chest. La Llorona's warning that the bruja would be sacrificing the children tonight echoed in her thoughts. She *had* to find this barn and free the children. Once she was in the thick copse of trees, Isabella had to slow her pace considerably, so as not to trip and fall in the dark.

Her small flashlight was only able to illuminate a few feet in front of her, so Isabella had to choose each step carefully or risk twisting an ankle. It was then, as she slowly made her way in the dark, that Isabella heard the most frightful noise she had ever heard in her life. A dreadful and alarming howl made her blood run cold. Isabella had heard wolves before. Whatever made that terrible cry may have been wolf-like, but it was most definitely no wolf. Isabella wasn't even sure it was of this world.

"Demonios," she whispered as she made the sign of the cross. She shut off her flashlight, not wanting to attract the attention of whatever horrible creature made that sound, and headed off in the opposite direction as quickly and quietly as she could manage. Isabella came to a clearing where there was a small cornfield and a vegetable garden. Behind that was a large, dilapidated barn.

As Isabella made her way closer, she could see an orangish-red light shining from within. The light escaping through the small spaces between the old weathered wooden planks was clearly visible in the dark. Because of that light, she was able to spot a tripwire in front of the barn door just before she almost stumbled into it, springing whatever trap the bruja had laid for her.

"You crafty perra," Isabella mumbled under her breath. She carefully stepped over the wire, alert for any other surprises the bruja had waiting for her. Creeping up as silently as possible, Isabella put her eye to the barn's door and peered through a space between the planks.

Inside, Isabella could see a big bonfire. The bruja was prancing around it, chanting. She was in the process of casting a spell, no doubt. The children were huddled together nearby, their hands and feet tied together with rope. The bruja seemed preoccupied with her incantations. Perhaps she could sneak in and blow her away with the shotgun before she knew what hit her.

Isabella gingerly pushed the door, careful to make no sound as she tried to open it. The entryway held fast. "Nope. That would be too easy wouldn't it?" she muttered to herself. Upon closer inspection, Isabella noticed a section of the door where no light was shining through. Something just below eye level was blocking it. A wooden latch perhaps? It made sense. That's what you'd expect on a barn door. Out here in the boonies, one wouldn't expect any thievery. Having already booby-trapped the only entrance with a tripwire, perhaps the only other precaution the witch took was latching the door.

Isabella took out her hunting knife. Maybe she could jimmy the lock, so to speak. People did it with credit cards on TV so why couldn't she? Carefully, she slid the blade into the space between the wooden planks just below the wooden latch. It was a tight fit, but she was able to manage it. She simply lifted up with her knife. It worked like a charm! She unlatched the door, now able to enter.

Isabella sheathed her knife and grabbed the shotgun. She kept the stock firmly seated in her shoulder and her cheek near the receiver so she would be ready to fire in an instant. Using the barrel of the weapon, she slowly pushed open the barn door.

The scene before her was shocking and horrifying, assaulting her senses. Swaying from the barn ceiling, at the end of ropes, were the newly butchered carcasses of several dead animals. Dogs, cats, goats, and pigs; their entrails dangling from their eviscerated bellies. Copious amounts of blood cascaded down into narrow channels dug into the dirt floor of the barn. The sight was appalling to behold, but the stench! The stench was revolting! Isabella could not only smell it, but almost taste it as the fetid stink of blood and whatever had been digesting in the animals' bellies caught in the back of her throat. It made her want to retch.

On the dirt floor, the narrow channels formed an intricate pattern of arcane symbols. At the center of this gruesome network of crimson canals was a massive bonfire. The bruja danced around it, completely naked, brandishing a huge knife with an upswept blade and bone handle. At her feet was one of the children, also naked. Her arms and legs were tied to wooden stakes pounded into the ground, forcing her limbs spread-eagled, leaving her completely helpless and vulnerable.

The witch spun and whirled about, her arms spread wide in a ritualistic dance. She tilted her head back, chanting and singing. As she sang her spell, the channels of blood suddenly ignited, erupting forth into crimson flames. Sparks showered like burning trails of gunpowder. The bonfire at their center swelled in size and changed color from orangish yellow to blood red. It began to belch black smoke into the air which gathered in a massive cloud at the ceiling and engulfed the dead animals hanging from the rafters.

The dark, vaporous mass roiled like a turbulent storm cloud, obscuring the dead animals from view. Although Isabella was glad she was spared the repugnant sight of the butchered animals, the horrible scene was replaced by something equally disturbing. Unearthly sounds of tearing and chomping, followed by disgusting slurping and sucking noises, bounced off the walls. The dark cloud erupted forth, spewing several smaller versions of itself into the air, like some monstrous beast spawning vile young. There were half a dozen of the things, roughly man-sized black shadowy spheres that shot about the room. They zoomed back and forth, trailing long tendrils of black smoke behind them. The things were bestial but had vaguely human faces with glowing red eyes. They wore angry, wrathful expressions. Their gaping maws were dripping blood. Isabella realized that, in the short time she'd been watching the horrific spectacle, the shadow creatures had completely devoured the butchered animals. They had picked the carcasses clean. Now, it was naught but bloody skeletons that hung from the rafters.

The shadow creatures were terrifying to behold, but what frightened and enraged Isabella even more was the sight of Chumana wielding that enormous knife. She loomed ominously over the poor helpless child, bound and staked to the ground at the witch's feet. The exposed and defenseless youth was sobbing. Chumana glanced down and chided the poor girl in a tone dripping with ridicule and mockery. "Hush child. Soon the darkness will rise from the deep and carry you down into sleep."

Perhaps it was all the time she'd been spending with Gideon lately. His constant quoting of movie lines was wearing off on her. Images from that new movie *Aliens*, when Ripley confronted the Alien Queen, came flashing to mind. Channeling her inner Sigourney Weaver, Isabella shouted, "Get away from her, you BITCH!" Although she wasn't wearing a huge mechanized suit with hydraulic pincers like the movie heroine, she did brandish a large shotgun. That made her an intimidating figure to behold.

Chumana froze mid-step, eyes growing wide at the sight of the gun-wielding curandera. Muttering something in a now-dead language, the witch made a sweeping gesture. One of the shadow creatures swooped down in front of Chumana just as Isabella squeezed the trigger of the Remington 12-gauge shotgun. A deafening blast erupted forth.

Chapter 38

Dancing with Shadows

Isabella aimed at the witch, not the demonic shadow creature. Whether intentionally or accidentally, the thing threw itself into the line of fire and took the armor-piercing shotgun shell to the face. The blessed projectile struck with incredible force, penetrating deeply into the protoplasmic mass of the thing. A revolting mixture of blood and black ichor spewed forth.

The creature crashed to the ground where it screamed and thrashed about on the floor, bleeding profusely. The shadow creature's cries were an unnerving mixture of a deep demonic roar and the higher-pitched squeals of an enraged wild pig. As if in the throes of electrocution, the horrendous thing convulsed violently. Black smoke billowed from its wound, in addition to the profuse amounts of charcoal-colored ichor and blood.

Isabella was transfixed, staring with morbid curiosity as the vile thing bled out and spewed black smoke into the air. To her surprise, the thing began to deflate like a balloon. In the space of a few seconds, it rapidly shrank before her eyes. All that remained of the sizable shadow creature was one of the tiny, ugly, misshapen Nadir fetishes sitting in a disgusting puddle of blood and ebony ooze.

While Isabella was distracted by the sight of the expiring demon, Chumana started bellowing incantations. Her voice was far too deep for a female, too deep for a human being for that matter. In response, the remaining five shadow creatures swooped down from the rafters and landed in front of the witch. Once on the ground, the spherical creatures erupted into a dense cloud of black smoke and rematerialized as large black humanoid figures. They had broad shoulders and thick limbs, standing close to seven feet tall, with glowing red eyes and black smoky auras. In unison they advanced on Isabella, their glowing red eyes emanating pure hatred.

Isabella held her ground instead of cowering in fear, emboldened by her first kill. She pointed the barrel of her shotgun towards Chumana once more, trying to re-acquire the bruja in her sights. The shadow creatures rushed her en masse, moving incredibly fast. They were on her in an instant, but not before Isabella squeezed the trigger and the thunderous boom of the shotgun echoed through the barn once more.

One of the shadow creatures staggered backwards and tumbled to the ground, struck in the chest center-mass by the shotgun slug. It thrashed about as its counterpart had done earlier, wildly flailing as it hemorrhaged ooze, blood, and smoke. Isabella heard screeching as it did so, despite this particular iteration of the creature having no discernible mouth from which to scream.

Enraged, the other four monsters set upon her. Isabella aimed the shotgun at the closest creature. The fiend grabbed hold of the shotgun barrel and pushed it downward, redirecting her aim just as she pulled the trigger. The slug slammed ineffectually into the floor, doing little more than spraying the creature with dirt.

Isabella struggled mightily to raise the shotgun barrel up again, but the creature was too strong. It prevented her from raising it even a fraction of an inch. Suddenly Isabella's head exploded with pain. She saw stars as one of the other creatures pummeled her with a vicious blow to the side of the head with its massive fist.

Isabella staggered, rocked by the blow, but retained her grip on the shotgun. It was the only reason she remained standing. As if sensing this, the shadow creature wrestling for control of the shotgun wrenched backwards. Savagely tearing the shotgun from Isabella's grasp, it flung the weapon aside, well out of her reach. As a result, Isabella fell to her hands and knees.

Immediately, another shadow creature moved in and landed a brutal kick to her side. The force of the blow lifted her clean off the ground and Isabella felt her ribs crack. Gasping for air, she curled into the fetal position as the monsters encircled her, closing in for the kill. While curled up in a ball, Isabella stealthily unsheathed her hunting knife. One of the shadow creatures moved in to kick her again. Moving faster than a striking cobra, Isabella lashed out and slashed the big knife across the creature's shins. Squealing like a stuck pig, the creature recoiled. Smoke billowed out of the wound.

Taking advantage of the space the retreating creature provided, Isabella immediately scrambled back to her feet. In response, the three uninjured shadow creatures rushed in, but Isabella didn't allow them to engulf her. Dealing with multiple attackers was something she practiced in her martial arts training. Singling out one of the demons, she advanced towards it, aggressively brandishing her knife. This created some distance for herself while simultaneously positioning it between the other shadow creatures and herself. They couldn't attack en masse, instead having to maneuver around their friends to get to her.

Maneuver they did, jockeying for positions from which to strike. When one creature seemed to be closing in, Isabella would pivot. This allowed her to use the new opponent as her shield, putting it between herself and the other shadows. The remaining creatures were forced to re-configure and start all over again.

The group angled back and forth, with Isabella dodging and feinting or threatening with her knife, in a deadly dance. Chumana watched, enthralled, as the combatants contended with each other. Isabella tried to steer towards the bonfire, but the bruja's shadow minions would have none of it. Instead, they tried to corral her into a corner, only to have the girl slip away. There was a definite stratagem to the ebb and flow. This girl was giving a good account of herself. Like her grandmother before her, she was proving to be a worthy opponent. Begrudgingly, Chumana found herself respecting the young curandera.

The witch smiled as she watched the conflict unfold. She recognized not only the combative aspect of the struggle, but the finesse. This bruja, who used dance as part of her spell craft, saw the grace hidden in it all. As they shuffled back and forth, as they leapt and spun about, Chumana saw it for what it was. It was a dance! More than that, it was her favorite kind of dance; a dance of death.

Chapter 39

Struggling with Skinwalkers

As I sprinted through the trees, I struggled to recall Father Dom's lessons about werewolves. What were their weaknesses? I could think of two. One was Wolf's Bane, a type of plant with blue flowers. I doubt I'd recognize it, even if I saw it up close. The other was silver bullets. Of course, I didn't have any. Things were definitely looking grim.

At that moment, I burst from the trees into a large clearing. There was a cornfield in front of a big barn constructed of wooden planks. I heard the menacing howl of the skinwalker as it smashed its way through the trees behind me. It was alarmingly close. The beast was practically on top of me. I could feel a spike of adrenaline. Although I was already running at breakneck speed, I dug deep down into that well of reserves we all have. I tapped into that extra bit of energy, pushing myself beyond my normal limits as I sprinted for the cover of the cornfield. Maybe I could lose it in the sea of tall green stalks.

As I dove into their midst, there was a resulting cloud of pollen. The crop was at the stage of development where the tassels of corn silk were visible, but no kernels of corn had developed yet. Stifling a sneeze, I remained perfectly still, quiet as a mouse, not wanting to give my position away. I heard the skinwalker noisily crashing through brush, followed by an eerie silence when it reached the clearing.

I caught glimpses of the beast between the stalks of corn as it paced back and forth. Somehow it guessed where I was hiding but, for some reason, seemed reluctant to come into the cornfield after me. I remained rooted in place. I desperately wanted to go further into the cornfield, but the slightest noise might give me away.

Moving painstakingly slow, I silently drew my pistol from its shoulder rig and did a quick press-check. A handgun press-check is a simple technique for ensuring a pistol is loaded and has a round in the chamber, ready to fire. I'd done this technique hundreds of times over the years. Muscle memory took over as I moved the slide back far enough to expose the round in the chamber but not far enough to eject the round.

Cornfields were a new experience to me, so I accidentally brushed against some nearby stalks. Pollen floated down to coat the exposed round and my face. This most likely wouldn't affect the pistol's ability to function. Unfortunately, being inhaled and making direct contact with my eyes, it resulted in a loud sneeze, alerting the skinwalker to my presence. The beast dropped down, galloping on all fours, and charged into the cornfield.

I barely had time to bring my pistol to bear and squeeze off a shot before the skinwalker crashed into me. After 15 years in the martial arts, I reacted instinctively. My body is well trained to go with the energy of a blow, rather than try to fight it. Over the years I've taken countless falls and strikes. As a private eye, I'd been tackled by a member of the Oakland Raiders. I played football in high school and I *thought* I knew what it was like to take a hit. When the six-foot-five, two hundred and sixty pound man brought me down, I updated my definition.

After being struck by the skinwalker, I definitely needed to re-define my notion of a hard hit once more. On a case last year, I was struck by a demon. That colossal blow sent me flying through some heavy wooden doors. Despite being highly skilled already, I started incorporating more dynamic throws and breakfalls into my training regime after the incident. As a result, the skinwalker rang my bell but didn't take me out of the fight.

The forceful impact knocked the gun from my hand, but I used a judo breakfall to smoothly roll back to my feet, relatively none the worse for wear. I was cognizant enough to realize the skinwalker had yelped in pain. The sound was much like a dog that had been unexpectedly hurt, albeit much deeper and with more bass.

Thanks to the light of the full moon, I saw I'd managed to injure the creature. The beast was bleeding! Not the dark red blood you'd expect, it was instead a thick yellowish liquid oozing from a wound in its shoulder. Why did this shot hit when my earlier shots couldn't penetrate the monster's hide? There was no time to ponder the question as the skinwalker took a swipe at me with one of its massive hands.

Although it was lightning fast, I saw the attack coming and leapt backwards to avoid the blow. Because of its elongated arms, the skinwalker still managed to rake its claws across my chest. I gritted my teeth against the searing pain. Not wanting to be on the receiving end of that again, when the skinwalker drew its arm back for another swipe, I rushed in. Ducking under the attack, I maneuvered around my adversary.

The skinwalker was a predator in the truest sense of the word and thus was used to his victims acting like prey. They would either run in terror or cower frozen with fear. Clearly, none had ever rushed to attack. My unexpectedly aggressive response gave it pause, allowing me just enough time to stomp down with all my might. I delivered a vicious kick to the side of the beast's knee, striking it at a ninety-degree angle in relation to how the creature's leg was designed to bend backwards. There was an audible snap as ligaments tore and bones broke.

The skinwalker howled in pain. I quickly maneuvered behind the monster, positioning myself where I could attack with no fear of a counterstrike. I unleashed a flurry of punches, hammering for all I was worth, at where I hoped the beast's kidneys were located. All my training maximizes my weight, strength, and body mechanics. I channeled my energy into a punch powerful enough to snap bones and rupture organs.

I let out a long and mighty kiai. I poured all my primal will to survive into the blows and vented my rage upon the foul beast threatening my life. The skinwalker arched its back and let out another yelp of pain. The monster tried to whirl about so it could swipe at me with its deadly claws again. Its wounded leg couldn't support the beast's considerable weight. The skinwalker collapsed to the ground, yowling in agony as it curled into the fetal position, clutching its ruined limb close to its body.

Although I lost one of my pistols when the skinwalker tackled me, I still had three left. Taking advantage of the fact that my enemy was down, I reached into my trench coat. I simultaneously drew two Colt 1911s. Fueled by adrenaline, I pulled the triggers so fast it sounded like I was firing a Thompson machine gun.

"Yeah! Get some, you ugly son of a bitch!" I whooped as I riddled the skinwalker with .45 caliber bullets.

As the beast writhed on the ground in agony, I smoothly ejected the spent magazines and slammed home new ones. To my dismay, I noticed these new gunshots hadn't drawn blood as my earlier shot in the cornfield had. Then, as if to add insult to this lack of injury, the skinwalker snapped its broken leg back into place and stood back up.

The creature fixed me with a murderous stare. Thanks to the skinwalker's mix of human features, I was able to read the expression on the beast's face. It seemed to convey something along the lines of, 'you're going to pay for that'.

Unblinking, I returned the fiend's stare. "Yeah? Well fuck you too!" Adjusting my aim, I raised both pistols and fired into the beast's face. As an afterthought, I emptied the last few rounds into the skinwalker's groin for good measure.

Although the beast was in obvious pain from being shot at point-blank range, once again the gunfire failed to produce any wounds. Deciding that discretion was the better part of valor, I tucked my proverbial tail between my legs. I turned on my heel and sprinted for all my worth towards the barn.

As I ran for my life my mind raced as well. Why had the first bullet in the cornfield drawn blood while all the others hadn't? My train of thought was broken, however, as the skinwalker brutally slammed into me from behind, knocking me to the ground.

Chapter 40

Shadow Stratagem

Chumana studied the struggle between Isabella and her shadow minions much like a general watching troop formations as a battle raged back and forth. As she did so, the witch took note that the three unharmed shadow creatures menaced the curandera constantly. However, the one Isabella wounded hung back a bit, not actively participating in the fray as much as the others. It seemed none too eager to suffer another slash from curandera's big knife.

The bruja started mumbling a spell under her breath, quietly at first but steadily increasing in volume. Chumana's eyes rolled back in her head until only the whites were visible. Apparently still able to see, the witch took a step forward while gesturing with her own sizable, curved blade at the wounded shadow creature. In a great booming voice, too deep and too loud for any human, she bellowed commands in that long-forgotten language.

In response, the wounded shadow creature charged Isabella. The curandera brandished her weapon menacingly, threatening the fiend, but it rushed in heedless of the risk. Outstretched otherworldly arms were ready to seize Isabella in their deadly embrace. At the last second, the curandera side-stepped off the line of attack at a forty-five-degree angle. Simultaneously, she slashed one of the creature's outstretched arms with her knife. The shadow creature emitted a high-pitched wail, still so unnerving to hear without a mouth to produce the sound, as it bled smoke and that viscous ooze.

Almost instantly, the thing whirled back on Isabella. This time she slashed it across the chest. The shadow creature screamed upon being cut again but continued to press forward despite being wounded. It seized Isabella in a bear hug and pulled her in close. The massive shadow creature began squeezing for all it was worth, crushing the much smaller woman in its powerful grasp. Although her upper arms were now pinned to her sides, Isabella could still move her arms from the elbow down. Desperately, the curandera stabbed the monster repeatedly in its mid-section. The thing shrieked and collapsed on her, billowing forth clouds of black smoke.

At first, Isabella staggered under the weight of the creature. The burden quickly lessened as the cloud of black smoke increased in volume. Soon there was no creature sagging upon her at all, just one of the ugly little Nadir fetishes on the ground at her feet, sitting in a puddle of blood and black goo. Using her distraction to their advantage, the other shadows moved in and surrounded Isabella.

The monster to her left seized her arm, clamping down around her wrist in a vice-like grip. The pain was excruciating. The fiend was crushing down on the bite wound Chumana gave her while in her dog form. Isabella immediately moved to slash her assailant, but another shadow creature grabbed her right wrist and held her fast before she could do it. As she struggled to break free, the third shadow creature moved forward, arm raised high. Just as it closed in, Isabela brought both of her knees up to her chest, letting her captors support her weight. She kicked out with everything she had, striking the shadow creature under the chin with both of her heels simultaneously.

The monster was knocked backwards from the force of the blow. Flailing about wildly, it backpedaled at a surprising rate of speed, desperately trying to regain its balance.

Chapter 41

Low Blow

The air forcefully expelled from my lungs as the skinwalker slammed into me from behind. The beast hit me so hard, I thought my lungs might just sail out of my mouth! One of the monster's muscular arms was wrapped around my waist, so I couldn't get into a judo roll. I did a forward breakfall instead. I turned my head to the side, so my face didn't smack into the ground. Then, I slapped the ground with my palms and forearms to let them absorb the brunt of the fall.

Tucking my head and rolling over my shoulder would have been less jarring, but the forward breakfall was better than doing a faceplant. Regrettably, I had to drop my pistols to perform the technique. I crashed into the ground so hard, I rebounded like a bounced ball. Twisting at the waist, I used the momentum to deliver an elbow strike with my left arm into the skinwalker's temple while I drew my last pistol with my right.

The attack didn't do any real damage to the creature, but it did create enough space for me to squirm into a position I could fire from. Fire I did, pulling the trigger as fast as he could, quickly emptying the entire magazine of .45 caliber rounds into the monster's face.

Howling in a mixture of pain and rage, the skinwalker recoiled, covering its face in a futile attempt to avoid being hit. I used the opportunity to scramble to my feet and run away. I mumbled a few choice profanities under my breath. Once again, the bullets failed to puncture the beast's seemingly impervious hide. Well, one bullet somehow managed to do the trick. How, damnit? *Maybe it's just a matter of finding the right spot*, I thought to myself. As I raced off, I ejected the spent magazine and reached for a new one.

Empty! I was out of ammo. "Shit, fuck, son of a bitch!" I swore as I grabbed my stiletto switchblade instead. Thumbing the release, I snapped the blade into place. Like a cat with its tail on fire, I tore off through the cornfield, smashing my way through the stalks. I squinted against the resulting clouds of pollen. If augmented .45 ACP ammunition failed to bring the monster down, how could a switchblade manage to do the trick?

Although my heart pounded in my chest as I ran for dear life, I could also feel it sink. Was this the end? I don't know whether it was an instant or an eternity later, but suddenly I was out the other side of the cornfield. Before me stood a huge, very old, weathered-looking barn. It was maybe fifty yards away. I could cover that distance in about six seconds. Channeling my inner Carl Lewis, I took off like a shot towards the barn. About two seconds into my run, I heard the skinwalker burst out of the cornfield behind me. In my heart of hearts, I knew I wouldn't make it all the way to the barn before the beast caught me.

Well, if this is how I check out, I'm going down fighting, I thought to myself. Skidding to a halt, I spun around to face the skinwalker. "Come on, let's dance!" I shouted, running straight at the charging behemoth.

It answered my challenge with a howl of its own, exposing a mouth full of razor-sharp teeth. Lumbering forward, the skinwalker lifted its arms high, claws ready to slash and tear.

We both charged towards each other. Just an instant before we collided, I dropped down and slid feet first towards the monster, like a baseball player trying to steal home plate. I slipped underneath the fiend's attempt to rake me with its claws and slid right between the monster's legs. As I slid along, I held my switchblade aloft and delivered a deep gash to the skinwalker's groin. The beast shrieked out in pain. To my great satisfaction, I saw my knife was covered in a thick and sticky yellowish goo.

Over the years, as a youth during my schooling and later as an adult throughout my career as a private eye, I've upset more than a few people. I've witnessed enough annoyed, irate, and even downright furious folks that I consider myself an expert on the subject of anger. Upon seeing the skinwalker howling and hopping around while clutching its genitalia, I decided that one couldn't *fully* understand angry until they had sliced open the scrotum of a murderous monster.

Taking advantage of my enemy's distraction, I moved in for the kill and plunged my knife into the side of the skinwalker's neck where the carotid artery would be on a human. It felt like stabbing a brick wall, not flesh and blood! Although the knife managed to penetrate the beast's tough hide about an inch and a half, the blade snapped in two. Instead of delivering a killing blow like I planned, I merely diverted the monster's attention from its mangled testicles back to me.

The skinwalker whirled to face me, a seven-foot-tall, five hundred pound personification of rage with long claws and sharp teeth. There are certain circumstances when one doesn't have time to think matters through and ponder options. For instance, when human beings are faced with something terrifying. It triggers a fight or flight response. My amygdala, or lizard brain, the part of the brain responsible for primitive survival instincts, told me to run. I dutifully obeyed.

Skinwalkers are incredibly fast, faster than horses. They are greatly feared among the Navajo tribe. People are reluctant to even talk about the shapeshifting witches and wizards, especially to outsiders. It's said that just talking about them can draw their unwanted attention. The younger generation of Navajo are less superstitious than their elders and don't believe merely mentioning a skinwalker will summon the foul thing. There are whispers of skinwalkers so fast they can keep pace with automobiles going sixty miles per hour. Lucky for me, if you slash a skinwalker's testicles it slows them down considerably!

I raced for the barn, the beast hot on my heels. As I got closer, I noticed the barn door was ajar. Reddish light from within spilled out into the night. I wasn't sure why, but the light had a foreboding quality to it. Seeing as I was being pursued by a five hundred pound monster intent on ripping me to shreds, I didn't give the eerie light much thought. My whole world narrowed down to reaching the barn before the skinwalker could catch me.

Seeing my frenetic pace, it was hardly a surprise I failed to notice the tripwire Chumana had set until the witch's trap was sprung. So it was a tad bit too late. Give me a little credit for realizing what was happening as soon as I felt my ankle snag the wire! In that instant, time slowed to a crawl, just like those slow-motion scenes in the movies. I fully understood that tensing up was counterproductive in survival situations, but I couldn't help puckering my sphincter just a little. Everyone knows nothing good ever happens in slow-mo.

Although I didn't know why, my instincts told me the danger would be coming from above. I immediately tucked into a dive roll. An eleven-inch long spike affixed to an axe handle came swinging down with incredible force from where it was spring-loaded above the other side of the door. Had I been running instead of executing the roll, the spike would have impaled me right through the face.

Instead, the sharp spike dug a shallow gash along the top of my head. It hurt like hell but wasn't fatal. The skinwalker, however, was right behind me and didn't fare as well. Being a good bit taller than me, the spike struck the beast right in the jugular.

Chapter 42

Barnyard Battle

Sailing through the open barn door catapulted me right into chaos. A strange shadowy creature was staggering around like it was trying to regain balance. Tucked into a forward dive roll, I bowled into the creature from behind, colliding with the thing below its knees. The monster toppled over backwards into the skinwalker, who was attempting to withdraw the large spike from its neck. The unexpected collision of the two behemoths resulted in the spike tearing through the side of the skinwalker's neck in a spray of yellow mucus-like gore.

Startled and disoriented, the two monsters began fighting each other. The shadow creature pummeled the skinwalker with sledgehammer-like blows from its massive fists and the skinwalker ripped and tore with its terrible claws. As the pair rolled about the dirt floor, they were enveloped in a cloud of black smoke. The haze billowed out from the shadow creature's wounds. Although the combatants could no longer be seen, their terrible cries echoed through the barn as they savaged each other.

Abruptly, the noise ceased and the smoke dissipated. It revealed a naked Navajo man with a ghastly wound to his head instead of his neck. He lay sprawled on a blood-stained wolf pelt with a Nadir fetish sitting upon his chest, in a puddle of black and yellow goo.

I watched the battle with morbid curiosity. Once it was over, I looked away and took in the rest of the nightmarish scene. Swaying from the rafters were the gory skeletons of dozens of animals. About ten feet in front of me were two more of the big black ...*things* with glowing red eyes. They held a struggling Isabella. Further back in the barn was a massive bonfire. For some reason, it burned an eerie blood red instead of the normal orangish-yellow one normally associated with fire.

Standing in front of the huge blaze was a middle-aged Native American woman, buck naked, holding an immense knife with a wicked-looking upswept blade. Staked to the ground at her feet was one of the missing children, a little girl, also naked. She bawled like a baby, understandably terrified. The rest of the kids were huddled together nearby, many of them sobbing as well, their hands and feet tied together with rope.

At this point, I was willing to admit I had feelings for Isabella. I also knew she was far from helpless. The same could not be said about the little girl staked to the ground at the witch's feet. Seeing the poor child in that dreadful condition, I could feel the righteous rage of angels boiling up inside me. I stared daggers at the witch. I was going to make that bitch pay! Without thinking, I broke into a run, heading straight for her.

Chumana saw me glaring at her. She looked shocked. Clearly, I was not supposed to survive an encounter with a skinwalker. This ritual wasn't meant to be disturbed. The witch gathered her power and pantomimed the act of throwing something at me. Even though I couldn't see anything sailing through the air towards me, I instinctively raised my hands to protect my face. Damn good thing, because a fraction of a second later, an invisible force slammed into me, knocking me off my feet and sending me flying backwards.

The blow would have rendered most men unconscious. My instinctive flinch response and training served me well. I went with the force of the blow. When I struck the ground, I automatically transitioned into a breakfall. I was back on my feet in an instant, relatively none the worse for wear.

I landed close to Isabella and the shadow creatures. On a hunch, I dug into one of my trench coat pockets and took out a vial of holy water. I threw it at the shadow creature holding Isabella's right arm. The vial shattered as it struck the creature in the chest. Squealing like a stuck pig, the thing released its hold of Isabella as black smoke erupted from its chest.

Her knife hand now free, Isabella slashed the shadow creature holding her left arm. It too released its hold and retreated a few steps backwards as smoke and black blood poured from the wound. The retreating demon gave Isabella the opening she was looking for. She made a mad dash for Chumana. Fleet of foot as the curandera was, the shadow overtook her and punched her with one of its massive fists. The blow landed right between her shoulder blades causing her to stumble and fall at the bruja's feet. Chumana savagely kicked Isabella in the face.

The blow from the shadow creature hurt more, but the fact that the bruja had kicked her when she was down infuriated Isabella. Springing back up to her feet, she took a running step and leapt at the witch, knife held high and ready to strike. The monster grabbed her hair and roughly yanked backwards, causing her to fall once more. The creature stomped down with its colossal foot to squash the curandera's head like a bug. At the last second, Isabella rolled aside, narrowly avoiding the blow. Countering, she slashed the creature across its shins with her knife. The resulting wound produced more black blood and smoke. Though the shadow retreated, Isabella pursued. Running towards the demon, she could move faster than it was able to backtrack away.

The fiend raised its hands in an attempt to ward her off, but Isabella slashed as soon as it did. When the creature instinctually brought its hands back close to its body upon being wounded, she took advantage and pressed in closer, stabbing the monster repeatedly. The shadow shrieked and squealed as it bled profusely and billowed clouds of black smoke. Isabella was relentless and did not stop until she had reduced the shadow creature back into a Nadir fetish sitting in a puddle of putrid ooze.

Since the first vial of holy water proved so effective, I dug back into my trench coat and withdrew another. Like a grenade, I lobbed it at the shadow creature, striking it on the shoulder. The blessed liquid immediately began eating away at the thing like a super acid. Shrieking, it ran away trailing black smoke behind it. I chased after it and threw my next bottle at the creature's feet.

The holy water melted the monster's limbs. Unable to run on its ruined appendages, the shadow creature tumbled. It fell to the ground, billowing more smoke. Desperate, the thing tried to crawl away, dragging its considerable weight with its powerful arms. It was a total sitting duck now. The last vial reduced the shadow back to a Nadir fetish.

Having defeated her shadow creature, Isabella whirled to face Chumana. The bruja had already hurled a spell at her and the phantasmal force hit the curandera like a Mac truck. She was slammed to the ground, where she stayed, unmoving. I charged the witch like an enraged bull. Chumana hit me with a similar spell before I could reach her. The blow rocked my world. I would've liked nothing better than to lie there for a while, but I could hear the little girl's frantic sobbing.

Doggedly, I pulled myself back up. After spitting out a mouthful of blood, I taunted the witch. "Is that the best you can do?"

In answer, Chumana me him again. This time her attack not only knocked me down, but it also sent me sliding across the ground several yards.

Still on my back, I groaned but then started laughing. "That's the spirit!" I got back up, albeit slower this time, and fixed Chumana with a steely stare. Menacingly, I stalked forward. "I've done in scarier things than you, witch! You'd best make the next hit count, cause I'm gonna END you for what you've done to those kids."

Chumana closed her eyes and drew in a deep breath. The witch's visage changed, and she seemed to grow in stature. Her eyelids snapped back open, revealing glowing green eyes. She spoke with an unearthly deep voice that human vocal cords could not possibly make. "Arrogant fool! I will make you beg for death before I am through!"

With a bestial sneer on her face, Chumana stretched out her arms and began flexing her hands and fingers like she was squeezing the life out of some invisible thing. I immediately dropped to my knees, clutching at my throat and gasping for air. I couldn't breathe! Chumana laughed as she continued to work her spell. I collapsed to the ground. My lungs cried out for air I could no longer take in. Like a fish out of water, I thrashed about on the ground, flailing my limbs in panic. The pain was awful.

The witch advanced forward until she was looming over me, a look of smug and malicious satisfaction upon her face. My vision began to narrow. All was fading to black. There are few people in this world as stubborn as Gideon Jones! Despite the terrible pain, I haltingly pulled myself up off the ground. Mirroring the witch's stance, I stretched out my arms so I could choke the life out of her. Chumana arched an eyebrow. Was she impressed with my herculean act? Even if she was, she quickly redoubled her efforts. Triumphantly, she watched as I collapsed again. The witch didn't let up on her magical onslaught, wanting to ensure I didn't rise again.

Chumana's concentration was broken, however, as a ringing CRACK split the air. Her head exploded with searing pain, the result of Isabella unleashing her whip and the deadly lug nuts braided into the whip's end. Traveling faster than the speed of sound, they created a small sonic boom as they slammed into the back of the witch's head. Chumana stumbled and fell face-first onto the ground.

Isabella knew the bruja wouldn't be getting up after that. She broke hundreds of cinder blocks practicing with her enhanced whip. Such a blow would have fractured the witch's skull like an eggshell.

I lay still for a moment, my eyes closed. Abruptly, I sat up, eyes wide, and began gasping. Inhaling loud and deep, I felt like a swimmer submerged underwater for too long. It was panicked at first but then slower, like relishing the scent of fresh flowers.

I gazed up at Isabella and smiled. "Thanks for the assist, darlin', but another second and I would have had her."

"Oh really? From where I was standing, it looked like you were lying on your back, unconscious."

"I was simply lulling her into a false sense of security."

Laughing, Isabella extended her hand. I gladly accepted the help up. We quickly went to the little girl staked to the ground. Isabella cut her lose and held the sobbing child in her arms, comforting her. "Ssshh, it's going to be ok now."

I draped my trench coat around the girl, took Isabella's knife, and began to cut the other children free.

Chapter 43

Dire Straits

"Noooo!! No, no, no!" Chumana cried out in a voice filled with outrage and hate.

I stopped sawing at the rope binding the children and, filled with dread, glanced back over my shoulder. There was Chumana, trembling like a bookworm in gym class who was unaccustomed to doing pushups. The witch slowly raised herself up from the dirt floor despite bleeding profusely. The back of her head was split wide open, exposing the brain matter within. Looking up, she fixed me with a stare full of loathing and pain.

"They shall pay for what they have done! They shall pay until the end of time!"

Not knowing a thing about this witch's history, the remark filled me with moral outrage. I finished slicing through the last bit of rope like it was butter and turned to face her. Brandishing the knife as if it were a great sword, I stalked forward like an avenging angel. "These children have done nothing to you! It's YOUR time that is at an end, witch!"

In answer, Chumana began uttering a spell. Suddenly, the bruja began to convulse violently. Amidst dreadful tearing and popping noises, her body began to bulge and swell, as if a vile spore germinated deep within her. It grew and expanded at an alarming rate, twisting and deforming her body as it did so. At first, because she was hunched over, I couldn't really see the extent of the transformation. When I took a step closer, the witch stood erect. It was evident that, in the space of a few seconds, the slender Native American woman morphed into a hulking monstrosity.

Chumana now towered over me, standing nearly eight feet tall. Her back was hunched, with a protruding hump that was crisscrossed with numerous festering lacerations that oozed a vile mixture of blood and pus. Her arms were now overly muscled and ape-like, hanging past her knees. They ended in disproportionately big hands with elongated fingers and nails that looked more like talons. Her skin, which had been deeply tanned a moment earlier, was now cadaverously pale, with a sickly greyish hue to it.

Before, Chumana had the lean figure of an athlete in her early twenties. Now, she was so wrinkly it looked like she was constructed entirely of scrotal skin coated in slime. Her long black hair was much sparser now, as if she suffered from mange. What was left of it was plastered to her head in unsightly clumps, sopping wet and coated in more slime. Her face was so gaunt it was almost skeletal with her cheekbones threatening to tear right through the skin. Her nose was now several times longer and dangled past her lips like a rotting chili. Her eyes were sunken and withdrawn deep into their sockets but glowed with an eerie green light. Chumana sneered at me, her lips curling back to reveal stained decaying teeth.

I stared up at her, disgust all over my face. "You are one *ugly* bitch."

Chumana suddenly swiped at me with one of her massive hands, attempting to rake me with her claws. Using Isabella's big knife like a shield, I both blocked the blow and cut the attacking limb. Going on the offensive, I rushed in, closing the distance and negating the witch's reach advantage.

I lunged like an Olympic fencer, attempting to stab the witch in the heart, but Chumana batted the blade aside with the flat of her hand. Knocking it down and to the right, the knife plunged into her right abdomen, puncturing her oblique muscles instead of her heart. It wasn't a fatal blow, but the witch gritted her teeth and hissed in pain. Encouraged by this, I withdrew the blade to stab her again. Before I could, Chumana seized me by the throat. With one hand, she lifted me high over her head and slammed me to the ground.

I know from lots of experience that the ground hits you a heck of a lot harder than a man. I positioned my body to avoid injury in the fall. Seeing as I'd been hurled by an eight-foot-tall witch in possession of greater than human strength, it still hurt like hell. I lay there for a moment, stunned. My vision swam with stars.

A moment was all Chumana needed. The bruja savagely kicked me while I was down. The blow had such force, it lifted me clear off the ground. My side exploded with agony. When I landed, I tried to roll away. The witch ran after me. Stooping down, she raked her claws down my back. Her razor-sharp talons easily tore through the fabric of my shirt and into my flesh, drawing blood.

I let out an involuntary gasp of pain. Laughing, the witch raised her arm for another swipe. There was a resounding crack and Chumana growled. Isabella's whip coiled around the witch's wrist, holding it fast and preventing her from slashing at me again. Chumana fixed the curandera with a venomous stare. Grabbing hold of the whip with both hands the bruja yanked with all her might, trying to tear the whip from her grasp.

Isabella had a death grip on the whip. Instead of having her weapon taken from her, she was sent sailing through the air towards the witch. Chumana sidestepped at the last instant and Isabella crashed into me, just as I was regaining my feet. We were both stunned. I had no strength to fight as Chumana picked us up, each by the throat. Lifting us high above her head, she slammed us together like a pair of cymbals.

Supremely confident, the bruja let us squirm there for a moment. Dazed from the blow, I struggled like a worm impaled on a fishhook. Chumana slammed us together again. This time, we both dangled limply in her grasp. The witch sighed, apparently disappointed it was over so quickly. She simply opened her hands and let us drop to the ground. Isabella stayed there in a crumpled heap. I came up swinging, delivering two uppercuts to Chumana's lower abdomen. Unfazed, the witch grabbed my hair with her left hand and yanked my head backwards, exposing my throat. She swiped at me with the claws on her right hand.

I quickly raised my arms up in a classic boxer's defensive stance to take the slash across my forearms instead of my jugular. Twisting at the hips, I delivered a roundhouse kick, striking with my shin into the witch's thigh. I've toppled men with the surprisingly powerful and painful technique, but Chumana stoically ignored the blow. The witch opened her hands, exposing her palms to me. I barely had time to wonder what the heck she was doing before I got slammed by one of her spells.

The phantasmal force sent me flying a dozen feet. Crashing to the floor, I tumbled several feet more, not stopping until I banged my head against a wooden support beam. Light briefly filled my skull. When my vision returned, Chumana was already upon me. Picking me up by the throat again, she slammed the back of my head into the beam once more.

The jarring blow sent pain cascading through my body and made me black out momentarily. I knew, in this new twisted form, the witch's arms were much longer than mine. There would be no opportunity to land a punch. I kicked out, striking the witch right on one of her sagging breasts. Gritting her teeth in pain, Chumana snorted a breath out through her nose. The sound was bursting with rage and congealed hate.

Still holding me up against the beam, she stepped in closer so I could no longer effectively kick her. She stopped just short of my punching range. Taking advantage of her longer arms, she drove one of her ghastly four-inch long fingernails into my pectoral muscle. Searing pain shot through my chest. A red stain appeared on my white shirt. Laughing, Chumana twisted her finger back and forth in the wound.

I thought the initial injury hurt but this new development was redefining pain for me. The first abuse had been a tidal wave, but this new trauma was a colossal tsunami! Gritting my teeth, I stubbornly refused to give the witch the satisfaction of crying out. Irked by my lack of reaction, Chumana brutally ripped the nail out sideways, shredding the muscle in the process.

I cried out. The entirety of my existence in that moment was a frenzied need to escape the torturous agony. I thrashed and desperately began hammering down on the brawny arm that held me by the throat. Pinned to the support beam, I might as well have been trying to push over a mountain. The thick, sinewy limb remained unmoved and didn't so much as acknowledge my effort with a slight wobble. I kicked at the witch again. Since she had moved closer, my attacks were impotent and had little more effect than slugging the bruja with a foam pillow.

Cackling with perverse glee at my feeble attacks, Chumana moved her free hand up close to my face. She stopped mere inches away and began wriggling her elongated fingers before my eyes, tauntingly, like a cat toying with its prey. One by one, she curled her fingers back, except for her index finger. It slowly crept forward, bit by bit, until her nail was pressed into my cheekbone just below my left eye. The bruja kept going until her nail had punctured my flesh and struck bone. I locked eyes with the witch as blood trickled down my cheek, giving no indication of fear. Chumana smirked and snorted contemptuously as if to say, 'we'll see how long this bravado lasts.' Her smug smile broadened as she slowly and deliberately dragged her finger down my face. Her nasty claw tore through my flesh as she did.

I grimaced and my body shook with pain, but again I refused to cry out. Chumana presented her bloodstained hand before my face again and slowly lowered it, making sure I was following her with my gaze. She stopped at my abdomen and held it there palm up. All her ghastly fingers pointed towards me. She kept her hand there for several seconds, relishing the trepidation evident in my expression.

The witch spoke in a guttural voice befitting her new hulking form. "Know this, white dog! Even after I rip out your entrails, death will not come quickly. I think, strong as you are, it might take hours. You will live long enough to see me sacrifice the children. As you hear their pitiful cries, you will know you have utterly failed them."

Chapter 44

Colossal Clash

My blood ran cold and I shivered, not with fear, but from a sudden drop in temperature. I could actually see the fog of my breath. An eerie and mournful wail echoed through the barn as the translucent apparition of a woman materialized behind Chumana. The specter hovered about three feet off the ground, so her head was level with that of the giant deformed witch.

Where Chumana was a grotesque and twisted thing, this creature was hauntingly beautiful, with porcelain white skin and raven black hair. She wore a white dress of antiquity and emanated a faint blue light. Her hair and dress fanned out as if she were submerged under water or stirred by a gentle breeze. There was no wind in the barn and the air hung heavy and still.

Chumana turned to face the specter. Upon seeing it, she snorted contemptuously. "Why are you here? I am through with you, *Llorona!*" Chumana said the last word with such derision and scorn. She practically spat it out, as if it left a bad taste in her mouth.

I really needed to learn more Spanish. I assumed the bruja was hurling insults, partially because of her tone and inflection, but mostly because of the phantom's reaction.

The ghost's face morphed from a picture of serene beauty to an ugly and contorted mask of horror, conveying burning hatred. Her eyes turned milky white with no discernible pupils.

Tears, black as tar, stained her face as they rolled down her cheeks. Long, sharp, obsidian-like fangs that dripped with saliva, black as pitch, lined a mouth opened impossibly wide. Her hands doubled in size with elongated fingers and freakishly long claw-like fingernails.

She roared in a great booming voice like a thunderclap. It had a strange repetitive quality like the soundwaves were being reflected from the bottom of a deep well. **"BUT *I* AM NOT FINISHED WITH *YOU*, BRUJA!!!"** With that, the ghost flew at Chumana, moving so fast she was a blur, covering the space between them in an instant.

Chumana's face was raked with grotesquely long claws before she fully realized what was happening. The witch tried to tear the ghost off her but, as soon as she raised her arms, La Llorona was already astride the bruja's back. She sank her black fangs into the side of the witch's head. Chumana reached back, trying to grab hold of the specter. Before she could pry her off, La Llorona tore off the bruja's ear. Chumana let out a deafening roar of agony. Like a big clump of bananas, one of the witch's massive hands clamped down around La Llorona's wrist. Seizing hold of the specter, Chumana swung her over her head like a sack of potatoes and slammed her to the ground repeatedly, like she was beating the dust out of a small throw rug.

When the colossal Chumana released her hold of La Llorona, the ghost lay stunned. The bruja seized the opportunity. She kicked the phantom so hard, the specter went sailing through the air like a punted football and crashed into the wall several feet away. Bellowing a challenge, the huge witch lumbered after her. Springing back to her feet, La Llorona answered the bruja's roar with a piercing cry of her own. Wailing like a banshee, she charged out to meet the witch. Instead of colliding with her, La Llorona circled Chumana like a cyclone, moving impossibly fast, and slashed the witch repeatedly with her deadly claws.

Roaring like an incensed bear swatting at bees, Chumana swiped again and again at the ghost with her own powerful talons. The ghost managed to avoid every blow. Soon, the bruja bled from numerous heinous wounds. Staggering under La Llorona's assault, Chumana careened like a drunken flamenco dancer into the raging inferno of the immense bonfire and was engulfed in its terrible flames.

There was a look of perverse satisfaction on La Llorona's face as the ghost hovered over the flames, delighting in Chumana's cries of agony. Suddenly, a thick sinewy limb shot out of the blaze, grabbed hold of the specter's throat, and dragged her screaming into the fire. The high-pitched wail of La Llorona intermingled with the bellowing roars of Chumana to create a vile chorus that assaulted the ears.

It carried on for a distressingly long period of time. I remembered stories from Catholic School about souls being tortured in Hell. That's what the screaming sounded like. Finally, the dreadful cries stopped. I sighed with relief, finally willing to take a breath. I had no idea what kind of creature the big witch had been fighting or what Chumana had done to piss it off, but I knew it was bad news. The pair had done each other in and that was the best outcome I could have asked for.

I limped over to Isabella and knelt by her side. I saw her ample bosom slowly rise and fall, so she was still breathing at least. "Hey darlin'. You ok?"

Isabella groaned loudly before answering. "You sure do have a hard head. Did you know that?"

I smiled. "I might have been told once or twice."

"Yeah? Well, they weren't kidding," Isabella chided while returning my smile.

I was extending her a helping hand when the smile fell off her face. Her eyes grew wide with fear. The children started screaming again. I quickly spun around. The hulking form of Chumana was staggering out of the blood-red inferno. The colossal bruja shambled forward, her body covered in third-degree burns. Her entire epidermis was a leathery mass of angry red open sores dotted with charred black patches.

"They will pay! They will pay until the end of time," the witch hissed as she stalked menacingly towards the children.

"It's you who'll pay!" I shouted. Bellowing a kiai like a mighty war cry of old, I charged the massive witch and launched myself into a flying side kick. I sailed through the air like a two hundred and five pound hurled javelin and struck the bruja in the mid-section with my heel. She doubled over in pain.

I followed up with a flurry of punches, putting my entire body into the powerful barrage of strikes. Chumana staggered backwards and fell but I didn't stop. Venting my rage upon her, repaying the bruja for her earlier sadistic cruelty, I continued to rain down blows. Chumana unleashed her most powerful spell yet on me. The force slammed into me like a freight train. I flew through the air and tumbled across the floor.

As if the blunt force trauma wasn't bad enough, Chumana's spell sent a wave of intense and excruciating pain coursing through my body. I felt like I was being eaten alive by an angry swarm of fire ants! It was such terrible agony I didn't even feel myself slam into the ground. Only brief flashes of floor and ceiling passed before my eyes as I tumbled end over end.

I came to a stop with my cheek laying on the dirt floor, staring at Chumana as the giant witch stomped towards the children. I fought to raise myself off the ground, but my arms and legs wouldn't obey. It was as if they couldn't hear me through the intense pain. I couldn't move. I could barely think. Helpless as my body started to shut down, all I could do was watch.

No! I refused to let it end that way. I couldn't just leave Isabella and the children to a horrific fate. Maybe I could distract Chumana to draw the witch's attention away from them. Hopefully, it would buy them time to escape. I yelled out for all I was worth, hurling insults at the bruja that would've made a sailor blush. At least... that was my intent. It came out as a faint wheezing sound, barely audible. My vision blurred and I was vaguely aware of Isabella calling my name, but it sounded muffled and far off. Everything faded to black.

Isabella cried out to Gideon, but he was still as a statue, sprawled upon the ground. She glanced at the frightened children huddled together. For an instant, panic showed on her face. The realization that there would be no cavalry coming to the rescue dawned on her. Isabella hardened her jaw and squared her shoulders as she turned to face Chumana.

The curandera boldly stepped between the advancing witch and the children, barring the way. "You will not lay a hand on them!" she shouted. Uncoiling her whip, Isabella lashed out with the weapon like a striking cobra aiming, for the bruja's face.

For such a big brute, the witch moved deceptively fast. She quickly tucked into a defensive stance, taking the blow on her meaty forearms instead. Chumana's eyes flashed with an eerie green light as she uttered a spell. The whip burst into flames. The durable kangaroo hide was instantly reduced to ash and Isabella dropped the iron handle, now glowing red hot.

Isabella remained rooted in place, even though she was weaponless, boldly standing between the bruja and the children. When the mammoth witch took a step closer, the curandera turned into a spinning back kick, striking Chumana in the knee. She beamed with fierce satisfaction as the bruja cried out in pain. The colossal Chumana countered with a devastating punch that overpowered Isabella's attempted block and sent the curandera flying. She crashed painfully to the ground, her vision swimming with stars.

The children sobbed pitifully as Chumana loomed over them. In a great booming voice, she bellowed, "PAY! Pay until the end of time!"

Galvanized into action, Isabella snatched the axe handle with the eleven-inch long spike from Chumana's booby trap. Brandishing it over her head, she charged forward screaming at the top of her lungs, "Toma esto, perra malvada!!"

Chumana spun around and caught the improvised club by the handle, just below the protruding spike, stopping it cold mere inches before it struck her jugular. Flexing her massively muscled arm, the huge witch snapped the wood handle in two. Her other arm shot out and seized Isabella by the throat. She frantically beat upon the witch's gigantic limb in a desperate attempt to break free of the bruja's iron grip. Chumana laughed, completely unfazed. "Time for you to die, curandera!"

Just as the bruja uttered the last syllable there was a thunderous boom. Chumana's head exploded in a crimson spray of gore. Releasing its hold of Isabella, the now headless body crashed to the floor like a giant tree hacked down by a lumberjack. Wondering what just happened, Isabella scanned the room to see Gideon still on the ground. Instead of sprawled unconscious, he was in a prone firing position, the Remington shotgun cradled in his arms and his face pressed up close to the rear sight.

Lifting my head up from where I sighted in on the witch, I flashed Isabella a roguish smile. Then, all the energy left my body and my shoulders slumped. Everything went black for a moment. I woke up to Isabella shaking me gently. After she helped me up, we limped over to the children.

The massive, headless body of Chumana shrunk back to human size. As we continued to stare, it aged rapidly before our eyes. In the span of a few seconds, it decayed into a dry, shriveled husk, like a mummy.

I nudged the corpse with my foot to make sure it was truly dead and no longer posed a threat. Satisfied, I turned to the children. "Come on, kids. Let's get you home."

Chapter 45

Loose Ends

As we bumped along on the dirt road on our way into town Isabella turned to me. "We should take them to the police, right?"

"Yeah, but we should get our story straight first."

"What do you mean?"

"Best not to mention anything about a witch casting spells, shadow creatures, her turning into a giant and then fighting with a ghost, or anything about the werewolf thing I was fighting. Or how we found the children in the first place, for that matter. In fact, it's best if we don't mention anything supernatural at all," I said.

"So, we just make something up then?"

"No. We tell them the truth, just not all of it. We omit the parts they won't believe."

"You mean we censor the truth," Isabella asked.

"Trust me. If you want to avoid any prolonged stays at the psychiatric ward, you'd best be mindful of what you say to the authorities."

"Ok, so what's the edited version of the truth we tell them?"

"That I'm a private investigator hired to find the missing children. During the course of my investigation, I learned Bruce

Ortiz was providing the names and addresses of certain children to a mysterious Pueblo woman. You helped me find Bruce, who gave us the location of the Pueblo woman. We arrived at her residence and heard the screams of children coming from the barn. Of course, we had to investigate. When we got to the barn, we saw the crazy scene with the dangling skeletons. She was about to slit the throat of one of the children. To save the child's life, I was forced to shoot the woman with the shotgun."

"Sounds plausible. How do we explain how you got that cut on your face?"

"Bruce wasn't immediately forthcoming with the information. In fact, he attacked me with a knife instead."

"Up until that last part, the police pretty much have to take our word for what happened. If they do their due diligence and try to get Bruce's side of the story, that could poke holes in our story."

"Don't worry. That's a loose end I'll be tying up shortly."

"What do you mean?"

"I'll drop you and the kids off at the police station and then I'll pay Bruce a little visit." There was a darkness in my voice when I spoke. I knew Isabella caught it.

"What are you up to, Gideon?"

"You see Isabella, I'm what you might call old school. I live my life by a certain code. In my book, you never, EVER, mess with children. If you do... well, some sins shouldn't go unpunished in this life, if you know what I mean. Besides, I made a promise to a boy named David that Bruce would pay for turning those kids over to the witch. Gideon Jones keeps his promises. If I can borrow your Jeep, that is."

"You can on one condition."

"What's that?"

"You hit Bruce once for me," Isabella demanded.

"Oh, I'll be hitting him more than once."

"You can borrow the Jeep."

I pulled into Bruce's driveway, right behind the black Chevy Impala. I took several deep breaths. The effects of the bruja's spell had worn off. Instead of hammered shit I just felt like shit. Adrenaline got me through some tight spots in that fight, but adrenaline only lasts so long. Though I felt beat down and worn out, I needed to demand a bit more from my overtaxed body. The warrior monks of the Hikari order pushed their bodies beyond normal human limits. I utilized Master Onosai's lessons now, focusing my Qi and tapping into reserves most people didn't even know they had, let alone how to access.

I marshaled up what was left of my strength and marched to Bruce's front door. After briefly examining the door with my flashlight I pounded loudly on it. When there was no immediate answer I pounded louder. After a few minutes of relentless knocking, I heard Bruce yell from inside.

"Who the fuck is it?!"

In answer, I just banged some more. The front door flew open to reveal Bruce holding a shotgun. Like most front doors, Bruce's opened inwards. Before I even started knocking, I was standing on the balls of my feet with my weight forward, poised to move the instant the door started to open. Shining the light in Bruce's eyes, I sprang forward and knocked the barrel of the shotgun aside before the shocked man fully registered what was happening.

With my right hand, I held the shotgun barrel pointed safely away from me. With my left hand, I jabbed Bruce in the face with the flashlight. Moving forward, I hooked my left foot behind Bruce's right ankle and struck him under the chin with my left elbow, in an upper cut-like motion. Bruce went down and left me holding the shotgun.

"I have a message from the Indian woman, Bruce."

"What does that crazy bitch want? I sent the boy to the river just like she asked. I did everything she said!"

"You're a liability, Bruce. She needs a scapegoat and you're it."

"Oh, hell no! If I go down, I'm taking that bitch with me!"

I didn't need to say anything else. The seed was planted in Bruce's mind and I knew the jackass would now tell the police everything. Of course, he would try to paint a picture that he was a mere lackey following Chumana's orders in an attempt to save his own hide, like the cockroach he was. That would still incriminate him and unwittingly substantiate our story. It was now time to deliver some payback for the kids. The police would lock Bruce up, sure, but he might get off in a few years with good behavior. Those kids would be scarred for life.

In my mind, that was *not* justice. Nothing less than justice would do. Thusly, I gave a *savage* beating to Bruce, one that would not just batter his body but scar him emotionally as well. I snapped joints and broke bones. When Bruce cried out for mercy, I thought of the screaming children and kept on going.

When Bruce finally lost consciousness, I took out a knife. Using a handkerchief, I wiped my prints from the handle. Gritting my teeth, I pinched my cheek until I re-opened the wound from the witch's fingernail. Blood dripped onto the blade. Still gripping it with the handkerchief, I placed it into Bruce's hand. Lastly, I took Bruce's shotgun and left. On my way to reunite with Isabella, I stopped at a payphone. I called in an anonymous tip to the police that Bruce was connected to the missing kids and gave them his address.

When I finished, I drove to the police station to corroborate Isabella's story. The police took our statements and did the requisite red tape bureaucracy demanded, but everyone was happy the children had been found. Isabella and I were the heroes of the day. We were free to go. It was a long drive back to Isabella's house in Glorieta. As we pulled into the driveway the sun was rising.

Isabella glanced over at me after cutting the ignition. I was slumped in the seat and probably looked more than tired. I was utterly spent and felt more like a casualty than a triumphant hero.

"You ok?"

"Yeah," I lied.

"You sure?"

"It's been a rough night. I'm bone tired. I did some things that needed to be done, but I sure didn't enjoy doing them."

"Well, we saved the children. That's something."

The beginnings of a smile creased the corners of my mouth. "Yeah, that it is."

"It's been a long night and neither you nor your car is in any shape to drive. How about you crash here?"

My smile broadened. "Yeah, that sounds nice. That sounds really nice."

We walked hand in hand up to the front door, silhouetted by a beautiful sunrise.

Epilogue

I blinked as gentle rays of morning sun filtered in through the blinds. I yawned and stretched lazily but remained lying down, in no hurry to leave the comfort of the bed. The scent of bacon and eggs tickled my nose and brought a smile to my face. After the harrowing ordeal at Chumana's, I decided to take some well-deserved time off and vacation a bit in New Mexico before returning to San Francisco.

As far as I was concerned, it was one of the best decisions I'd ever made. The past few days have been glorious. Isabella acts as a tour guide by day, showing me the sights and rich history of New Mexico. I'm really enjoying it. I can see why the state is called the Land of Enchantment. At night, Isabella shows me other delights I'm positive few tourists, if any, are lucky enough to experience.

I let out a deep sigh of contentment and contemplated staying in bed a bit longer, but the aroma of bacon proved to be too enticing. I hopped out of bed and trotted down the hallway to the kitchen. Before entering the room, I took a moment to admire Isabella's form as she stood in front of the stove preparing breakfast. She was wearing a t-shirt and ankle socks but somehow managed to make the casual attire look stunning.

I wolf-whistled. "Good morning, beautiful."

Isabella glanced over her shoulder, smiling. "Good morning, sleepyhead."

I walked over to where she was standing and leaned in close to kiss her on the cheek. "Anything I can do to help?"

"You're too late. I'm just finishing up."

"Ah, my timing is perfect then."

"Go sit down. I've already set the table," Isabella chuckled.

I did as I was told. Picking up a fork and knife, I felt my mouth begin to water as Isabella scooped food from the frying pan onto my plate. It was standard fare actually, just fried eggs and hash browns with a side of bacon. The addition of New Mexico green chili was the piece de resistance that, in my humble opinion, made it extraordinary. I greedily shoveled several spoonsful into my mouth before complimenting the chef in between loud chomps.

"Mmm, this is delicious, darlin'!"

"Mastica."

"Ma-tee-what? Is that you're welcome in Spanish?"

"No. It means chew."

"Oooh…" I got a little red in the face as I swallowed. "Sorry," I added sheepishly.

Isabella laughed. "No worries, I'm glad you like it. Just slow down. You'll enjoy it more if you chew instead of inhale." She sat down across from me at the kitchen table. "Take a look at today's paper," she said, sliding the folded periodical over to me.

I beamed with elation as I opened it up to the front page. The headline was in bold print:

SAN FRANCISCO PRIVATE EYE SOLVES CASE AND FINDS MISSING CHILDREN

"Oh my God! I'm going to have this matted, framed, and prominently displayed in my office!"

"I thought you might like it," Isabella said as she began to dig into her own plate of food.

I excitedly scanned the article, then put the paper down. "Hey, there's no mention of you in here."

"That's ok. I have no desire for fame. Fortune is enough for me."

"I'd hardly say me splitting my fee with you constitutes a fortune."

"First of all, you didn't have to do it. Second, twenty-nine hundred dollars is more money than I make in two months!"

"You earned it. I told you, I wouldn't have been able to save the kids without you. Hell, I might not be *alive* if it wasn't for you. Giving you half the fee is the least I can do. Not all my clients pay as well as the Order of Saint George. I'm lucky if I make over sixty-five thousand a year."

"In San Francisco that may not be a lot. Here in northern New Mexico, that's good money," Isabella exclaimed.

"Well, maybe you should consider moving to San Francisco then. The pay is better."

"Maybe you should consider moving to New Mexico. The cost of living is less," she countered.

I stared at her for a moment. "The scenery is better out here, that's for sure."

"Hey mister! I'm more than just a pretty face!"

"True. You are a wealth of knowledge. I wish I'd had time to consult with you before we raided the witch's lair. Tell me more about that Navajo werewolf."

"They're called skinwalkers and you're lucky you survived your encounter with one."

"You can say that again. Why could I only hurt it some of the time," I asked curiously.

"Skinwalkers have very few weaknesses. They can heal and regenerate from almost any injury, unless wounded by silver weapons or weapons dusted with white ash or corn pollen. From what you told me, when you did the press-check in the cornfield, that bullet got coated in corn pollen. The skinwalker couldn't heal from that wound. Similarly, when you ran through the cornfield with the knife, the blade must've been covered in pollen as well. When you slashed it in the groin it couldn't heal.

"Also, it's said you must fatally wound the neck to kill a skinwalker. First, you broke its neck. Later, the bruja's trap drove a spike through its neck. When that spike got torn out so forcefully, combined with all its other wounds, it must have finally been enough to do the creature in."

"Now why did that La Yorona ghost help us?" That really had me puzzled.

Isabella winced at my Anglo pronunciation of the name. "La *Llorona*," she said, rolling the r in the correct Spanish pronunciation. "She's an evil spirit. I don't think she was helping us so much as she was getting back at Chumana for binding her spirit into servitude."

"You really know your stuff. I let the Order of Saint George know just how crucial you were in solving this case. If you want, I can also tell them I think you would be a valuable ally in the fight against dark forces. It's dangerous work, but it's for a good cause and it pays well."

"I have to give that one some thought before I say yes."

"Fair enough."

"Yeah. For now, let's be patient and give it some time."

I nodded my head in agreement. *A man would be wise to take his time with a woman like this,* I thought as I sipped my coffee. No need to rush things. Life is short and one should take time to savor the good times when they came along. Sometimes when you dance, it's to a slow song.

Glossary...ish

Dear reader,

Most of Gideon's adventure takes place in New Mexico, the land of enchantment. It is a beautiful place with a rich history and diverse culture. Part of that culture includes Spanish and Native American language influences. It occurred to me that not all my readers will be fluent in these languages, so I have included this glossary. A warning to my readers with delicate sensibilities; there are swear words, as some of the more colorful characters in the book have a knack for profanity.

abuela – grandmother

adobe – sun-dried brick made of clay and straw, commonly used in areas having little rainfall

arroyo – a small, steep-sided watercourse or gulch with a nearly flat floor, usually dry except after heavy rains

bruja – witch

cabrónes – bastards or assholes

callate cabrón – shut up bastard or shut up asshole

chingate cabrón – fuck you bastard or fuck you asshole

chorizo – a type of spicy sausage

chota – a negative New Mexican slang for police, like calling police pigs in English slang

Chumana – snake woman

cuidado – watch out

curandera - female folk healer or medicine woman who uses herbs, psychoactive plants, magic, and spiritualism to treat illness, induce visions, impart traditional wisdom, etc.; a female shaman

demonios – demons

Española – the Spanish maiden

excelente – excellent

gringo – a person who is not Hispanic or Latino

hijo de puta – son of a bitch

huevitos – little eggs

iss cheetz ay yah - you piss me off

juralo – swear

kiva – a large chamber, often wholly or partly underground in a Pueblo village, used for religious ceremonies and other purposes

La Llorona – the weeping or wailing woman or the crier. An infamous Latin American legend of a malevolent spirt who haunts riverbanks and other places.

limpia – cleaning or cleansing

loca – crazy

Lo juro, juro por Dios, juro por las almas de mis hijos! – I swear, I swear to God, I swear on the souls of my children!

mastica – chew

mierda – shit

mija – a colloquial word for 'mi hija', my daughter. While primarily used by parents to address their daughters, it is also a term of endearment from any relative, or someone older and not necessarily related, towards a younger woman or girl. The same happens for younger men or boys: mijo for 'mi hijo'.

Me cago en tu puta madre! Hija de la grand puta! – I shit on your whore of a mother! Daughter of the grand whore!

melika – dog

melika wattsida – white dog

mucho gusto – pleased to meet you

Norteño – an inhabitant or native of northern New Mexico

Ojito Seco – the little dry eye

padre – father

pedazo de mierda – piece of shit

perra – female dog or bitch

pinche – a strong swear word variously meaning goddamned, shitty, or fucking, among others (the latter being the most common)

puta – slut

que no? – This one is a bit tricky. In Spanish, it depends on the context and what part of the world you're in. In New Mexican slang it's used like the English 'don't you think so?'

Rio Grande – Big River. Nowadays, much of the Rio Grande is not a very impressive sight and one might wonder how it earned its name. It's been harnessed and dammed, utilizing the water for drinking and irrigation purposes, as much of New Mexico is an arid landscape. When the first Spanish settlers laid eyes on it, however, it was a grandiose sight to behold.

San Miguel – Saint Michael

sucio – dirty

Toma esto, perra malvada!! – Take this, evil bitch!

www.ingramcontent.com/pod-product-compliance
Lightning Source LLC
Chambersburg PA
CBHW071728190726
48292CB00003B/650